OVERKILL

A LOU THORNE THRILLER

KORY M. SHRUM

TIMBERLANE
PRESS

OVERKILL

AN EXCLUSIVE OFFER FOR YOU

Connecting with my readers is the best part of my job as a writer. One way that I like to connect is by sending 2–3 newsletters a month with a subscribers-only giveaway, free stories from your favorite series, and personal updates (read: pictures of my dog).

When you first sign up for the mailing list, I send you at least three free stories right away. If free stories and exclusive giveaways sound like something you're interested in, please look for the special offer in the back of this book.

Happy reading,

Kory M. Shrum

For my fellow horsemen:
Angela, Katie, and Monica

May your pens stay sharp
and the caffeine strong.

1

____

The killer crossed the street. Louie Thorne watched him weave between the oncoming cars from her patch of shadow beneath the dance club's awning. A drunk couple, arm in arm, stumbled past her, laughing. A car door slammed shut and rude instructions were barked at the valet. A group of women stood to one side, smoking. Snowflakes drifted from the lavender sky, sparking gold as they fell through the streetlights.

None of this distracted Lou. Not the people. Not the rowdy energy of the night. Not the cold settling into her exposed hands and turning her knuckles red.

Her eyes remained fixed on the killer and the prey he'd hooked his arm around.

She didn't cross the street to follow him as King or any other detective might have done. Instead, she took a step backward into the shadows, her leather jacket scraping against the concrete wall. The darkness folded around her, embraced her as one embraced an old friend. Another step back and the alleyway changed altogether. The club she'd been standing beside was across the street now. The women smoking stamped their cigarette butts out against the side-walk and turned to go back inside.

The killer passed Lou, his silhouette thrown across the alleyway where she hid. He was close enough to touch. So close that she could smell his cologne, a cheap synthetic musk. Overdone, in her opinion. He might as well have bathed in it.

When he moved through the streetlamp's halo, she saw the snow collected in his soft brown hair, his bearded jaw.

She did not take him.

It was tempting. She wanted to reach out and grab him by the back of his neck and pull him into the alley. Instead, she stilled her hunger.

But she couldn't wait forever.

The killer already had his next victim. A smaller man, walking hip to hip, was tucked into the crook of the killer's arm. He chatted companionably, unaware of the danger he was in. Lou recognized the prey's Spanish accent and recalled something the man had said in the bar, not long after Lou had first spotted them in the chaos of flashing lights and a generous thumping bass.

She'd ordered a drink, her back inches from the killer's, and listened to his would-be victim talk about Puerto Rico, his home, and how he missed it, no matter how nice NYC's charms might be.

Earlier, Lou had watched the killer spot him, cross the room to the shorter man with sparkles on his cheeks, his clothes tight and showing an appealing amount of skin.

The killer had approached him, offered to buy him a drink.

He'd smiled at the right moments. Laughed when expected.

I miss it, but I'll be home by the end of the month, the prey had said with a pout. He'd placed a hand on the killer's chest then. *Too bad I didn't meet you earlier.*

That's when the killer had bent and said something into his ear, had provided an invitation seductive enough to coax his mark away from the safety of the club and out into the snowy night.

Maybe he's genuinely interested in sex, Lou considered. *Maybe he doesn't plan to rape and strangle him like the others.*

Maybe the Puerto Rican with sparkles on his cheeks would go home happy, satisfied.

More importantly, alive.

The couple hooked a left at the end of the next block, disappearing from Lou's line of sight.

She softened into the darkness again, letting the world blur at its edges, making enough room for her to move through it as she pleased.

When she rematerialized, she found herself in a parked car. She kept low in the seat, unmoving, until she spotted the killer again.

He stood outside a townhouse, fishing a key from his pocket. He was trying to fit it into the lock.

The car was cold, thickly shadowed, and quiet. It offered the perfect vantage point. Lou could even see that the killer's hands trembled.

"Yeah, it's pretty chilly out here." The tourist came up onto his toes. "Let's get you inside and warm you up."

He leaned his weight against the killer's side. He bit his lip, turning his face up as if for a kiss. But the killer hardly noticed this flirtation. All of his concentration was on the door.

Are you shaking from the cold or from excitement? Lou wondered.

She knew where she'd place her bet.

Lou rested her back against the leather seat of the BMW

she'd temporarily commandeered and watched as the killer finally opened the door and ushered his companion inside.

The door slammed shut behind them. A moment later, the light clicked on in the first-floor window. The glow thrown by the lamp seemed deceptively warm and inviting against the winter blazing outside.

Lou didn't make her move. The curtains were open. Anyone from the street could simply look in and see the pair together.

Surely the killer wouldn't be so stupid as to murder someone with the curtains open.

As she sat in the car, her gaze slid back to the curtains every moment or so. Otherwise, she watched the snow fall, soft and slow, and thought of another snowy night, the one that started this hunt.

She'd been restless then too, as she often was. She'd climbed from her bed with the intention of quelling that unease within her. She'd told her compass, *Find me a body. Someone who needs to go home.*

Not that she had planned to drop a corpse on someone's step. They had a good system for giving families peace now. Lou found the bodies. Dani used her media contacts across the country to break the stories wide open. King and Piper lent the technical and logistical support needed to identify the killers and the victims and get the cases into a court of law.

Not one of them knew better than King what evidence was needed to convict someone.

Lou had activated the team five nights ago when she'd stepped from her apartment's closet into a moonlit forest.

The pines had been heavy with snow. The air thick with the sort of silence only possible in winter. In the distance, she'd seen the lights of a house and wondered if she was on someone's property.

But the pull had been unmistakable. As the moon shone down on her through the bare winter branches, she'd noticed the exposed earth beneath her feet where the snow was thinnest.

Not that it mattered. Lou would've known where to dig no matter what.

She always did.

Just like she always knew how to find the killers responsible.

The first night Lou found the New York killer, he was in a different club in Manhattan, talking to a slender man with thick hair and sharp almond eyes. But he hadn't managed to get the man to leave with him.

On the second night, he'd been at the same club but had set his sights on a dark-haired man with large, soulful eyes. This one would have left with the killer if his friends hadn't stepped in at the last minute and pulled him away.

Now here Lou was, on the third night, watching the killer successfully lure an innocent man back to his place.

She looked away from the falling snow to the townhouse's windows.

The curtains were closed.

The twin chords of terror and urgency clanged within her. She slipped reactively through the darkness and into the townhouse.

Clothes hung all around her. Shirts and pressed pants brushed her face. Shoes in neat rows surrounded her feet. Through the slats in a closet door she saw the bed, the victim face down and seemingly asleep.

Asleep, she told herself, sounding a great deal more like a command or prayer than a fact. *Not dead.*

The killer was behind him. Naked from the waist up, his chest heaving with barely controlled...what?

Arousal? He did have an erection, which he exposed and stroked eagerly with one hand as he watched the other man.

The killer's face pulled into a grimace, the hand working harder.

Because of the lamp in one corner of the room, there was no way to get closer without revealing herself. She couldn't appear behind him as she preferred, and slipping under his bed would be useless, if not terrifying.

She would have to step out and face him directly.

Lou threw open the door.

The killer froze, the hand holding his erection faltering.

She wasn't sure if it was the sight of her—a woman dressed head to toe in black leather and mirror shades—or the fact that a stranger had just emerged from his bedroom closet.

Whatever the case, the hunger and excitement that had filled his face the moment before was now gone. Only the rage remained.

He charged her, throwing his weight against her body as if he thought he could overpower her by sheer force alone.

This was his mistake.

Because of Lou's gift with darkness, her body had a different relationship with gravity.

If she'd kept her feet firmly planted, he would've been knocked back against the bed, probably rousing the sleeping tourist.

However, she decided to step back at the last moment. Again and again, leading him to believe he was shoving her back into the closet.

She wondered what he'd thought when she grabbed the door handle and shut him inside with her.

Perhaps nothing. The snarling man trying to wrap his hands around her throat likely had no thoughts at all.

Few killers did in the heated moment of an attack. What they felt was their compulsion. Their all-consuming need.

Being a killer herself, Lou would know that better than anyone.

His hold on her throat faltered as the darkness shifted and he was pulled through it with her. His grip slackened. His arms reached out as if to steady himself.

Hadn't it been King who had said traveling with her like this gave one a drop-kicked feeling? Like a rollercoaster cresting its largest hill?

But there was nothing for the killer to grab on to but her. His hands latched on to her forearms reflexively, nails digging into the unforgiving leather of her jacket, as the closet fell away and in its place the Alaskan night bloomed.

And here it was.

Her favorite place.

The small, placid lake held a perfect reflection of the moon. Coyotes yipped in the distance. A light fog hung over the water. Tall grasses framed its edge. There was nothing but snow-covered land as far as the eye could see, broken up by the large, looming conifers and Sitka pines.

The best part was that the sun wouldn't rise here. At least, not for several weeks.

As the killer cried out, something startled from the edge of the lake and Lou heard hooves pounding the earth. Caribou? A moose or deer? It was hard to say.

Her attention remained on the killer, who was trying to right himself. His bare feet slipped across the snow.

Lou stood where she was, waiting to see what kind of person he'd turn out to be.

Was he someone who believed what he saw and thought she was a witch or demon? Or would he disbelieve his eyes, taking one look at the Alaskan wilderness stretching around him on all sides, its blistering cold and slow, rumbling wind, and be certain he was in a dream?

"Did you already kill him?" she asked. "The man you brought home."

He righted himself. He'd tucked his dick back into his pants at least.

"A man?" he asked, his eyes struggling to fix on any one thing.

He finally met her gaze. The rage was gone. He was in control of himself again.

"You left the club with a man. Short. Cute. Sparkling cheeks. You took him home, and then what?"

"Is this a dream?" he asked. He opened and closed his hands in front of him as if he'd never seen them before.

"Sure. Now tell me, did you give him something or is he dead?"

"Liquid G," he said. "I just gave him liquid G."

She recognized the name, and knew that it was something often slipped into drinks at clubs. Maybe he'd even drugged the man before they'd left together. It would explain their hasty departure.

He wasn't dead then, the tourist. Not yet.

Lou relaxed. "How many people have you killed?"

"I don't know," he said.

"How many?"

"Why the hell is it so cold? What kind of place is this?"

"How *many*?" she asked again.

"I don't know. It doesn't matter. Who cares?"

Who cares? Their families, Lou thought. *Their friends. The people who loved them.*

He pinched his eyes shut and wrapped his arms around himself. "I want to wake up. Wake up now, Elliot. Wake up."

Elliot. Lou filed the name away.

She hated when they thought it was all a dream. It wasn't

as fun to play with them when they believed they would just wake up from it all, safe and warm in their beds, not a scratch on their pretty heads. In those cases, they weren't as scared as they deserved to be.

She took a step toward him, leaned her hip into his like his victim had.

"Do you want to tell me what you do to the men you bring home? Don't you want to tell someone?"

"Yes," he said, his voice low and husky. Konstantine's voice got like that sometimes.

"Did you always find them in clubs?" she asked.

"No," he said, licking his lips. "I found one at a grocery store."

"And he, what, came back to the car with you?"

"We fucked in the backseat," he said, his shoulders shivering.

"And?"

"I forced him to swallow it."

Lou needed to be more specific in her questions. She didn't want a play-by-play of this man's assaults. She wanted to gather what she could about his murders, anything that might help King and the others build a case.

"He came back to my place with me after that. Left his groceries in the car and everything. They like when you make them do what you want. Fucking faggots."

Lou arched her brow. *We have some repression here.*

"Do you always drug them?" she asked.

"No. Sometimes I choke them and don't stop."

"*Then* you rape them?"

The glassy, aroused look in his eyes sharpened. "It's not rape. They want it."

King isn't going to like this.

Lou pulled the gun from beneath her leather jacket and pressed the barrel to his chin. She pulled the trigger.

The killer's head snapped up as if punched, the body lifting up before collapsing to the shore.

When the gunshot stopped ringing through the still night, she said, "Oops."

The coyotes began yipping again.

She holstered her gun and bent to grab his pale ankle. It was cold against her palm. It didn't matter. The lake water was colder.

Still, she stepped from the frozen shore, and ripples flowed from her chest across the water's slate-gray surface, disturbing the starlight gathered there.

Lou marveled, not for the first time, that this lake didn't freeze over in winter. This was Alaska. It was winter, where endless nights never surrendered to the day. Yet it didn't freeze over. She saw ice gather at its corners from time to time, but the lake itself remained clear.

Was that by some natural design? Or was it because of what she'd done to it? By her own particular use, had she changed the waters somehow?

She wondered.

She questioned everything now that Konstantine's tests had come back, telling them just how strange her alien world really was.

Her world.

Lou dipped her head beneath the surface of the water, still holding tight to the killer's ankle, and loosed a breath underwater.

As the bubbles rose to the surface, the water shifted from midnight gray to red. From icy cold to bathwater, warmer.

This was her cue to kick until she broke the surface. Blinking the water from her eyes, she cleared it with a swipe of her hands.

La Loon. She took it in.

Its monstrous landscape. An irrationally purple sky, twin

milky moons. Smoke-yellow mountains in the distance, obscured by a menacing haze.

She pulled herself out of the blood-red waters, which she had unimaginatively named Blood Lake as a child, and onto its black shore. Unceremoniously, she dumped the killer's body onto the embankment.

Then she waited.

She waited for the death screech, waited for the serpentine beast with skin the color of tar, scaly and six-footed, to burst through the trees and greet her as it always did.

The beast was always excited for Lou's arrival but even more thrilled to consume the offerings Lou brought her.

Lou scanned the black foliage and tall oil-black grasses, looking for movement.

Nothing stirred. There was no sound.

No yellow eyes looked back at her. There was no welcoming screech.

"Hello?" she cried out.

Her voice echoed across the valley, before ricocheting off the rock face and thinning into a dull whine.

"I'm back," she called, feeling more than a little silly considering she'd never had to announce her arrival before.

Jabbers had always been here. She'd always known when Lou was coming and had been there waiting.

But this time was different.

This time the air remained silent. The beast did not come.

2

———

Takeshita Street was packed. The schools had let out twenty minutes before and that was more than enough time for the street to fill with teenagers in their school uniforms. They clustered in groups outside the dessert crepe stalls and the cheese dog stands. They ate and laughed, and a few, feeling bold enough away from the eyes of their parents, dared to smoke, their collars loose and postures slouched.

Riku Yamamoto liked the look of children in school uniforms, especially girls, with their bare legs exposed beneath their pleated skirts.

He looked his fill as he made his way through the crowd. He noted more than bare legs, of course. There were cute keychains fixed to matching backpacks and the lilting singsong of J-pop music floating through the streets. Two girls holding hands stopped in front of a store to admire the action figurines lined in the windows, characters from shows that Riku didn't know.

The crowd thinned the longer he walked.

Toward the end of the street, past the shops and dessert stalls, there were few students.

Still, Riku found what he wanted in the second-to-last store on the right.

He stopped, facing it.

In the window display were lines of sneakers, showcasing the current style and trending taste in footwear. He stood there, in the middle of the road, looking at the sneakers without really seeing them. He pulled out a cigarette, lit it, and waited.

A Nigerian man, large and intimidating, loomed in the doorway of the shop. He saw Riku, nodded, and Riku returned the gesture.

This was the sign. If there was a language barrier, it didn't matter. No words would be needed for this exchange.

The Nigerian went inside.

As Riku smoked, girls began to exit the shop, but none approached Riku directly. One cleaned the window. Another began to sweep up the sidewalk, collecting trash from careless tourists and uncaring teens. Two more worked on adjusting a sales display, moving the sneakers from one end to the other and back again.

Riku watched these girls. As he exhaled thin gray smoke toward the sky, his eyes finally fixed on a girl still inside the store. She was in the large display window, trying to wrestle a new shoe onto a mannequin's foot.

Her hair was bleached white and pulled up into twin high ponytails. Sparkles had been added to the corners of her eyes and her makeup done in soft pinks. The baby doll dress also accentuated her childlike features.

Riku finished his cigarette and nodded at the girl in the window. The Nigerian nodded in return and disappeared into the shop. The girl was still in the window when he bent and grabbed her arm, hauling her up and out of sight.

He kept holding on to her until they were both outside, stopping just short of where Riku stood. Then he waited, clearly expecting something of Riku. Of course, this wasn't Riku's first trip to this second, lesser-known world of Takeshita Street.

So he slid his hand into the inner pocket of his suit and pulled out an envelope. The broad man opened it, counted the bills with swift, dark fingers. Then nodded. "Okay."

Riku wasn't worried about the price. That money would make its way back into his pockets soon, and there was no need to let these people know who Riku was or what hold he had over their pathetic lives.

Let them believe he was simply another Japanese businessman hoping to kill a few hours pleasantly.

The girl was pushed forward.

She bowed to Riku, her long ponytails grazing her shoulders. Riku put his hand softly on her elbow and led her away.

Halfway up the street, he released her.

She didn't scream. She didn't run. She continued at his side, one step behind, matching her pace to his.

He considered offering her his coat. She had to be cold in such little clothing. January in Tokyo could be a brutal affair. He didn't think it was more than five degrees Celsius today.

Yet she didn't complain. Even though her platform shoes were not made for walking.

That was the wonderful thing about these girls.

They were obedient.

After four blocks, his hotel came into view.

It was a blessed relief, the warm lobby. It offered his iced cheeks a reprieve from the blistering wind. He crossed the elegant red-and-gold carpet to the elevator, nodding to the receptionists he passed. The cleaning personnel. Everyone knew him, or at least, knew who owned the building.

That was why none of them looked too closely at the girl.

Riku held the elevator door open for her and waited until she was on the lift before he pushed the button for the penthouse suite. In the small space he could smell her sweat even beneath the generous dose of cheap perfume she'd splashed on.

It made him dizzy. He didn't like it.

The elevator opened on the foyer, the holding space between the elevator and the front door to his apartment.

Riku noted who was on guard duty tonight.

Kenchi and Shibu.

Shibu sat on the sofa, scrolling through his phone with a rapid flick of his thumb. Kenchi stood by the door, his back bent in the image of nonchalance.

"Good evening, Mr. Yamamoto," Kenchi called out.

Riku closed the door behind them without so much as a hello.

Here, the girl began to show a semblance of autonomy.

She slipped off her shoes and wandered across the wide expanse of his well-furnished living room in only her white socks. From the back, with her pigtails, baby doll dress, and socked feet, she looked more like a child than ever.

She was perfect.

She went to the window and gazed out at the beautiful night forming beyond. The sun had fallen behind the horizon, leaving the winter sky an icy blue folding into gray. Soft white flakes floated on the wind.

Riku went to the bathroom, turned on the shower, and put a towel on the sink.

Then he went back to the window. She was still looking out over the bustling streets far below, until he took her elbow and guided her to the shower.

"Get in," he said in Japanese. "This towel is for you."

She reached for the button on his shirt with uncertain hands.

He tried Chinese, both Mandarin and Cantonese. No response. Was she Thai, maybe? Malaysian?

He stopped her and shook his head. When she frowned, her confusion obvious, he nudged her toward the shower stall.

She nodded and began to remove her clothes. When she saw him watching, she did it slowly, tilting her eyes up to meet his.

He watched her reveal herself, piece by piece.

A slender throat. Small high breasts, a flat stomach. Thin arms and legs. A non-existent ass.

He noted each attribute in turn but felt nothing.

She stepped into the shower and began to wet her body. She did not close the door. Did she expect him to climb in after her? Or to watch?

He didn't. Still standing outside the shower, he wet and soaped his hands in the hot stream, making sure they were clean before he slid them between her legs. He probed each fold as he washed it.

It was not sexual. He simply wanted to make sure she was clean.

She'd remained still until he slid his fingers inside her, one hole then the other, giving each a little twist before withdrawing. She sucked in a surprised breath but said nothing.

Satisfied that she would be clean, he closed the door, allowing her some privacy to do the rest of the work on her own.

At the sink he washed his hands again, before going to the kitchen to make himself a drink.

He decided on a Kirin Lager tonight, using the opener from the drawer to remove the bottlecap.

He took a deep drink, felt the burn at the back of his throat.

He drank half the bottle before he went to the large armoire in his bedroom and opened it.

The rack was covered with baby doll dresses and pinafores. Lacy socks and ribbons for the hair.

Stuffed animals and bows.

Riku pushed each hanger along the metallic bar, regarding them in turn, before deciding on a pink dress with white kittens on it. The kittens, some sitting, some cleaning their paws or stretching for a nap, seemed indifferent to his inspection.

He selected two white ribbons to match as well as soft cotton panties with a ruffled trim on the ass. He laid all of this on the bed, then took a seat by the expansive window, the night blooming behind him.

He drank his beer and looked at the clothes.

Still he felt nothing. No heat. No building tension.

Disappointment grew in his chest.

After the shower turned off and only a slight drip from the faucet could be heard against the ceramic tile, the girl appeared, wrapped in a towel, her hair only partially dried.

As soon as she saw him sitting in the chair, she dropped the towel.

He pointed at the clothes, made a series of gestures that suggested she put them on.

She seemed confused that she was being asked to put clothes on, but she did as she was told, pulling on the underwear first and then the dress. When she began to brush out her hair, he stopped her, pushing her down on the bench in front of the vanity. She kept her eyes lowered as he dried her hair with the blower and restyled it into the pigtails that had first caught his attention, securing each with one of the white ribbons, which he lovingly tied into a bow.

Then he led her to the bed. She climbed into the sheets without being told.

Again he surprised her, by not climbing in after her but tucking her in tightly.

When her brows pinched in confusion, he pressed his fingertips to her eyes, forcing her to close them. She lay still, her body a mimicry of a little girl asleep in his bed.

It still wasn't enough.

He went to the armoire again and selected one of the bears. This one white to match the ribbons. He tucked it into the crook of her arm.

She snuggled it, almost instinctually, before he motioned for her to close her eyes again.

Then he waited.

He drank his beer and watched the girl sleep, or pretend to.

It's her, he told himself. *It's not some girl you picked up from Takeshita Street, it's her. It's Mai.*

Nothing.

It's Mai, he pleaded, trying to will his desire into being. *It's Mai. My sweet little Mai.*

He set the beer down on the table beside his chair and rose, going to the bedside. The girl, to her credit, did not stir, did not move as Riku peeled back the covers, exposing her bare legs.

She remained perfectly still even after he traced the side of her thigh with his fingertips, moving the dress higher, and higher, exposing the ruffled backside of her panties.

Perhaps she understood the game after all.

He peeled back the fabric and slid the underwear down to reveal the curve of her buttocks.

Here she rolled over, looked up at him questioningly.

She shouldn't have done that. She should have remained on her side, perfectly still.

His anger spiked and he slapped her. Her eyes went wide. The teddy fell to the floor.

Her hand went to her cheek, but she did not cry out. Did not scream.

And he hated her for it.

He grabbed her shoulders, shook her, thrusting her back against the mattress over and over again.

"Cry!" he demanded.

The girl did begin to cry, even though he suspected it had little to do with his command and was more the natural result of being slapped and shaken.

He grabbed her hair, pulling it.

Now the tears were real.

"Tell me to stop," he said. "Say, 'Brother, please. Stop.'"

She screamed.

He grabbed one of her pigtails and dragged her from the bed.

She twisted in his grip, her fingernails clawing frantically at his wrists. He threw her to the ground and slipped a hand into his pocket. The switchblade was thin but sharp. A press of a button and it extended from its resting position.

Riku grabbed the girl's pigtails and twisted her neck sharply to one side. She cried out, but the sound was cut short as he drew the blade across her throat.

"That's for leaving me!" he snarled. "How dare you! How *dare* you!"

Her hands stopped fighting with his and instead went to her throat. She pressed against the split skin. Gurgling, crying. She tried to pull herself away from him, inching slowly toward the door.

She's getting blood all over the dress. My carpet, he thought with disgust.

It wasn't Mai.

It wasn't his Mai. His beautiful though vicious little sister.

He kicked her corpse until he'd exhausted himself with the effort.

Panting, out of breath, he fell back into his chair. He pulled a handkerchief from his suit pocket and cleaned the blood off the blade before closing it and returning it to his pocket.

Then he drank his beer, refusing to look at the mess he'd made on the floor.

He kept drinking.

It wasn't her.

Why wasn't it her?

He wanted his Mai. No one else would do.

When the beer was finished and the silence had grown unbearable again, he called out for the bodyguards. He listened to the sounds of the apartment door opening, and shoes hitting the floor by the door. Riku tracked their footfall crossing the living area and into the bedroom.

When they saw the girl on the floor, they stopped, but said nothing.

"Get rid of it," Riku said. "And make sure there isn't a drop of blood left on my carpet."

"Careful, Shibu," Kenchi said, pushing the second guard back with a hand. "You'll get the blood on your socks."

It was true that Shibu, all muscle, little brain, had been standing too close to the body. And he wasn't as good at hiding his disappointment as Kenchi was.

"You can still have her if you want," Riku said with a snide laugh.

Shibu looked up, horrified. Kenchi kept his mask in place. Now that Riku thought about it, had he ever seen Kenchi take his leftovers? Shibu, yes. Several times. But Kenchi...

Riku searched for a memory but found none. Perhaps women were not to his taste. Or certainly not ones soaked in their own blood.

"Get rid of it," Riku said again, before rising from his seat and going into the bathroom.

Kenchi bowed as Riku passed. Shibu did the same.

The last thing Riku saw before he shut the bathroom door tight was the two of them standing over the dead girl, neither one of them wanting to touch her first.

3

———

"I understand," Paolo Konstantine said into the warm phone pressed to his ear. "*Si, amico mio.* I will do my best."

The call ended. Konstantine turned away from his desk and regarded the fireplace, watching the flames dance and swirl, offering their own magic against the cold night pressing in on them from outside. It could be worse. Compared to winters past, this January had been mild in Florence.

January.

Lou's birthday was just weeks away and he hadn't decided on her gift yet.

His gaze slid to the phone in his hand, the troubling sound of the man's tears ringing through his mind.

And there are more pressing concerns, he thought.

A rough knock on his office door made him look up.

It was Stefano, Konstantine's second-in-command, with his hair damp from the light rain, the shoulders of his Armani suit splattered with its droplets.

"What is it?" Konstantine asked.

"It's almost two in the morning," Stefano said. His eyes

flicked around the room, to its dark corners. He was looking for Lou, Konstantine was sure of that. "When are you going home for the night?"

"Soon," Konstantine promised. "I'm almost done here."

Stefano gave him a doubtful look, his brow rising.

"If you say so," he said, and then closed the door, leaving Konstantine to his thoughts.

Konstantine bent and placed another log on the dying fire. As he stirred its embers, coaxing it to new heights, his ears popped, the pressure snapping under some weight.

When he looked up from the fire, brushing wood dust from his hands, there she was.

Louie Thorne.

Her hair was wet. Her eyes hidden behind her mirrored shades.

"Did you get caught in the rain too?" he asked. "Or did you hunt tonight?"

"Jabbers isn't there," she said.

There was something in her tone that caused him to stop his incessant thinking. In his mind, he'd been working over the problem consuming his thoughts, his dear Somchai in trouble.

Now something else was wrong.

"What do you mean?" he asked, pushing his sleeves up to the elbow.

"I brought the killer to La Loon, and she wasn't there," she said. She shrugged off her jacket and hung it on the hook by the fireplace.

"It isn't as if she can leave, *amore mio*," Konstantine assured her. "Perhaps she was sleeping. Or hunting like you."

"Every time I've ever crossed in the past, no matter the day, hour, season, she was there. She was always on the shore or near to it when I came."

It wasn't that Konstantine himself was worried for the

beast. It was hard to feel concern for a creature that looked like it had been spawned from the bowels of Hell and crafted by Satan's own hands, but Lou's concern was clear.

Considering how rarely she showed concern, it added gravity to the situation.

"You think something's wrong with her?" he asked. "Maybe she's hurt?"

"I should go look for her."

"Or perhaps it was simply the first time you came and she was busy, *amore mio*." He reached for her. He wanted her close to him.

The skin between her brows softened. "Maybe."

"Maybe," he mimicked her. "What did you do with the body? Was it the hunt you just began or another?"

"It was him. The one from New York."

Last night, from the flat of her back in his bed, she'd told him about the murdering rapist in New York City.

"I left his body on the shore," she said. "If I'd known she wasn't coming I'd have left it in the water. There are other things in the lake that can eat the body."

He placed his hands on her hips and squeezed them. Moisture welled between his fingers. She was soaked and reeked of the other world.

"You came straight here," he said. *You must truly be upset.*

"I thought you would be at your apartment," she said. The last of the tension melted from her shoulders.

Konstantine's thoughts turned to his dilemma again. "I got a phone call as I was about to leave."

"Bad news?"

"A friend is missing his daughter."

Lou shifted her weight to the other hip, seeming to press it into Konstantine's palm. "She was kidnapped or she ran away?"

"It would seem she was kidnapped."

"What's her name?" she asked.

"Busaba Chen," he said. "Her father is Somchai. We have known each other a long time."

He saw the way she was standing there, lingering because she did not want to put her wet body on his desk.

"Sit here, by the fire," he said, offering her his seat. "It will keep you warm until we go home."

Home.

His stomach tightened. He hadn't meant to say it like that.

"I have one drawer at your place," she said with a twitch of her lips. "We aren't living together yet."

Yet.

He tried to hide how much the idea pleased him.

She sat on his lap, pinning him against the chair's leather, the high back.

He turned his eyes up to look at her. "That's not what I meant. I wanted you to have the chair."

"Are you worried I've gotten your clothes dirty?" she asked, her smile amused. "Always so fussy about your clothes."

It was true that he liked his clothes pristine, but he enjoyed having her body on his more.

"Now that you're dirty, too, I guess we'll have to take a shower together," she said.

Her face was relaxed and voice easy, but Konstantine had not overlooked the tight set of her lips. The tension running along her upper back.

She is very worried about her beast, he knew. The only thing he could do for her in that respect was distract her.

"It will be a terrible punishment, to share the shower with you," he said, playing along. "Should we head back now?"

"Your fire is too high to leave it," she said. "And I want to hear about your friend."

"Somchai and I met as boys at a computer campo—"

"Camp."

"Yes," he said. *A camp.* "Padre Leo knew that I loved computers and encouraged that love. Somchai's family was poor. His whole village scraped together the money to send him, in hopes he would use his knowledge to get them out of poverty. We struck up a friendship that summer and have stayed in touch, more or less, over the years since. Padre brought him to Florence twice so I could spend time with him."

"Did he save his village?" she asked.

"He did. He has more than enough to take care of himself and his family, and his businesses provide many jobs in his town."

"Does he know who you are? What you do?"

"He knows that my father was a bad man, and that Padre Leo looked after me. He knows that I have connections to crime families across Europe. He does not blame or hate me for it, which I appreciate. He sees it as something I was born into."

"If he called you, then he must be having a criminal problem," she said, her eyes on the fire.

Konstantine enjoyed watching the flames dance across her cheeks.

"Somchai believes Busaba was taken by traffickers."

"What do you think?"

"I think he's right. At least, I hope he is."

Lou arched a brow, turning away from the flames. The side of her throat glowed. "You *hope* she's a sex slave?"

Konstantine tilted his head. "Because it means she's *alive*. I don't want to tell my friend that his daughter is dead."

"How old is she?"

"Seventeen."

Lou searched his face. "Are you going to ask me? Or are you too proud?"

He'd wondered when they would arrive at this point. Ever since Lou had discovered that Konstantine would rather sacrifice little Matteo—one of the many street boys in Konstantine's care—than ask her to help him resolve his conflict with the Albanians, she'd teased him ruthlessly.

Well, first she'd pressed a blade to his throat and dared him to ever put a child in harm's way again. *Then* she'd teased him. For months, she would bring it up at every opportunity.

Can you ask me to pass you the cream, or is it too much?

Can you ask me for this pillow, or will it kill you?

Should I pick up dinner, or maybe you'd rather starve than ask me?

She had never mentioned Matteo, blessedly. She seemed to understand that he had not forgiven himself for that miscalculation.

"Ask," she said. "It will be easier for me to find her than you."

"I know." He sighed. It was still difficult for him to ask anything of her, but he was getting better at it. "Will you please go and get her for me?"

"Yes," she said, lifting from his lap. "The shower can wait."

4

Melandra Durand was dreaming. She'd realized it as soon as the bangles on her wrist did not make a sound. In her waking life, they always made a soft, bell-like ring whenever she moved her hands or arms. The music was a calm reminder to be here *now*, in this body and time.

Except that now, no matter how she turned her wrists or lifted her arms, the golden rings remained silent. It wasn't only her bangles that had helped her achieve this lucidity. It was also the bird and the empty French Quarter street.

Mel stood in the center of the road without another soul in sight. Shop windows were dark, their doors shut tight. The stoops vacant.

Everything was too still, too silent. All except for that bird.

A cardinal.

Beaming, its chest out to convey its authority.

A cardinal in New Orleans. Mel wasn't sure she'd ever seen one in the city. Of course, she hadn't spent as much time in the parks as she should. She tended to stick to the urban areas, where greenery was more sparse.

The bird took flight then, pushing itself up and away from the concrete. It flew ahead of her, and when she did not immediately follow, it circled back for her.

"All right, Mr. Bird," she called up. "I'm comin'."

Mel kept pace with that flash and blur of red despite the strange warping of time and space. They'd begun on Royal Street, just outside of King's detective agency. Now they were down by the French Market, overlooking the Mississippi River. It was a long walk, completed in seconds.

With a flap and flourish of its wings, the cardinal dropped down and landed on its little black feet. Its wings snapped closed.

It wasn't looking at Mel. It was looking at the girl.

The girl was alone, overlooking the Mississippi River, her back to Mel.

No older than Piper, she had strawberry-blond hair. It whipped in the wind rolling off the river. A wind that Mel couldn't feel, only hear and see.

The girl pulled her green coat tighter around her body and shifted uneasily in her furry boots.

The cardinal chirped, sharp and urgent.

The girl didn't turn.

It chirped again, and this time, as if in a dream herself, she turned, her eyes glassy, gaze unfocused with some deep, wretched emotion like grief.

The girl raised her gaze to meet Mel's.

That's when Mel saw the blood on her chest. From throat to navel, the cream-colored shirt she wore beneath the coat was soaked with it.

"I'm sorry," the girl said, tears spilling from the corners of her eyes. "I didn't mean to."

Mel stepped forward, her sole desire to hug this poor

child. Tell her it would be all right, that whatever had happened was over.

Before Mel could reach her, the girl fell, her body tumbling off the riverwalk and into the slate-gray waters of the Mississippi.

Mel jolted forward to grab her, to pull her out of the icy waves.

She bolted upright in her dark bedroom, the shadows dull gray and retreating from the early-morning light.

There was no girl. No platform. No winter river. No brilliant red bird.

"It really was a dream," she said to the Belgian Malinois placing its worried head on Mel's covered legs.

Mel rubbed the fur between Lady's gentle brown eyes.

"Just a dream," she said again, though her body still thrummed with residual panic.

Tap. Tap. Tap.

Mel's hand stilled on the dog's head as she looked to the balcony window.

There on the wrought-iron railing was a cardinal. Bright red.

It chirped once. Twice. A sharp, pleading cry.

Mel raised her hand as if to protect herself from it. The bangles on her wrist tinkled lightly like a forgotten song.

That's when Mel knew she was in trouble.

FED, DRESSED, HOT GREEN TEA IN HER BELLY, MEL LOCKED the door of her apartment and took the stairs that would lead down to her occult shop, Melandra's Fortunes and Fixes. Lady was on her heels as the metal stairs rattled and shook.

The shop looked ready for the day. The shelves well stocked, the glass cases clean.

Piper was already there, earbuds in her ears as she opened a shipping box and began unpacking new inventory.

Mel pressed a hand to her shoulder and the girl shrieked. Lady's ears went flat against her head.

"Oh man," Piper moaned, pulling the earbuds out. Her bright eyes pinched shut dramatically before rolling open again. "I just lost two of my nine lives. Why you gotta creep up on me like that?"

"I just wanted you to know I was here," Mel said.

Piper wrapped her arms around the dog's neck and graciously accepted several wet kisses on her cheeks. "Thanks, but I'm listening to this scary story and you about gave me a heart attack."

Mel went around to the register and opened it. The drawer had already been counted out and was ready to go. Mel was going to acknowledge this, thank Piper for getting the shop ready for the day, but she was still going on about the story she'd been listening to.

"I was rooting around in this box, hoping it wasn't full of parasite worms, and—"

"Worms?" Mel wrinkled her nose.

"This book is about alien worms. Their sole purpose is to invade our planet by possessing us. They get inside you and make you eat until you literally explode. It sounds dumb, but if you're a germaphobe it's *horrifying*. You can't imagine all the terrible ways these things can get inside you."

Piper shuddered.

"It looks like you've already done all the opening chores," Mel said, unable to keep the frown off her face.

Piper didn't miss it. "Was I not supposed to?"

"No, no," Mel said, waving her hand away. "You did good. Thank you."

Lady came around the register and spun three times

before lying down on her cushion, her customary position while in the shop.

"Then why do you have that look on your face?" Piper stood, still holding the pricing gun in one hand. "Last time you looked like that your ex-husband had gotten out of prison and was extorting you for money. Shit, is he back from the dead? Is his ghost haunting you right now? Do we need to smudge up in here?"

"No." Mel shook her head. "There's no dead husband."

Piper abandoned the inventory box and came to the counter. She laid the pricing gun on the glass. "Then what is it? You know I'm just going to pester you until you tell me."

Mel searched her earnest face. It was true that if Mel didn't say something, Piper's next move would be to recruit King. They'd start checking up on her, looking for clues as to what was going on, as they had when Terry, her bastard of an ex-husband, had come back.

"I'm having a debt dream," she said quietly.

"Oh yeah," Piper said knowingly. "I have those all the time. Usually someone is coming to repossess my car, and I'm like, 'No, don't. I can't get anywhere without it,' which is *ridiculous* because I've never owned a car in my life. I get along fine without one. Where this fear is coming from, I've *no* idea."

"Not that kind of debt." Mel lifted her wrist and pretended to fuss over the pens in the cup by the register. The truth was she just wanted to make sure she was awake. That her bangles would ring, as she'd hoped they would.

They did.

Mel's shoulders relaxed. "It was Grandmamie who called them debt dreams. She said they came from God. You dream about someone. Someone who is going to get hurt, or die, and God leaves it up to you to change that fate."

Piper whistled. "Shit. That's a lot of pressure. Does something terrible happen if you screw it up?"

"No," Mel said, adjusting the scarf tied across her forehead, following it down where it wrapped around her braids. "No, it wasn't like you were punished if you failed. It was just a calling, and you were supposed to help if you could. It's the price of having your gifts. If God gives you a gift, then you pay your debt. That's what she meant."

Piper seemed to consider this, twisting the silver ring on her thumb as she did. "So what are you going to do? Call this person up and tell them to look both ways before crossing the road? Don't buy that lotto ticket? What?"

"I can't call her. I don't know who she is. I don't have a name. I don't even know where she is."

"*What?*" Piper scoffed. "You're expected to save someone you don't even know? Geez, that is a hell of a mission. How in the world are you supposed to save a stranger?"

"I know what she looks like," Mel said. "I might dream about her again. If I do, maybe I can get her name."

Piper rubbed a fist across her forehead. "I think King is friends with the sketch artist at the station. Maybe he will draw you a sketch and we can try to ID her from that. Luke is pretty good. Luke is the artist."

"We could give it a try," Mel said. "I'm not sure how else to move forward. Unless the girl comes into this shop or I spot her in the street, there's no way for me to know if she's even real."

"And what the heck do you say if you do see her? Oh, wait!" Piper snapped her fingers. "Maybe Lou can locate her using her inner compass thingy."

"Maybe." The idea appealed to Melandra.

The sense of urgency was still very fresh in her mind.

But no. She couldn't do that. The last time Lou had been

brought into Melandra's business, Mel had accidentally shot her. She still hadn't completely forgiven herself for that.

Besides, Grandmamie had said a debt dream was meant for the dreamer. Mel was the one who could save the girl. The responsibility lay with her. Somehow she held the key to getting the girl out of harm's way.

"Let's not ask Lou yet. I don't want to rely on her unless I have to," Mel said.

Piper looked ready to protest but then saw something in Mel's face.

"Okay," she said. "Then we'll start with the sketch."

Mel placed her hand over Piper's and squeezed. The bangles rang against the glass countertop. "Thank you."

I'm awake. I have time. I can still save her.

LOU HAD LEARNED OVER THE YEARS OF TRYING TO USE HER gift that her questions had to be precise.

If she asked the wrong one, or if there was too much ambiguity, vagueness, or possibility in her question, then the compass could deliver unclear results.

It was true that Lou didn't know much about Thailand, but Konstantine had said Chen was a common name, and that was why Lou chose not to use it. Who knew how many Somchai or Busaba Chens there were in the world?

If she'd asked, *Take me to Busaba Chen*, she might find any number of girls.

Instead, she thought, *Take me to the girl Konstantine promised to find.*

The compass inside her whirled and clicked before snagging to a stop. The pull rose up to seize her, a current moving her, directing her to her desired point in time and space.

She moved through the black, becoming one with it, formless and unbound.

Her next step brought her to a strange, curtained room.

It took her a moment to understand where she was. A dark digital screen lit up in front of her, activated by her movement. It showed cute Japanese girls holding up peace signs to their eyes and smiling. The booth—the one in the short film—took pictures of the girls in different poses before spitting the images out into the silver receiving slot.

Only then did she realize she was in a photo booth. The black curtain was drawn closed on her left.

She pulled it back and stepped out into the day.

Takeshita Street burned bright with cheerful morning light, but the crowd was thin. The kiosk signs were mostly dark. Workers were dragging out display tables and unlocking doors, but there was not much laughter. No music.

A young man carrying a box bumped into Lou and stopped, his face pinched in irritation.

Then he saw her.

The leather jacket, the mirrored shades.

His face softened and he dipped his head in apology before stepping around her.

Lou had seen Takeshita Street at night and knew how lively it could be. This stillness was strange.

She rolled her wrist to check her GPS watch. She waited for it to acclimate itself to the new time, new place, before spitting out a time with its fluorescent green numbers.

It was almost ten in the morning in Tokyo. That's why it looked the way it did. She didn't think the majority of these stores opened until eleven.

The compass in Lou pulled her further down the street, toward the shops at the end.

She moved slowly, hands in her pockets, as if she were simply a tourist waiting for the day to begin. In truth, she was trying to get a good lock on the Chen girl.

There was a lot of light here. Even in winter, the sun was

at its strongest at midday. Lou suspected that there had not been a patch of darkness close to the girl. Not a closet or bathroom.

That's why she'd been forced to use the photo booth as her entry point.

This meant the extraction would be tricky. Taking the girl without causing a fight or being seen might not be possible.

Lou touched her jacket, making sure her gun was where she'd left it.

Satisfied, she moved on, pretending to look into the shop windows and shuttered food stalls with mild interest as she passed.

She appreciated the warmth of her coat, but her damp hair was irritating her. She secured it with an elastic from her wrist.

Nothing else to do about it now.

Her mind noted the irritation, suspicious of it. When was the last time something as simple as wet hair had irritated her? Or her toes being soaked and boots soggy? In fact, now that she thought about it, her muscles ached. She felt heavy in her limbs, sluggish.

Maybe I'm hungry, she thought.

She tried to remember the last time she'd eaten. She often forgot to eat when she was working. It had been something that had driven her aunt Lucy crazy when she'd been alive.

As far as Lou was concerned, taking care of herself wasn't the priority.

Konstantine couldn't simply tell her about a girl kidnapped and trafficked then expect her to go have a hot shower, hearty meal, and good night's sleep.

Lou understood that she couldn't be everything to everyone. She couldn't save every tortured soul in the world.

Still, every second enslaved must feel like an eternity. Lou refused to add to that nightmare.

A snag pulled at Lou's heart and she stopped, her boots scuffing the concrete.

A girl was sweeping the steps of a clothing store with a battered broom that had seen better days.

Her long black braid was loose and hung over one shoulder.

Someone had put makeup on her, but it didn't sit right. The colors were wrong, and it did nothing to hide the puffiness beneath her eyes, the swollen, dark bags collected there.

As if she sensed Lou's eyes on her, she looked up, the broom faltering in her hands.

It is very cold to be in so little clothing, Lou thought. "Who the hell dressed you?"

No answer.

Lou saw the bruise partially hidden by the shoulder strap of the dress.

The compass tugged again, and that was all Lou needed to know that she had found the right girl.

"Busaba," she said.

The girl's eyes widened.

"Come with me." Lou waved toward herself. The girl's forehead creased. "Come on. Your father sent me."

A white lie, but close enough.

"Somchai," Lou said, and pointed at her chest, waving the girl toward her again. *"Let's go."*

Lou knew that Somchai and Konstantine had spoken in English, though how much his daughter understood of the language was unclear.

The broom fell from her hands. *"Phaw?"*

She rushed into Lou's arms.

A curtain in the display window rustled.

Lou took Busaba's arm and pulled her down a side street, past the clothing store that Lou had a feeling wasn't a clothing store at all. A brothel, maybe.

The alley wasn't quite dark enough for her to slip. There was too much space between this building and the next. Lou couldn't stop, her eyes searching each nook and corner for an exit.

Footsteps pounded the alleyway behind them, echoing off the building's walls.

We're out of time.

"Run to *there*," Lou said. She pointed at the shadowed corner up ahead. "Wait for me by that door."

The girl had opened her mouth to speak, but the first assailant arrived, swinging.

As soon as he saw Lou, he snarled, trying to split her skull with his fists.

Lou pulled the Browning from the holster beneath her jacket and shot the man in the face. His head knocked back. Once, twice.

Busaba screeched, surprised.

Lou pushed her toward their exit. "*Run.*"

She didn't have to be told a third time. Busaba ran.

Two more men lurched into sight, and Lou pulled the trigger without hesitation.

One held his gushing throat, blood seeping from between his fingers. The other man's skullcap was torn off the top of his head. He collapsed first to his knees, then to his stomach, face down.

With the alleyway quiet again, Lou turned, hoping to find Busaba waiting for her in the pocket of shadow beside the door she'd pointed out.

Busaba wasn't there.

She'd run past their exit. She was *still* running.

"Shit." Lou went after her, her own feet pounding the pavement. Again she was reminded of the cold in her arms and legs that she couldn't quite shake. The weakness in her limbs. The way her stomach rolled.

Not now.

As if to prove her point, a gun went off behind her, and concrete from the building on her right splintered, spraying dust and debris across her shoulders.

Faced with a T at the end of the alleyway, Busaba went right.

Lou gained ground on her and caught her just as she reached the edge of the next building.

Busaba screamed and Lou put a hand over her mouth, pulling her against the wall.

Lou could only vaguely note their surroundings. Where were they? It wasn't so much a park as a thin collection of green abutting commercial buildings on all sides.

There were trees. A bench.

More importantly, there was enough shadow for them to escape. Lou felt the world thinning at her back as she held Busaba close.

The girl squirmed, panting, her heart hammering as fast as a caught rabbit's against the arm Lou used to hold her tight.

Two men stepped into view, searching for them. Lou took a moment to get a good look at their faces. She wanted to remember them for later.

She already knew she was coming back.

The man in front, closest to them, was Japanese. The side of his neck was tattooed with an elaborate design, his long black hair pulled back loosely in a bun at the base of his neck to reveal it.

The second had a shaved head, a deep gash in his cheek reminding her of Konstantine's own scar.

The man with the neck tattoo saw them first. His eyes met Lou's and he raised his gun, taking aim. Busaba opened her mouth to scream but the sound of it was swallowed by the shadows as Lou pulled them both through the dark.

5

T he doorbell chimed, and Piper waltzed into the
Crescent City Detective Agency, hoisting a paper
bag over her head into the air. "Order up."
Then she saw the man in tears at King's desk.

King never looked up. He remained focused on the client
in front of him. Piper understood the solemn *I'm sorry but
your partner is a cheating scumbag* look well and took that as
her cue.

Piper lowered the sandwich bag and tiptoed into the
room. She went to her desk as quietly as she could as to not
intrude on the moment.

"I just don't understand how she could do this," the man
said. "We've been married for sixteen years. We have two children. Twin boys!"

"I'm so sorry this has happened to you," King said with
true empathy.

Piper always admired that about him, the way he was
comfortable with the emotions of others. You wouldn't think
it, given the fact he was a burly ex-cop type of dude. But
somehow he was really good at it.

King pushed the tissue box across his desk. "You've every right to be upset."

"How am I going to move past this?" The man took a tissue and dabbed at his red-rimmed eyes. "What am I going to tell the kids?"

"How old are they?" King asked.

"Thirteen."

"Maybe the reason for your divorce is something you can explain later," King offered, his face remaining a mask of sympathy. "When they're old enough to understand."

"Divorce," he said. "Lord help me, I haven't even thought about divorce and what that will do to the kids. Who will get the house? Where will everyone live? What if she tries to take the children?"

King reached into his desk and grabbed a card.

"I know a good divorce attorney if you decide to go that route. She's very good at what she does. Yvonka Pearl. If you tell her you want to keep the kids, she will fight hard to make that happen. You should give her a call."

King slid the card across the desk and the man took it. He looked at it disbelievingly.

"Divorce," he murmured. "I don't want a divorce."

"Then maybe you can work it out," King offered. "Plenty of couples survive infidelity."

Piper knew full and well King had not been one of them, that his first marriage had ended because his wife had cheated on him. Of course, they hadn't had kids. Maybe that had made it easier to walk away.

"I have to go," the man said, rising from his seat. "I have to pick the boys up from school."

"If you need anything else, we'll be here," King said, getting up from his chair.

The man extended his hand. "Thank you for all you've done Mr. King."

King shook it. "I'm sorry I couldn't give you better news."

"I got what I asked for," he said with a forced smile, then was gone.

It wasn't until the bell rang again and the man disappeared into the busy French Quarter street that Piper opened the Gino's bag.

"My bad," she said, casting a nervous glance at the closing door. "The sun was on the glass so I couldn't see what was happening inside. I usually check. For obvious reasons."

"He won't think twice about it," King assured her. "He's got other things on his mind."

King used the edge of a manila folder to sweep the used tissues off his desk into the trash can.

Piper dug a fresh cookie out of the bag and took a big bite. "Ugh, cheating is the worst. Have you ever cheated on someone?"

"Once," King admitted.

Piper raised both her brows. "Really? Why?"

"Revenge. She'd already cheated on me. I'd thought that I'd feel vindicated or that somehow we would be even then. Or maybe that I'd realize it wasn't such a big deal sleeping with someone else and we could get past it. But it was a big deal. To me anyway."

Piper had never cheated on anyone before, but that could be because she'd also never really committed to anyone either. Dani was her first serious relationship.

King unwrapped his BLT and took a big bite. "Delicious. Hard to beat a good BLT. It's the perfect blend of salty and sweet."

"I'll make a fresh pot of coffee," Piper said, trying to ignore the slight panic she felt at thinking of her commitment to Dani.

"No need." He wiped mayo from the corner of his lips. "I just did for Mr. Cruz."

He pointed at the untouched mug of coffee on his desk.

Piper poured herself a cup and doctored it with cream and sugar. "If that wraps up the Cruz case, what do we have left?"

She sank into the chair behind her desk and opened her laptop.

"We're down to nine cases, right?"

"Eight," King corrected, before taking another bite. He took a drink of his own coffee before elaborating. "I closed one of the robbery cases before Cruz arrived. That leaves us with two suspected infidelities, three thefts, the stalking case, and the two DA assists."

"How *is* the DA lately?" Piper dipped the last of her cookie into her coffee before slipping it into her mouth.

She wiggled her eyebrows at King.

He was not amused. "Ms. Miller is just fine."

Piper's grin only deepened. "I bet she is."

"Can we maintain professionalism while in this office?"

"I think it's lovely that you've managed to find love as an old guy," Piper said. "When I'm old I hope I'm still in love."

"It isn't love," King said. "We've been—"

"Go on." Piper was unable to hide her excitement. "Say it. *Having sex.*"

King took a breath before answering. "We've been spending time together. That's it. Probably because we are both so *old.*"

They weren't that old. Piper knew Beth Miller was in her sixties, like King. But she'd stop picking on him.

For now.

She brushed cookie crumbs from her hands and checked her phone. "We've got about three hours before we close up. What do you want me to do?"

"I need you to call Bennigan back and see if he's had any luck finding an offshore account for the fraud case. Then you can call the DA's office and give them these updates."

He tossed the yellow legal pad across the office and she caught it, pinning it down to her desk.

"Are you sure *you* don't want to make the call to your not-girlfriend?"

He looked like he was trying very hard not to roll his eyes at her. "You can do it. You'll probably only get one of her assistants anyway. Don't be chatty."

She placed a hand over her chest in mock offense. "When am I chatty?"

King ignored this. "After that, I need you to go through the database again for any known phone numbers and addresses for Hathaway."

"That's one of the thieves, right?"

"Alleged," he countered. "Alleged until convicted."

"Fine. Is she the *alleged* thief who took the company computer, or is it the guy who cleared out Bethel's safe?"

"The computer."

"Got it," she said, making notes to herself. She read everything back to him for confirmation.

"One more thing," he said. "How do you feel about doing the stalker case? Solo."

"Are you serious?" Piper sat up straighter. "Really?"

He was smiling now. "Really."

"Like the *whole* case?"

"The whole case," he said, sipping his coffee.

"Evidence collection, interviews and testimonies—"

"All of it," he said.

She was ready to burst.

Piper had been begging him for weeks to trust her to do more of the investigative work on her own. He took her to interviews, of course, but he rarely sent her out to collect evidence or do interviews on her own. It was dangerous. People didn't like it when you snuck up on them.

King had tried to explain that he was good at diffusing

confrontational situations because he'd worked as a DEA agent for decades, and that even if his skills failed him, he could take a punch.

That was usually the point where he also emphasized that Piper was half his size, and though he knew she could handle herself, it didn't mean he wanted to put her in danger.

Now he was talking about letting her take the lead on a case. Her very own case.

She couldn't wait to tell Dani.

"I'd rather you took someone with you," King was saying. "Lou is best, but I'd settle for Dani."

She felt like her face was going to split in half from smiling. "I've been practicing the surveillance techniques you showed me."

A short laugh escaped him. "On who?"

"Randos in the Quarter. I'm getting pretty good."

"Just remember we need good pictures. Anything that proves he's hanging around her place, following her. As long as your camera hand is steady and he doesn't suspect you, you'll be fine."

"Aye, aye!" She was bouncing in her seat.

"Oh, and don't forget that unless evidence is obtained lawfully, we can't use it in court."

She saluted him. "I'll start tonight."

"Just make me one promise," he said, leveling her with one of his serious stares.

"Anything."

"Promise me you'll be careful and that if you run into trouble, you will tell me."

"I will," she said. "I absolutely a hundred percent *will*."

King watched Piper sail through the rest of the day with a pep in her step. He loved that he'd put her in such a great mood. He'd known for a while how much a case of her own would mean to the girl. She'd made her intentions to pursue criminal justice clear. She was taking classes at Delgado with plans to transfer to a bigger school to finish out her degree. More importantly, he could tell her interest in the subject was genuine. She asked him endless questions and was extremely meticulous in her legwork. She'd only been working at the agency for two years, but she'd come a long way in that time. More than that, she often surprised him with her ideas and methods for handling their roadblocks.

He couldn't deny it. She was good at this.

The only problem was the last time he'd been a mentor—to Lou's father, Jack Thorne—it had ended with his charge being brutally murdered in front of his daughter.

King didn't want to make the same mistake twice.

His good feeling abruptly vanished when Mel walked through the agency door at 4:30, twisting the bangles on her wrist nervously.

"What's wrong?" he asked as soon as he saw her.

Lady was there too, the Belgian Malinois tucked close to Mel's side, looking up at her. The dog kept flicking her ears back against her head.

"I need to talk to you about something," Mel said, still touching her wrists self-consciously. "If you have a minute."

"Alone?" King asked. His eyes flicked to Piper.

Piper paused in her typing, looking up from her computer. "Is it about the dream?"

Mel nodded.

Piper closed the laptop. "I'll finish this upstairs, then I'll head out to do the surveillance on the stalker."

King wasn't sure why Piper was giving them space to talk about a dream that she already knew about, but he didn't question her decision. "All right. But remember my cell will be on all night if something comes up. You better call me if you need me."

Piper gave him a thumbs up. "You got it, boss."

As she gathered up her stuff and cleared her desk, Mel sank into the chair that Cruz had occupied earlier.

King took the moment to look her over, trying to gain a sense of how she was.

She looked tired. The circles under her eyes were dark, as if she hadn't slept well the night before. By the way she kept playing with the bangles on her wrist, he knew she was bothered, but how serious was this?

The door at the end of the office clicked shut, and Piper's footsteps echoed on the carpeted stairs as she climbed them to the apartment above the agency she and Dani shared.

When Mel didn't say anything, fidgeting with the deep purple scarf wrapped around her head, he asked, "What's this about a dream? Are you having nightmares about Terry?"

"No, it's not Terry," she said, clasping her hands in her lap. "And it's not a nightmare, it's an omen."

King arched his brow. Melandra knew that he wasn't a superstitious man. He liked to believe in an afterlife, if only so that he could hold on to the ideas that he'd see Lucy again someday and that the assholes of the world would get what was coming to them.

He knew what Mel's faith was to her. That *she* was superstitious and that she had a set of occult beliefs, like her faith in that battered deck of tarot cards, a centuries-old family heirloom that her grandmother had passed down to her. She also had her instincts and intuitions, and she'd been right more than a few times. He knew that too.

But she'd never talked about dreams before.

"What kind of omen?" he said. "Is someone going to get hurt?"

"Yes," she said simply. "If I don't do something about it."

King's heart kicked. "Is it Piper?"

"No," Mel said, and loosed a breath, seeming to share and understand his apprehension. "Nor Dani. We never can tell with Lou, but she wasn't in this dream and I didn't get the Death card when I did a spread."

"No Death card," he said, knowing only what Mel had told him about tarot, which wasn't much. "That's good news, right?"

"Maybe." Here she tried for a smile.

Lady rested her head on Mel's lap, and the woman placed a dark hand on the dog's head and began to pet it gently, absentmindedly.

"*Ma grande*," she cooed.

Lady's tail thumped against the floor.

"Grandmamie put a lot of stock in dreams," Mel said at last, still stroking Lady's head. "She said it was either one of two things. God was talkin' to you, or *you* were talkin' to you. And whichever it may be, you'd best pay attention."

King didn't interrupt.

"I've been having a dream about a girl. It's the same dream for several nights now. I'm down by the market, by the river, and I see her, looking out over the water. She's young and pretty and just looking out at the waves until she turns around. That's when I see she's covered in blood. Just the whole front of her. She's soaked with it. Then she says she's sorry. *I'm sorry, I'm sorry, I didn't mean to.* Then she falls off the walkway and into the river. I always try to catch her but I'm never quick enough."

Lady whined.

"Have you ever had dreams like this before?" King asked.

"No, not like this. I would have reoccurring nightmares about Terry, of course—but I've slept like a baby since he's been dead."

Terry, Mel's abusive ex-husband. Now there was someone King hoped there was a hell for.

"If I can ask, why are you worried about this dream? What makes it different than the others?"

"It feels different. Heck, I know it's different because of how clear it is. Grandmamie said these are what we call debt dreams. They're from God."

"God," King repeated, and hoped he didn't sound condescending.

"Yes. He wants me to save this girl. And I gotta try."

King rose and went to the coffee pot to make himself a fresh cup. "Can I make you a coffee?"

"Sure," she said. "Black, two sugars."

King did as he was told and placed the sky-blue ceramic mug in front of her.

"Are you telling me because you want me to help you save this girl?" King asked.

She looked at him over the rim of the mug. "I know you don't believe what I believe—"

"We've been over this," he interrupted. "You believe it and that's enough for me."

Her shoulders relaxed a little but not enough.

"Just look at Lou," King said. "She does incredible things I'd have never believed, even if Jack had told me himself."

Jack hadn't. King's protégé had been a loving and protective father until the day he'd died. It hadn't mattered how close the two of them had been, Jack would've never shared his daughter's secrets.

"I might not *understand* what you see or what you do," he told her, "but I believe in *you*. You're my friend. I'll help if I can."

Her shoulders slumped back against the chair. "I don't know where to start. I don't have a name or an address. Piper said that we could use a sketch artist to make a picture of her and that from there, maybe you can identify her."

King was impressed, feeling more sure than ever that Piper was capable of investigating on her own. "That's a pretty good idea. You want me to walk you down to see Luke Landry?"

"Yes, please. That would be nice," she said, taking another drink of coffee.

The color was returning to her face. King hoped it wasn't just the steam from the coffee and that she was actually feeling better about all of this.

"Once we get the sketch done, what's next?" she said. "I'd be lying if I said it didn't feel hopeless."

"There's plenty of databases with public photos to check against. I'll have Piper help us sort through the possible matches. I'd say stick to New Orleans, but we might have to widen the search. We get a lot of tourists here, and you don't have any idea of where she's from, do you?"

"I feel like I've been asked to find a needle in a haystack."

King drank his coffee. "If the dreams *are* from God, you'd have to believe that he'd put her on your path, right? Otherwise, how else will you have the chance to help her?"

Mel tilted her head to one side. "Sometimes he doesn't make it so easy."

"Landry will be down there until six. Let's finish our coffees and go."

Mel finished first. That left King rushing to catch up.

He packed up his satchel, checked that his keys were in the pocket of his duster jacket, and stood to leave.

On the stoop of 777 Royal Street, King locked up the agency a few minutes before their usual five p.m. closing time. The cool January wind rolled down the street and blew Mel's hair into her face. She pulled her coat tighter around her.

Lady didn't mind the cold, her tail thumping happily against King's leg.

"After you," he said, gesturing up Royal Street in the direction of the precinct.

King hated to see the worry in Mel's eyes. She hadn't been like this in a long time. He hoped that whatever *this* was, it would resolve soon. Mel had an unhealthy habit of blaming herself for things that weren't her fault. For most of her adult life, she'd thought she'd hit and killed a woman, a lie her ex-husband had perpetuated because it kept his pockets flush and Mel under his thumb.

But there had been no woman.

Then she'd accidentally shot Lou and it had taken them months to convince her that it truly was an accident, that anyone could've done the same. How was she to know Lou was about to materialize in the path of her bullet?

Please let us find the girl, King thought. *Let her be alive and well.*

If this went sideways, if somehow they found the girl but it was too late, if she got hurt or killed, he didn't want this to be one more thing that Mel could use like a weapon against herself.

6

———

When Lou found herself in Konstantine's office again, he wasn't alone. Stefano was mid-sentence, gesturing emphatically about something, when Lou stepped from the dark corner into the room with Busaba in her arms.

Konstantine looked to her immediately.

Busaba saw him and rushed across the office to him. *"Lung!"*

Lou arched a brow as the girl threw her arms around his neck.

"It means uncle. She knows me as Uncle Konstantine," he said plainly, stroking her hair.

The girl was sobbing now, a deep, pitiful release. Konstantine held her, cooing reassurances in her ears.

"I need a shower," Lou said, unwilling to endure her wet, cold toes a minute longer.

Stefano inclined his head to her, a subtle acknowledgment of her before she left.

Lou returned it, amused. Things had started off hostile between them, Lou and Konstantine's right-hand man. But he'd seemed to soften to her ever since she'd killed the Albanians threatening Konstantine with war. At least now he didn't look like he wanted to put a bullet in her every time she walked into a room.

Stepping from the dark, Lou pushed open the door to her emptied linen closet and found her apartment.

It was after seven in the evening, the winter night made purple by the glow of artificial light. The cloud cover made seeing the stars impossible, but the river still shone beneath the illuminated arch that stood guard over its waters. The wind caused white waves to form on the gunmetal-gray surface.

Reluctantly, she gave up the view for a shower. She ran the water as hot as she could stand it and stood beneath its pounding stream until her skin had turned bright red from the assault.

Her fatigue grew stronger. In addition to that unwelcome heaviness in her limbs, her head was beginning to buzz at the edges.

I'm just hungry, she told herself. *I can't even remember the last time I stopped to eat.*

Once the water began to turn cold, Lou climbed out and dried herself. She chose thicker clothes than usual. A black t-shirt and one of her father's faded flannels over thick black cargo pants. Her socks were wool that went all the way up to the knees.

She checked her fridge and found half of a box of Pad Thai with beef. When had she gotten this? Two days ago? Three?

She ate it with the wooden chopsticks the restaurant in LA had provided and drank a tall glass of water from the sink.

Her mind turned to La Loon then. To that empty, silent beach where she'd left the killer's corpse. Lou hoped that Konstantine was right. That Jabbers had simply been out hunting or sleeping, or otherwise preoccupied. And hadn't it struck her as strange that the creature had always been there when she'd arrived? No matter the hour or day?

She will be there when I go back, she assured herself. *She will be on the shore as if she hadn't gone missing at all.*

It was strange to be worrying about such a beast. Given its nightmarish size, its speed, its ferocity, it seemed as invincible as a creature could be.

Yet she *was* worried.

Lou could always just dump the bodies in Blood Lake, and they would be eaten by the strange orca-like creatures that patrolled its depths.

But there was no replacing Jabbers.

Who would have thought I'd grow to care so much about her, she marveled as she stepped back into the linen closet. If she'd told her ten-year-old self, *Hey, that creature that just took a huge bite out of your shoulder will be like a best friend one day*, she'd have never believed it.

She would've run away screaming.

Lou pressed her back against the bare closet wall and exhaled. Her headache had softened a little at its edges, probably because of the water she drank.

And the darkness helped too.

When she stepped into the world again, they were still in Konstantine's office.

Lou wasn't sure what she'd walked in on, but Busaba was on her knees, pleading with her hands clasped in front of her. Tears streamed down her cheeks as she begged Konstantine for—what?

Whatever it was, Stefano was unimpressed. He rubbed the crease between his brows, his unhappiness as apparent as ever.

Konstantine's expression remained unreadable as he

looked up from the girl. His eyes held the dancing flame from the last of the firelight.

Lou couldn't read his face. Though who he was hiding his emotions from, she couldn't be sure. The girl or Stefano? Or maybe even her.

Busaba followed Konstantine's gaze, and when she saw Lou lingering in the shadows, she lit up and rushed over to her, grabbing her hands.

"Please," Busaba pleaded, her brown eyes bright. "*Please.*"

Lou looked to Konstantine.

He said, "She wants you to save the other girls."

Lou looked to Stefano. "You don't?"

Stefano loosed a controlled breath. "If the prostitution ring belongs to who I believe it belongs to, it will be big trouble for us."

"We don't know it belongs to him," Konstantine said.

Stefano gave him a look as if he thought Konstantine the stupidest man in the world. To Lou, he said, "You took this one from Takeshita Street, no?"

"Yes."

Busaba was still holding Lou's hands and crying. Lou guided her to the fireplace and eased her down into the empty chair beside Konstantine's. But she wouldn't let go of Lou's hand.

Lou was too tired to fight her for it, so she let the girl hold it.

"Riku Yamamoto owns most of Tokyo, and our relationship—"

"We don't need to discuss this now." Konstantine gave Stefano a cold look. "Not while we have company."

Lou knew he wasn't shutting Stefano up for her sake. There was little Konstantine did—or any mob boss in this world, for that matter—that Lou didn't know about or couldn't uncover with a bit of digging. She could only assume he didn't want to talk about it in front of Busaba.

Lou suspected that while Somchai might be a good friend, it didn't mean Konstantine wanted to share intimate details of his business with him.

"Please," Busaba said again, her tears wet on Lou's hand. "Please help them."

She sniffed, and Stefano pulled the purple handkerchief from his front suit pocket and handed it to her.

What a gentleman, Lou thought.

The girl's dark eyes were huge and wet. With her round face and uptilted nose, she still looked like a child.

A child, Lou thought coldly. *She's a fucking child.*

She was going to murder Riku and all his men regardless of what Konstantine decided.

"We will help," Konstantine assured her. When she didn't seem to understand, he said, "Yes. Yes."

Lou's and Konstantine's eyes met.

"Busaba, your father misses you very much. You need to go home now," Konstantine said. "*Amore mio*, may I ask you to take Busaba home? You are the quickest."

Irritation spiked in her mind. She didn't want to run any more errands. She wanted to lie down and put a pillow over her face. The slight lift she'd felt from the shower, water, and beef Pad Thai seemed to be losing its power already. She was fading fast.

"It's almost three in the morning," she said, wondering if she sounded short.

"It will be after eight in the morning there." Konstantine must've seen something in her expression because he hesitated. "Meet me at the apartment after?"

His apartment.

"Fine," she said. Lou melded with the shadows of the

office, stepping away from the inviting heat of the fireplace with her hand on Busaba's arm.

Busaba let out a little cry of surprise as the tight space formed around them. Lou's elbows pressed against something, and as she turned, glass rattled. She turned again and found shelves that creaked on all sides. The smell of something sweet and earthy filled the space. Grain? Wheat?

She found a handle and turned it, pushing against the door.

The light spilled in and revealed that they were in a pantry. A sack of rice sat on the floor beneath the shelves, elevated on a crate as if to keep it off the tile.

Busaba stepped into the kitchen, calling out, *"Phaw! Phaw!"*

A man yelled in return. There was a thunder of footsteps on the ceiling above Lou's head and it seemed as if the whole house shook.

Then there were other voices. A woman screaming, children squealing.

Busaba took a moment to fuss with her hair, her dress, as if realizing for the first time what she was wearing and what her family would see her in.

A woman with a wiry body and gray in her dark hair burst into the kitchen first. She threw her arms around Busaba. Sobs erupted from her slender throat. She kept repeating the girl's name over and over again, cupping her cheeks and squeezing her shoulders.

The mother, Lou presumed, was still crushing Busaba against her and crying into her hair when the children arrived.

A boy and a girl hugged her legs, and Busaba tried to touch and hold each one in turn, but she only had so many arms and hands, and the woman clutching her was sobbing as if she'd never let her daughter go.

None of them took notice of Lou, who stood perfectly still in the doorway of the pantry.

Lou couldn't get a good sense of the size or shape of the house from where she stood, but the kitchen was decent, modern. The sunlight coming from the windows was bright and inviting. The street noise was loud, and the rip of a motorcycle blared past the window.

That's when Somchai entered the kitchen, his hair and shirt disheveled. His eyes wide and red-rimmed. He grabbed Busaba and looked her over as if to make sure she wasn't a ghost.

Somehow satisfied, he crushed her to him and spoke rapidly in the family language. Lou assumed it was some dialect of Thai.

Then Somchai looked up and saw Lou for the first time.

He started.

Lou wasn't sure why. Her guns were put away. Standing in the doorway of the pantry, Lou didn't think she looked particularly menacing.

"Thank you," he said. "Thank you. Thank you."

He kept repeating it like a prayer.

"Thank Konstantine," she said, and stepped back into the pantry, her job done.

Lou closed the door and was gone.

When the world formed around her again, she was in Konstantine's dark bedroom. Cold air was seeping through the crack around the window overlooking the Arno River. Conversations and music wafted up from the street below.

She was cold by the window. And her body ached.

It was rare that she felt chilled.

Was she getting sick? Was it spending all that time in soaking-wet socks in January? It couldn't be. She'd been doing it for years. Why in the world would she get sick now?

Lou fished an extra pair of socks out of her drawer.

She'd told Konstantine she'd wanted this drawer. He'd protested because it was smaller than the others in his dresser, but it was what she'd wanted so he'd been forced to acquiesce. Because of its size, she couldn't keep much in it. She usually only kept one change of clothes at a time. Plus an extra sweater and socks.

She shrugged out of the leather jacket, folding it over the arm of the wooden chair in the corner where Lou liked to watch Konstantine sit in the mornings and pull on his socks and lace his leather shoes. This was usually before he rolled up the sleeves of his dress shirts, revealing the muscular forearms she loved even more.

She pulled the sweater down over her father's flannel and tugged the second pair of thick socks on over the ones she already wore.

That's when she heard the door creak open, and Konstantine's familiar gait scuffing across the stone floor.

"*Amore mio?*" he called out.

She moved through the darkness and was hit first by the smell of him, even before she fully hooked her arms around his waist and buried her face in the crook of his neck.

"Here," she breathed along his skin.

"Your hands are cold," he said, placing his hands over hers.

"I'm cold," she admitted.

He turned then, concern in his eyes.

"Your cheeks are flushed. Do you have a fever?"

How was she to know? She hadn't taken her temperature. She wasn't even sure she owned a thermometer.

She could hear Aunt Lucy scolding her. *When was the last time you ate something green? Or slept for eight whole hours?*

Konstantine hung up his coat and stuffed his gloves into the pockets. Then he was pressing his hands to her face again.

"I think you have a fever."

"Make me a cup of coffee," she said. Because she still

hadn't figured out how his moka worked. His coffee was usually better than what she could get in a café, but she had yet to manifest the patience to fool with the device.

"I'll make you a cup, but I want to take your temperature before you drink it," he said. "Will you let me?"

Her irritation spiked again. That wasn't like her, to be so short-tempered. "Fine."

She sank down onto his sofa.

Taking the weight off her bones was a blessed release.

Konstantine got the moka started before running up the stairs to the bathroom.

She waited on the sofa, trying to keep her growing irritation in place.

I'm not sick, she thought. *I don't get sick.*

Konstantine reappeared with a little red bag, a medical cross stamped on its exterior. He rummaged inside it until he found the thermometer. It beeped when he turned it on.

"Open up," he said.

She lifted her tongue. While it rested between her pressed lips, she watched the numbers creep up. *Thirty-seven. Thirty-seven point two. Thirty-seven point four. Thirty-seven point six.*

How was she supposed to know if she had a fever when the numbers were in metric?

It beeped, and Konstantine pulled it from her mouth and frowned at it.

"It's thirty-eight degrees," he told her. "You have a fever, *amore mio.*"

The moka called for attention and Konstantine rose. He washed the thermometer in the sink before making her a cup of coffee.

"It's decaffeinated," he confessed, placing the warm mug in her extended hand. "Will you go to sleep after you drink it?"

When she didn't immediately answer, he added, "Please."

She wasn't ready to admit how delicious the idea of sleep was to her aching body.

Worse, she didn't want to ask that he come with her. That she liked the idea of curling up into the warmth of his back and sleeping like that, with him beside her.

"Do you need anything else?" He frowned down at her from where he stood with his hands on his hips. "Can you eat?"

"I ate a little after my shower. I'm just—I'm tired."

His frown deepened when she pulled back. "Come to bed. You can bring the coffee."

The shadows at her back softened, and she was through them and into Konstantine's bed before his first footfall rang on the steps.

She rested her head against his headboard and sipped the coffee, enjoying the way it warmed her chest. Once in his bedroom, Konstantine began to strip down for his own shower. He always showered before getting into bed. It didn't matter if it was after three in the morning, as it was tonight—he would still wash the day from his body first.

Lou admired the look of him. She sipped her coffee and let her eyes lazily trace the tattoos covering his arm from shoulder to elbow.

It reminded her suddenly of the Japanese man who'd almost shot her. He'd had a tattoo on his neck.

"I should go back to my apartment," she said.

His hands froze on the belt buckle. "Why?"

"If I'm sick, I shouldn't be in your bed, breathing on you and your pillows. You'll get sick too."

"Most viruses have an incubation period," he said. "You've been in my bed every night this week. If you were going to give me a virus, you would've done so already."

Lou wasn't sure his medical assessment was a sound one, but she was too tired to argue.

Konstantine disappeared into the bathroom and reappeared with two white pills in his hand.

"For the fever," he told her.

She wondered if he took off his shirt first just in hopes of getting her to take the pills. Did he really think her that easy?

"*Amore mio*," he pleaded. "Take them."

Octavia, the British Blue, chose that moment to jump onto the foot of the bed and make her presence known.

She'd been hiding somewhere. She did that when Lou came. But Konstantine's voice, low and soothing, had clearly been too much for her to resist.

"*Ciao, bella*," he said, and scratched Octavia behind her ears. The cat pushed her head into the palm of his offered hand.

Konstantine still held the pills in the other. Lou took them, washing them down with the coffee quickly so they wouldn't melt.

He bent and placed a kiss on her lips. His were cool on hers.

"Thank you," he said, and kissed her again.

Only then did he disappear into the bathroom.

Lou finished her coffee and placed the mug on the side table. She snuggled under the covers and listened to Konstantine sing some song in Italian while the cat stretched herself long at the foot of the bed, waiting for him to return. Lou didn't mind the cat.

It wasn't *her* face she tapped in the morning asking for food and attention.

Lou had almost dropped off to sleep when she felt the bed shift and Konstantine slide in beside her. She tightened reflexively, coming half out of the dream she'd been having. Something about Jabbers and the oil-black shores of La Loon.

"It's only me," Konstantine said, and pressed a hand to her forehead.

Her dream was fading out of focus no matter how hard she tried to hold on to it. There was something important, receding into the black.

"I'm sorry if I woke you when I took the call," he said.

Lou hadn't heard any call. She told him so.

"Somchai wanted to thank me. He wants you to know how grateful he is that Busaba is home safe."

"How badly was she hurt?" Lou said. It had been hard to tell at the time if the girl had been beaten or raped.

Konstantine's face tightened. "It's unclear. She won't tell them what happened except the details about how she was taken to Japan. She's given very little information for someone who has been gone for over a week."

"If she's leaving things out, we can assume—"

"I know," he said.

"I'm going to kill them."

Konstantine smoothed the hair away from her face. "You don't need to worry about that now. You need to rest."

"What about the other girls?" she said.

"You can't help anyone unless you get better. *Rest.*"

With a flash of clarity, Lou remembered her dream.

She'd been standing on the shore of La Loon, looking up at those twin moons in the yellow sky, when she'd heard a cry behind her. It had been so desperate, so mournful, that she'd turned away from the sky to see what pitiful creature had made it.

It was Jabbers.

She'd been torn apart by something. Her serpentine body had been ripped open at the abdomen, her insides spilling out of her.

Who could do such a thing to you? Lou thought. *What* could do such a thing?

"Something is wrong in La Loon," she said. "Something is wrong with Jabbers."

"It's the fever, *amore mio*." He pressed a cool hand to her forehead. "It gives everyone bad dreams."

"No," she said. "I can feel it. Something's happened."

He considered this.

She rolled her eyes up to meet him. The room was soft at the edges. There was something wrong with the light, or maybe her eyes.

"You said I'm full of the microbes from the water there." She licked her lips. "That they're the reason I always heal so quickly."

"*Sì*," he said.

"Then why am I sick?"

"I don't know."

"I don't get sick," she said.

In the ten years since she'd started hauling bodies to La Loon, Lou couldn't remember the last time she'd been sick.

"We could take a sample of your blood and see if something has changed," he said. "*After* you've slept."

She wondered if he was only saying something to calm her, anything to get her to close her eyes and go to sleep.

The throbbing in her temples intensified. She squeezed her eyes tight against it.

"Tomorrow," she said.

Her sleep was not restful. Her skin felt alive, itching, crawling with unease.

The nightmares continued.

All night long, Lou wandered the red shores of Blood Lake, looking for Jabbers, trying to follow the sound of the beast's screams.

7

———

King sat in the plastic chair across from Luke Landry's desk, while Mel did her best to describe the girl she'd seen in her dream.

King hoped it didn't look like he hated being here, or that he was annoyed to be helping Mel with this case, if he could call it a case.

The truth was, he blamed the chair.

It was little more than shapely swirls of plastic, meant for a much smaller person. Someone bigger than five feet tall and a hundred and forty pounds was in for a world of pain. The edges that were meant to slightly envelop the body for comfort dug into his back and ribs.

The bottom of the chair rose up a little, like the rising swoosh of the letter J, but instead of cradling his weight, it pressed mercilessly into the back of his thighs.

No matter what he did, he couldn't quite find a bearable position, and that meant he couldn't be still. Yet if he stood up, it might make Mel feel like he was in a hurry or signal that the interview should end.

"The hair was strawberry blond," Melandra said. "Mostly

blond, but it had this orange shade to it, if you know what I mean."

Once Mel's eyes cut to him for the sixteenth time, King gave up.

"I'm sorry," he confessed finally. "It's the chair."

"We're almost done," Landry said, barely glancing up from the pad in his hands.

For minutes, the only sounds filling the room were the squeak of King's chair and the scratch of Landry's pencil across the pad. Finally, he turned the sketch toward Melandra for approval.

"Very close," she told him. "Her chin is just a little pointier here at the end, and her eyes are darker. A very dark brown."

Though the sketch was black and white, King understood what she meant. Landry had only shaded the irises lightly, perhaps only to give the pupils distinction.

King stood, stretching. The small room was too warm.

"What about this?" Landry asked.

Mel straightened. "Why, you're very good at this, Mr. Landry. It looks just like her."

"And here my parents said my art degree would amount to nothing." Landry gave them both a friendly grin.

He looked pleased with himself as he tore the page from his sketchbook, slipped it into a sheath of protective plastic, and handed it over to Mel.

Mel accepted it.

King extended his hand across the desk toward Landry. "Thank you for your time. It's appreciated."

"It's no problem, Robbie. I owed you anyway."

It was true that King had agreed to tail Celine, Landry's oldest daughter, home from school for nearly a week last year. She'd been coming home later than usual, hanging out with new kids that her parents hadn't recognized, and had refused to give a clear answer on what she was doing in those missing hours of time.

Landry and his wife were blessedly relieved when King told them that it wasn't drugs or a secret boyfriend. It was rock 'n' roll. Celine was spending her hours after school in a friend's garage, learning how to drum.

"Better their house than mine," Landry had said.

"How much do we owe you?" King asked.

Landry shook his head and held up his palm. "I'm still on company time. I'm paid."

King touched the imaginary bill of his imaginary cap in a salute, and they slipped out of the overheated office into the frosty day.

On the steps of the police precinct he asked, "Are you happy with it?"

Because Mel wasn't above saying thank you for things she didn't like.

"He did a fine job," she said. "It looks just like her. I only wish it had a bit of color."

"We won't need it. There are programs that will pull the face and look for matches even without the color. It has to because sometimes photocopies or black-and-white footage is all we can get of a person."

"I'll leave that part to you then." Mel handed him the sketch. "How long does it usually take?"

"If she's been reported missing or has a record, no time at all. If she's been a good girl and nothing comes up, longer. Is that going to be all right with you?"

Mel exhaled a puff of breath. It fogged white in the air around them as she pulled her coat tighter, tucking her chin into the fur lining at its neck. They descended the steps together.

"I don't have much choice," she said. "Without a name or address, my only clue is the riverwalk, down by the French

Market. I'm already walking past there twice a day with Lady, just on the off chance I see her there. I haven't."

King threw an arm over her shoulder and squeezed. "We'll find her. Don't worry."

That was the exact moment, with Mel in his arms, that King looked up and saw Beth Miller, the DA, coming up the street.

King slowly slid his arm off of Mel's shoulder, controlling the moment to make it look purposeful and calm.

If he'd torn it off, he'd have looked guiltier.

You don't have to feel guilty, he reminded himself. *You're comforting a friend.*

Maybe Beth doesn't even care. You're having sex. You're not married to each other.

"Good evening, Robbie," Beth said with a smile. It seemed natural enough. She ran a hand down the front of her black suede coat. "Miss Melandra."

"Good evening to you too, Ms. Miller," Mel said.

Mel had taken one step away from King as if maybe she was thinking the same thing King was, how cozy they must've looked with his arm around her outside the police station.

Beth motioned at the precinct. "Everything all right? I saw you two come outta there."

Then her eyes went to the sketch in King's hand.

"You lookin' for somebody?"

King wet his lips. "A friend of Mel's."

"Oh, I'm sorry to hear it," Beth said, her face a mask of concern. "She's a pretty little thing. I hope you find her safe and sound."

"You and me both," Melandra said, burrowing her chin deeper into her coat.

"Yes, it's cold out here, isn't it?" Beth tugged at her gloves and adjusted the hat on her head. "We ought to get out of it while we can. You still coming over tonight, Robbie?"

Dinner. He'd almost forgotten.

The look in her eyes told him she realized it as soon as he did.

"Wouldn't miss it. I might just be a few minutes later than we'd agreed. I still need to go back to my apartment. Is that all right?"

She smiled up at him over the rim of her black glasses. "It's just fine by me. You have a good night, Ms. Durand."

"You too."

Beth disappeared into the police precinct as King and Mel started down Royal Street in the direction of home.

"I hope you've told her we're just friends," Melandra said, slipping her hands into her pocket.

"I have."

Mel glanced over her shoulder at the station, the furrow between her brow deepening. "It may bear repeating."

Piper had just submitted the final draft of her CRJU 160 paper when Dani walked through the door of their apartment. She'd heard Dani open the agency, the familiar bell above the door calling out, before the *clack clack clack* of her boot heels echoed across the polished wood. Then she was up the stairs and pushing open the door to their loft apartment above.

"Hey, baby," Piper called out from the sofa as the door clicked shut.

"Hey," she said, breathless from the stairs. "What were you thinking for dinner?"

Her thick dark hair was down and windswept from her walk home and her cheeks were red from the cool winter wind. She smelled like the outside as she bent and placed a cool kiss on Piper's lips.

As soon as she tried to pull back, Piper pulled her into another one.

"Dinner," Dani whispered. "I am starving."

"There's a sushi place across the street from Samantha's apartment."

Dani's forehead furrowed. "Who's Samantha?"

"The victim of the stalking case King gave me today," Piper said, closing her laptop.

Dani's brows went up. "He gave you a case?"

Piper was unable to hide her excitement. "The *whole* enchilada. I get to do all of it all by myself. Even the DA paperwork."

She wrapped Dani in her arms as soon as the girl had her coat off. She wore Piper's favorite top. A tight white turtleneck that accentuated her curves.

"I don't know who gets excited about paperwork, but if you're happy, I'm happy, baby." Dani's concern was clear, but so was her attempt to hide it away as to not dampen Piper's thrill of being in charge of her very own case for the first time.

"He wants me to take you or Lou with me," Piper added, knowing this would relax her. "So we could go to the sushi place across from her apartment together. If we can get a seat by the window, I can watch the building while we eat."

"I wouldn't mind some udon. I love a hot noodle soup on a cold day," Dani said, returning Piper's squeeze. "But tell me now who's paying because I'm not having another fight with you like what happened at that chicken wing place. I'm still embarrassed for that hostess."

It was true that a slight disagreement as to who was responsible for their meal led to a physical chase around the restaurant, with Piper holding Dani's card above her head like a battle flag.

If Piper was being honest, it was not her proudest moment.

"That's the best part. King's paying." Piper ran her fingers through Dani's hair. "He covers all food expenses while working, and I'll be working. Are you mad that it will be a working dinner?"

Dani tilted her head. "No, because I'm also technically on call. I haven't heard back from two of my contacts about the embezzlement piece I'm writing. I really need those testimonies before the story goes to print Friday."

"I will forgive your workaholism if you forgive mine," Piper said, releasing her. "Besides, I like it when we work together."

Dani smiled down at her. "Me too. It's sweet when I look up and you're there. We feel like a team."

"We *are* a team," Piper said.

Something in Dani's eyes softened. "Let me wash up for dinner, then we'll go."

Piper grabbed her again. "Kiss me again and then you can wash up."

Dani kissed her for real now. Not the sweet peck of a welcome home kiss, but a deep, lingering embrace. It warmed Piper to her toes and made her insides twist in on themselves.

When she finally pulled back, Dani's eyes were glassy with desire. "What time did you want to leave?"

She was biting her lip now. Piper knew what that meant.

"You said you were starving. And that you wanted a shower."

"I have competing needs," Dani admitted.

"We don't have time." Piper laughed.

"If we're quick—"

"We're never quick. You'll want to reciprocate and brush your hair, and if you can't you'll be pissed."

"I don't get *pissed* if I can't reciprocate." A snort escaped

Dani as she came up onto her toes to kiss Piper again. "And I definitely don't get mad if I can't brush my hair."

"Oh yes you do." Piper placed her hands on Dani's waist as she began backing them toward the bedroom. Fortunately, Piper knew this route well enough to make it with her eyes closed.

"Just you then," Dani said into Piper's mouth, the voice low enough to be a purr. "And I'll bring a hairbrush."

It was closer to 6:45 when they arrived at the sushi place in Fillmore. At this hour there were a lot of students still walking around, hats pulled down over their heads and coats held close as if this were actually cold weather. Piper had spent enough time slipping around the world with Lou to know that what touched New Orleans wasn't frigid by any measure, and she was happy about that. She wasn't made for colder climes.

Dani took another drink of green tea from one of the little cups that came with the pot they'd ordered upon arriving. Behind the steaming cup she wore a contented grin.

"I told you I wouldn't get mad," Dani said haughtily.

"Way to prove me wrong, babe." Piper smiled. "To be clear, I intend to finish what we started when we get home."

Dani's cheeks flushed. "I look forward to it."

Dani's phone went off and her face lit up. "This is my contact."

"Go on then."

Dani snatched her coat off the back of the chair and stepped out of the restaurant as she answered the phone.

"Daniella Allendale speaking." The glass door swung shut behind her.

Piper twisted the silver ring on her thumb and watched Dani pace beneath a live oak tree.

Her attention slid away when a light clicked on in the apartment building beyond Dani's head.

Piper counted the windows and realized the light was coming from Samantha's apartment.

The girl was home an hour earlier than her schedule said she'd be.

Piper searched the area, looking for any sign of the stalker, for anyone with a hat pulled down or a collar flipped up to hide their face. Dark sunglasses.

There was no one watching the building except for Piper.

Five minutes later, she spotted Samantha talking to someone by the door to the apartment building. The light in her window upstairs was still on.

"Here's your order of spring rolls," the waitress said, placing the fried rolls on the table with a smile.

"Thank you," Piper said, before her gaze slid to Samantha again.

The girl still wore her work uniform beneath her puffy black coat and the bedazzled messenger bag slung over one shoulder.

"Is she leaving again?" Piper muttered.

The light's still on. Maybe I should let her know I'll be hanging around outside her apartment tonight, in case she needs anything.

Abandoning her tea and spring rolls, Piper rose from the table and went outside just as Dani was ending her phone call.

Dani slipped the phone into her coat pocket. "What is it?"

"I'm going to let Samantha know we're here. Can you go back to the table so the waitress doesn't think we ditched?"

"Sure." Dani gave her arm a squeeze before going back inside.

Samantha had turned away from her friend, heading toward the double doors as Piper began jogging toward her.

"Samantha, hey!"

The girl's hand hesitated on the handle, her face pinched in a frown. The lines relaxed when she recognized Piper.

"Hey." She released the door. "You're that assistant from the detective agency."

"Piper." She extended her hand. "You're home early."

I shouldn't have said that, she thought. *It sounds creepy.*

Please. She knows you know her schedule. You're supposed to be looking out for her.

Yeah, but I didn't have to make it weird.

Piper shoved these voices down. "I just wanted to let you know that we'll be watching your place tonight, until midnight or so, if you need anything. I might interview some of your neighbors while I'm here too, if that's okay."

Samantha twisted the straps of her messenger bag. "Have you seen him?"

"No, but we've only been here for about twenty minutes. I saw when you turned your light on though."

Her brow furrowed. "When I turned my light on?"

Piper took a few steps and lifted her hand to point at Samantha's window. She faltered. The window was dark again.

"I guess you turned it off when you came back down."

"I haven't been up to my apartment yet."

Piper's heart kicked. "You haven't been up? Wait. That's your window, right?"

She pointed at the one where she'd seen light earlier.

"Yeah, but I just got here. I stopped to talk to Jaime, but I haven't been up."

"I'm guessing you don't have a timer or automatic lights set up or something, do you?" Piper was already pulling her phone out of her pocket and calling 911. "No friends with a key or a maid or—"

"No, nothing like that." Samantha's hand fell away from the handle as if it might catch fire.

Piper turned toward the restaurant and saw that Dani was watching her through the big window.

Piper held up her finger as if to say, *One minute*.

"911, what's your emergency?"

"Hi, yes. Someone broke into my friend's apartment and we think they're still inside."

She gave them Samantha's address.

Piper would sort out the not-really-a-friend details later. The important thing was that someone professional went through Samantha's apartment as soon as possible. Piper couldn't just send her up there if stalker guy was hiding under the bed or behind the shower curtain.

"We're sending a unit now," the operator said.

"You can wait inside where it's warm, if you want," Piper suggested, pointing at the table where Dani sat watching them. The restaurant looked so inviting compared to the cold, dark night.

Samantha agreed to wait in the restaurant, but she refused to eat.

Almost fifteen minutes had passed before a black-and-white rolled to a stop outside of Samantha's building and two officers got out. A man and a woman in NOPD uniforms looked the building over.

Piper didn't recognize either of them, so she was hesitant to introduce herself and her relationship to Samantha. In the end she caved. Then she waited with Samantha on the street while the police searched her apartment.

They came back twenty minutes later.

"The lock was broken on the apartment door," the female officer said. "It's not clear what they used to get into the apartment, but you'll want to get a new lock. I recommend a double deadbolt, or you could get a Yale Premier Single Cylinder YH 82. That's what I put on my daughter's door."

"Can you repeat that?" Piper asked, and wrote down the name of the lock. "Thanks."

"I've already called a locksmith," Dani said, coming to stand beside the three of them on the street outside the apartment building. She held the leftovers in one hand. "They can be here in ten."

"Thank you," Samantha said. "But maybe I should stay somewhere else. I don't know if I'll be able to sleep knowing he's been in my apartment and going through my stuff."

"I can't blame you there," Dani said. "Do you have someone you can stay with?"

"My sister is in Lakeview. She's been asking me to come stay with her and her kids until this is over. I'll call her and see if she can pick me up."

Samantha made the call and confirmed the details with her sister.

Piper made notes to include the two officers' names and testimonies for her report. She was going to talk to the locksmith too. His expertise on the broken lock might come in handy.

Under her breath, Dani said, "We should stay until she gets packed up and goes with the sister."

"And until the locks are done," Piper said.

"Should I go get us some warm drinks then?" Dani asked. "It looks like it's going to be a long night."

"The best long nights are the ones I spend with you," Piper said.

Dani laughed. "I'll take that as a *yes*."

8

Riku sat in his private garden, a fragrant clove cigarette burning between two fingers. One by one, girls were pushed forward for his inspection.

"No," he said, dismissing each in turn. "No. No. No."

Each girl was dragged away again.

Riku looked toward the sky and closed his eyes. He was tired today. No matter what he drank, ate, smoked, it seemed nothing could give him the energy he sought. Even his walk through Shinjuku Park, which usually invigorated him, had left him empty.

A cluster of ducks quacked beside the running water. It burbled gently as it passed beneath the stone bridge.

"No," he said again, to the girl with pink hair and silver platform shoes.

"No." He took a drag of his cigarette and dismissed the little dark girl who'd bowed at his feet.

I'll never find her, he thought dismally. *I'll never find my Mai again.*

He ground the cigarette out on his wrist. Even the pain

wasn't enough to wake him from the dull disappointment his life had become.

He pocketed the butt and stood.

That's when she stepped forward. Her face was wet with tears, the cheeks red from a hasty wiping. Someone had tried to make her presentable for him, with the cute dress and high pigtails.

The sparkles painted in the corners of her eyes had washed down to her cheeks. Her lip was bloody, either because she'd bitten it while crying or because she'd been slapped.

"How old are you?" Riku asked in Japanese, kneeling down in front of her.

She didn't understand. Where had they found her?

These girls came from everywhere. Poor villages in Japan or the city slums. But they also arrived on boats, and trains, and planes. Riku could never be sure.

He tapped her chest then counted on his fingers.

Ich, ni, san, shi...

She stopped him at ten.

Ten years old.

How old had Mai been the first time he'd touched her? Six, wasn't it? Maybe seven. It had been the night of the summer festival, after their parents had gone to bed.

She'd been frightened by the fireworks.

By ten, Mai had learned to touch him back. Maybe this one could learn too.

He motioned to his assistant Yui, holding the little girl's hand, and the child was pulled away in the direction of Riku's waiting car. Everyone else was dismissed and sent home.

Everyone except Watanabe, who lingered on the stone bridge beneath the maple tree.

"What is it?"

"The Triad has been waiting for your answer for over a week," Watanabe said.

"Whose fault is that?" Riku said testily.

"They will not sail from Macao without your confirmation, sir."

"What do they have?" Riku asked. "Drugs?"

"No, sir," Watanabe said. "Cargo."

Cargo. *People.*

Why did Watanabe never call them *people?*

Riku lit a second cigarette, a compulsive habit, and as the smoke rose thin and gray into the dull day, he considered his empire. He thought his drug holdings might be down to as little as ten percent of everything he bought and sold. There was so much more money in people. And the sustainability was better. He could sell a drug only once, and then it was gone. More had to be made.

With people, he could sell them a dozen times in a single night. And as long as they lived, and they were young enough to work, they had an excellent shelf life.

"The Song clan is still waiting for you to make a decision about the weapons in the port of Tai Pei. They don't want to try to cross the East China Sea until you can promise safe passage."

"Tell them to come," Riku said.

"Should I contact Sato then, Yamamoto-san?"

"No," Riku said, his attention turning toward the car waiting for him.

To the little girl sitting inside.

Watanabe was still whining. "If they are stopped and we haven't informed our contacts—"

"I won't waste my resources on it. Not for something as small as a weapons deal."

Watanabe's face was unreadable, but Riku heard the disapproval in his voice when he said, "If you do not protect your contacts, sir, others may come to believe you are not to be trusted."

"I'm to be feared, not trusted," Riku said, steel in his voice.

"Sir, I think—"

"Take care of it." Riku took his last drag on the cigarette, exhaling thin gray smoke into the sky.

"You should—"

Riku ground his cigarette into Watanabe's hand.

Watanabe flinched, moving to jerk his hand back, but Riku held it tight.

"It feels good, doesn't it?" Riku said, his eyes fixed on Watanabe's chin, on the tight mouth and jaw struggling to hold back emotion and words.

"Take care of it, Watanabe. Don't bother me with these small complaints anymore. My time is more valuable than that."

He turned his back on his second-in-command and followed the line of manicured trees to the idling black sedan.

Lou opened her eyes to find enormous golden eyes boring into hers. Octavia had succeeded in claiming Konstantine's chest and now lay against it, purring loudly. Konstantine's back rested against the headboard, a romance novel open in the hand that wasn't scratching Octavia's ears.

He saw Lou watching him and closed the book. "How do you feel?"

She tried to sit up. The room swam and her stomach lurched. She placed her head in her hand. "What time is it?"

"Almost two in the afternoon. Did you feel me get up earlier?"

She hadn't.

"You should be at the church," she said.

"Stefano can manage without me," he said, and placed the book on the bedside table. "Can you eat?"

Lou wasn't sure she could. Her stomach felt raw on the inside.

"Water then," he insisted, and handed her a tall glass of crystalline water. It was room temperature and slid past her parched lips easily. She finished the entire glass in one go, though her stomach cramped against the intrusion.

Here Konstantine placed Octavia gently on the bed, much to the cat's protest, and went to the bathroom. When he came back he had a warm washcloth in his hands, which he pressed to the back of Lou's neck, her cheeks, her forehead.

She allowed this.

It was nice, and she found her eyes wanting to drift shut again even though she'd only just awakened.

"I can ask a doctor to come examine you. Is that all right?" he asked.

Lou wasn't sure. "I assume this doctor won't be shocked to see all my scars."

He shook his head. "She patches up the Ravengers. She will overlook such things."

"How soon will he be here?"

"She. Isadora can be here in twenty minutes," he said.

"I want to shower," she said. If someone was going to do a physical exam, Lou would rather not be covered in a thin sheen of sweat.

"Should I help you?" One look from Lou made him laugh. "Of course not. I will only turn on the water then."

She undressed in the bathroom and stepped into the hot stream. Her shaking legs held, but they felt weak. She couldn't remember the last time she'd felt this depleted. She remembered getting sick a lot when she was a child. Her mother had called it *nerves*. But those were mostly stom-

achaches and headaches that caused her to spend the after-
noons in bed with books.

When she was fourteen she'd caught some bug at school.
Half of the students had been sent home over the course of
two weeks. Her aunt Lucy had plied her with chicken noodle
soup and electrolytes, and that had been that. But as an adult?

No. She couldn't remember a single time she'd had so
much as a sniffle.

She found herself letting the hot water pound her back
even after she'd finished washing up. She wanted to absorb
the heat, and the shower pressure felt good against the aches
in her muscles. She only begrudgingly got out once the water
began to cool.

She'd just managed to get into fresh clothes and make it
down to Konstantine's living room by the time the doctor
knocked on the door.

Konstantine put a fresh cup of warm coffee on the
desktop in front of Lou before crossing to open it.

A brisk woman entered, barely more than a smudge of
black clothing and thick spectacles. But the eyes behind them
were a fierce brown.

Isadora was short for a woman, with straight brown hair
pulled back into a neat bun on the top of her head. Her
glasses were black and they made her eyes slightly larger than
Lou suspected they actually were.

"*Buona sera, signora. Come si sente?*" she asked.

"In English, please. Your patient doesn't understand Italian," Konstantine said, and gestured toward Lou.

"No problem," Isadora said. To Lou she said, "How are
you feeling?"

"I've felt better," Lou admitted.

The woman opened her bag and pulled out a box of latex
gloves. "What are your symptoms?"

Lou did her best to describe the throbbing in her head,

the way her eyes hurt. How her muscles ached and her body felt heavy, all while the woman pulled on her gloves.

She took Lou's temperature, blood pressure, and pulse. She listened to her heart and lungs. Lastly, she swabbed Lou's nose and throat. Then she touched Lou's throat and lymph nodes and looked into her mouth and eyes with a penlight.

"Any stomach pain?" she asked after clicking the light off.

No point in lying now, Lou thought.

The doctor motioned to Konstantine's couch, and Lou lay down on it, allowing the doctor to lift her shirt and palpate her abdomen. Konstantine busied himself in the kitchen, arranging cut fruit and cheese on a plate.

"Do you drink a lot of coffee?" the doctor asked as the rubber gloves pushed against her stomach muscles.

"Yes," Lou said.

"On an empty stomach?"

Lou hesitated to admit that she almost always drank her coffee on an empty stomach. This felt like a setup for a lecture.

"Yes," she said finally.

"Do you sleep well? Eat often?"

Konstantine said something in Italian, a quick stream of words that Lou couldn't place. To this, the doctor clicked her tongue.

"No wonder you're sick, signora," the doctor said. "You do not take care of yourself."

Lou scowled at Konstantine. "I don't know what he told you but—"

"He said that you sleep erratically, day and night. That you often skip meals and work all the time. You drink a lot of coffee but no water, and your choice of food is usually takeaway."

She couldn't find any lie in what he'd said. "I don't cook, no."

The doctor frowned down at her. "I am not one to tell a young woman what to do. If you want to work, work. How you spend your nights is also your business—"

Does she think I'm a prostitute?

"But I am betting that your tests will tell me that you have nothing more than a cold and that the reason why you have a cold is because you are depleted."

"Depleted," Lou said.

"Yes. Overworked. *Esausta.*"

"Run down," Konstantine offered, and handed the doctor an espresso cup.

She threw this back in one go and thanked him.

"Oh, did you want me to take the blood sample to Gabriele's laboratory?"

Konstantine looked to Lou. "Do you still want to do another blood test? If you do, Isadora's clinic is near the lab."

"It's no trouble for me. I will be taking your other tests to the same laboratory," Isadora added, giving Konstantine her empty espresso cup.

Lou rolled up her sleeve to expose her bare forearm.

Isadora rummaged in her kit for the vials, pressure cord, and tubing that she would need to take Lou's blood.

Lou had a moment of thinking it was very weird to have a doctor draw blood in Konstantine's living room, but then she thought of the time she had given Konstantine a blood transfusion in her apartment after Nico had pumped him full of bullets. Isadora was likely used to unconventional treatment settings.

The fact that Isadora hadn't batted an eyelash made Lou curious about her. How many shot-up or stabbed people had he dragged to her door? Or because she seemed so comfortable with house calls, how many times had she come to the church to patch up one of Konstantine's people and send them on their way? Had she even saved Konstantine himself?

She knew where Konstantine lived, and Lou didn't think many did.

Lou considered these things while Isadora filled three vials with deep red blood from Lou's left arm and packed everything away.

"Add pressure to this, signora." She held a cotton ball to her skin until Lou did this for herself. Then she unwrapped a bandage and fixed the cotton ball in place.

"We are done here." Isadora stood, her knees popping.

Lou rolled down her sleeve.

"For now, the best I can tell you is that you need rest. Coffee is good, but please drink *water* also. And sleep. Sleep for days if you must."

Isadora gave Konstantine a sharp nod, which he returned, and then she was out the door.

Lou's body was heavy against the sofa, and she realized again that she was tired. Desperately tired. So tired, in fact, that she didn't even want to slip from the sofa back to Konstantine's bed. She wanted to lie where she was.

"Your eyes are glassy again," he said. He pressed cool hands to her cheeks. "How do you feel?"

She didn't care to admit that the short visit with Isadora had worn her out.

"Come on," Konstantine said, and before she could protest, he slipped his arms under her and lifted her to his chest.

He cradled her against him like a bride.

She tightened, but even that wasn't worth the effort, so she went soft in his arms and let her cheek rest against the base of his throat.

"Wow," he murmured into her hair. "You must really feel like shit if you are going to let me carry you."

"Shut up," she growled.

She felt rather than heard his laughter as a rumble in his chest.

She knew that she was heavy, given the strange relationship she had with gravity, but he carried her without complaint back to his dark bedroom.

He placed her on the bed gently. A moment later, he returned with a fresh, cool cloth for her face.

"My face is hot but my body is cold," she said.

He opened her drawer and looked for another pair of socks. When he did not find a pair to his liking, he grabbed one of his.

He looked at her disapprovingly as he pulled one black sock over the white one she wore, then the other.

"Whatever you want to say, say it." She dabbed the cloth against the back of her neck.

"Isadora is right. You don't take good care of yourself."

She'd never enjoyed being lectured. Her aunt Lucy had been a pro at it, complaining often that Lou didn't sleep enough, rest enough, eat enough, drink enough water or any of the teas from the endless parade of greens and herbals that Lucy had brought home.

It was probably why she'd never complained about Lou's love of books. It was one of the few activities Lou did that kept her stretched out on the sofa or her bed for any length of time.

Then there had been the yoga. She'd wanted Lou to go at least twice a week with her.

You can't possibly keep all that stress and violence stored up in your body, Lucy had said. *You need a way to release it.*

Considering how many bodies Lou had delivered to the shores of La Loon, she didn't think yoga, even *three* times a week, was going to cut it. Let alone a kale salad.

And here was Konstantine, giving her the same look her late aunt had. Chiding her in the same disappointed tone.

Not quite pleading and not quite angry, but full of an emotion that lay somewhere between.

"What do you want me to do? Eat more leaves?" she asked.

His hands faltered on her feet, where he'd been fussing over the socks. He cradled them. "I'm sorry. We don't have to talk about this now."

Now.

"I don't want to talk about it when I'm better either."

What if you won't get better? Maybe something serious is wrong with you and you'll die like Lucy did.

Like Lucy did.

Her stomach clenched.

Konstantine pursed his lips. "I simply want to say that you must take better care of your body. Just because it is stronger than most does not mean it shouldn't be cared for. This illness is simply another reminder that you are not indestructible, *amore mio.*"

He turned his attention to rubbing her feet. The gentle pressure lulled her into a doze, her head against the headboard and the rag on her forehead forgotten.

When she woke, there was a large bottle of water on the bedside table with a note.

I'm downstairs working. Call for me when you want me to heat your soup.

She listened and caught the sound of his fingers moving across a keyboard, then the clink of a cup returned to its saucer.

Her body relaxed. Keeping one ear tuned to the sound of him, she closed her eyes and sank back into sleep.

. . .

KING WAS SEVEN MINUTES LATE WHEN HE KNOCKED ON Beth Miller's door. When she opened it, he lifted the takeout bag holding two shrimp po'boys and salt and vinegar chips.

"Sorry I'm late," he said.

"Not a problem," she said, and opened the door for him.

He slipped his shoes off and gave her the bag of food. He'd learned that she liked to plate things a certain way.

He didn't mind. As long as he got to eat, he didn't care how it was arranged.

"The game already started. Do you mind if we eat in the living room?" she asked.

WNBA wasn't his favorite sport, but there wasn't another game on tonight that he wanted to see.

"Sure," he said. "Can I carry anything?"

"Of course."

In the kitchen, she arranged the takeout on her floral plates. Then she carried the plates one by one to the coffee table while she set up the TV and found the game she wanted.

King poured their sodas into large tumblers of ice and got the napkins together.

Eating on the sofa, side by side, they watched the game. They commented on the performance of the players, and often Beth cheered. Her team was doing well and it pleased him to see it. Once the game was over and their plates cleared, King took them to the sink and washed them without having to be asked.

It was their usual pattern to go up to Beth's bed after dinner and the game, but they stayed on the sofa, cuddled close, listening to each other's breathing as much as the rumble of Prytania Street outside.

"There's another game on Wednesday," she said, running her fingers through his hair. King loved the feel of her acrylic nails softly scraping his scalp. "Would you like to watch it at your place this time?"

"That's my lasagna night with Mel," he said.

As soon as he said it, he stiffened, wondering how that sounded.

"We watch *RuPaul's Drag Race* and eat lasagna," he said, trying not to sound guilty. "We've been doing it for five seasons now."

"*RuPaul's Drag Race*," she said, removing her fingers from his hair. "Now that's an interesting choice."

King wasn't sure what to say to that. His mind had wandered back to earlier that evening, when Beth had seen him holding Mel outside the police precinct.

"Beth," he said, his throat tightening. "I feel like I should tell you something."

"That you're sleeping with Ms. Durand?"

King choked. "What? No."

But Beth was smiling. "No? Somebody else then?"

He turned to face her. "I'm not sleeping with anyone else. Only you."

Her smile only broadened. "Then why so serious?"

"I just..." His sputtering mind tried to right itself. "I just know you saw us hugging outside the precinct and I didn't want you to think that—"

He broke off, unsure of how to finish the sentence.

"You didn't want me to think what?" She met his eyes over the rim of her glasses.

"That we were sleeping together. Or that we'd ever had. Or that I had something going on with her."

Beth placed one hand over King's. "Robbie, first of all, I wasn't aware that we were exclusive to each other."

King's face reddened. "You're right. We haven't talked about that."

"Second of all," she said, "I'm too old to be jealous. After two marriages, raising a kid, and my work, I can't afford to be. I don't have the time or energy to be chasing around a man, wasting my precious energy."

"I wouldn't ask you to," he said.

"Good." Her face was still gentle. Soft. "Then I should tell *you* something."

This is where I find out I'm only one of six boyfriends, he thought, and tried not to laugh.

"I'm going to retire sometime in the next five years. And when I do, I don't know where I'll be. If my son marries this girl he loves, and she's a good girl, so he might, then I could be a grandma by then. If so, you better believe I'll be in Orlando with those babies, no matter how cute you are."

Her whole face lit up when she said it. King laughed.

"It's no competition," he conceded.

She squeezed his hand. "So tell me why you were so worried I'd be upset."

Had he been worried? He had. He recognized that in the twisting of his guts and the tightness in his throat.

"Mel means a lot to me," he said finally. "She met me when I was in a bad place, and she was really good to me. My first real friend in a long time. Since then, we've only grown closer. We've been through a lot together."

This was a hell of an understatement.

They'd been kidnapped together, threatened at gunpoint together, and had faced down a Russian mob boss and her violent ex-husband together.

They were more than friends. They were family.

"And I like you too," he said. "So I didn't want there to be any friction between us or between you and Mel. I just wanted you to know that she means a lot to me. But not like that."

Beth searched his face, probably for sincerity or falsehood. King couldn't be sure what she saw, but whatever it was, she must've liked it.

She cupped his cheek. "I *am* glad you've got somebody like that in your life, Robbie. Good friends are hard to come by."

"They are," he said.

"Then don't you worry about me and Ms. Durand one bit. Like I said, I'd drop you in a heartbeat for a grandbaby."

King laughed.

"In the meantime, I'd like to keep spending time with you," Beth said.

His face flushed. "Me too. I'd like to keep spending time with you too."

"I'm glad to hear it." She grabbed his hand and pulled him toward the stairs that led up to her bedroom. "Why don't we spend a little time together right now?"

9

———

Lou woke in darkness. Konstantine was behind her, one arm stretched over her body, cradling her against him.

It felt late.

Only darkness oozed through the cracks around the large window overlooking the Arno River. She sat up and her head spun. She cradled it with a damp palm.

"What is it?" Konstantine asked, his voice thick with sleep.

Was something wrong? She did a quick check with her compass, but all was still. Quiet.

No, the trouble wasn't out there. The trouble was within her. Much to her dismay, she was still sick.

"I need the bathroom," she said, and untangled herself from the sheets.

She shut herself inside so the light wouldn't bother him. Her GPS watch was still on the sink where she'd left it, and she checked the time. It was four in the morning in Florence. No wonder it was still so quiet outside. Little more could be heard than the slapping of the Arno River against the walls of the canal.

Lou rubbed her face and tried to take measure of her body. It still felt shaky, weak.

She hated herself for it. How could this have happened? How did she get sick? The only people she came into close contact with were Konstantine, Piper, Dani, and King. Sometimes Melandra. None of *them* were sick.

Only her.

Was it one of her kills that had infected her with something? Some last-ditch revenge before she dragged them to their watery grave?

Konstantine knocked on the door. "Are you okay in there?"

She opened the door. "I'm dizzy."

Why had she said that? Why did she keep admitting to him that she didn't feel well? She'd never been a whiner.

Konstantine's lifted brow and the pout of his lips told her that he was just as surprised by her admission. "Drink water."

"Drink water," she said. "Why does everyone think drinking water cures everything?"

"You could be dizzy because you're dehydrated. Isadora told me to make sure that it didn't happen."

Lou turned on the tap and splashed cold water on her face. "When did you speak to her?"

"This evening, while you were sleeping. She called to say that you tested negative for the flu and that nothing has changed in your blood."

Lou's hand turned red in the cold water.

So the microbes in Blood Lake, the ones infesting her system, could speed up the healing of physical damage—knife wounds, gunshot wounds, cuts, torn muscles, bruises, and scratches—but not protect against viral ailments.

I better start making sure no one breathes on me then, she thought.

"It's as the doctor says, *amore mio*." He placed a tall glass of water on the sink beside the hand towel she used to dry off. "You're exhausted. That's all."

"A terrible time to be exhausted." Lou thought of Riku and her compass reacted, spinning to life within her. *It* wasn't exhausted.

Konstantine leaned his weight against the counter, watching her face. "You can still destroy him. *After* you feel better."

I will feel better, she assured herself. It had only been a few days. It wasn't like people had colds forever. The longest she'd ever seen someone with a cold was Piper, which she had for almost two weeks. She'd spent fourteen years hunting Angelo Martinelli.

Riku Yamamoto could wait two weeks.

"Do you think you can eat something?" he asked.

"Fine." She lifted the glass he'd placed by the towel and drank it down. It made her stomach cramp, but she finished it.

Then he was pulling her into his arms. "I know you hate this, but you will get better faster if you let me take care of you."

He was placing a cool hand on the back of her neck. "I said I'd eat, didn't I?"

He looked as if he was holding back laughter. "*Sì*. Get back in bed and I'll bring it up for you."

Lou had the covers pulled to her chest, trying to dodge the kitty claws attacking her toes, when her mind went to La Loon again. Taking down the traffickers wasn't her only bit of unfinished business. She also needed to get to La Loon as soon as she could.

What to do in the meantime?

Lou could take the girls, couldn't she? At least some of them? She could stick to the shadows and slip in and out without starting a fight. Then again, she'd tried to do that with Busaba and it had still been guns blazing.

Perhaps if she worded her questions carefully, something like *a girl they won't miss right away* or *a girl I can save without being noticed*, Lou could move most of the girls out of danger even while she was still sick. She didn't have to wait to be a hundred percent healed to help.

What if you give them a cold? a voice asked. It was her dead aunt's voice.

A cold is a small price to pay to escape enslavement, Lou thought.

That's what she would do. She'd eat Konstantine's soup and water, and sleep when she could, but she would also move as many girls out of Riku's clutches as possible. More than that, she could work with Dani to resolve the New York case. She hadn't forgotten about her last hunt either.

"*Why* are you smiling?" Konstantine placed the tray on the bed beside her. "Should I be worried?"

There was a large bowl of steaming soup, but also two bread rolls. He'd told her the name of them before and showed her the bakery where he liked to buy them fresh in the morning, but her brain wasn't able to recall the Italian word now.

Given how much the soup was steaming, she started with a roll.

"No reason," she said. "I'm feeling better."

He cocked his head. "Are you? Really?"

"Yes," she said. *And once I kill Riku, I'll feel great.*

· · ·

"Zoey Peterson," King said, looking up from his computer. He turned his laptop so Mel could see the picture on his screen. "Is this her?"

Mel grabbed her headband. "My Lord, yes! That's her."

King turned the computer toward himself again so he could read the police report.

"Zoey Peterson, a student from the University of Louisiana-Lafayette. Twenty years old. Was living in student housing with her roommates until two weeks ago."

"What happened two weeks ago?" Dani asked. She'd come to the agency to have lunch with Piper. Both girls were sitting behind Piper's desk, sharing red beans and rice and two large slabs of cornbread between them.

"She was reported missing. Her friends haven't seen her since."

"Missing for two weeks," Mel said. Her face fell.

"Missing people come back," King said, hoping to curb her disappointment. "It doesn't mean that something terrible has happened."

"Yet," Mel said.

Though he didn't want to admit that Mel knowing about a girl who was missing over a hundred and forty miles away had stopped his mind.

If he was being honest with himself, he hadn't expected them to find the girl at all. He'd hoped that Mel had simply had an unsettling nightmare and she'd let this go, but now the girl was real.

Not only was she real, but there was an active investigation.

Her family thought she'd been kidnapped.

Her friends thought she'd run off but hadn't given the local authorities a clear reason why.

"She's real," Melandra said, as if she'd been thinking the same thing King had. "She's a real person. My dream—"

"We'll figure this out," King assured her before the anxiety on her face could bloom into something more dangerous. A panic attack, maybe. He wondered if Melandra had her Xanax on her, and if she might need to take one now.

"Piper, how's your case load with the stalker?" he asked.

"It's fine," she said, almost reflexively. King chose to ignore this.

"Can I also get one of you to help with Zoey's case? We need statements from the friends who saw her last. They might be more willing to tell another female their age what really happened before she disappeared than some old guy who seems like a cop."

"I'll do it," Dani said. "I've had girls tell me things that they'd never tell the police."

"Yeah, you'd be surprised how often they think their friend is going to turn up and be mad at them for blabbing, so they don't say things that would've resolved the case sooner," King said.

"Anything we're looking for in particular?" Piper pulled a notepad out of the desk drawer.

"We want to know what happened two weeks ago, or thereabouts. If she did take off, it wasn't for no reason. There is usually a catalyst, some sort of breaking point that causes a person to run. See if you can find out what it was."

"Got it," Piper said, scribbling on the pad. "The report wouldn't happen to have the names of the friends that reported her missing, would it?"

King smiled. "You know it's not that easy. I've got Zoey's last-known address, so you can track down the roommates. I think there were four women to one unit."

"A quad," Dani said, taking a big bite of the sandwich. "Let's just hope that Zoey wasn't the type to stay in her room and not talk to anyone. With student housing, sometimes the university decides who rooms together, and there's no guarantee they'll gel."

Dani and Piper returned to their lunch, and King jotted down a few important details on Zoey—her parents' names and address, her place of employment, the make and model of her car—before closing the record.

When he met Mel's eyes again, they were still round with concern.

"Don't worry," he told her. "We found her. That's a good thing."

"Not if she's already dead," Mel said.

"Do they usually die before someone has these—" He searched for the word she'd used. "Debt dreams?"

She shook her head. "No. No, usually the dream comes first."

"And how many days ago did you start having these dreams?"

"Four. No, five."

"All we can do is keep going until something changes," King said. "In the meantime, stay optimistic. As far as we know, she's still alive."

Mel twisted the bangles on her wrist. "I hope you're right, Mr. King."

Piper's legs were *noodles*. She'd walked for hours today and couldn't guess how many flights of stairs she marched up and down, both in Samantha's apartment building and also at her school, as she interviewed her professors and a few classmates. Then she went to the coffee shop where the girl worked part-time as a barista and interviewed the working manager and a few employees who'd had a spare minute to talk to her. All had been concerned for Samantha, who struck them as a "sweet if quiet girl," and that just made Piper more desperate to protect her.

The one good thing on Piper's side was that the university, coffee shop, and apartment building were in the same part of town. Unfortunately, that meant they were spaced just far enough apart that it didn't make sense to hop on and off the bus when she could just walk and get there faster.

Her legs, however, clearly disagreed.

"Just two more," she told herself. "I just need to knock on two more doors and then I can go home and put my legs up."

Armed with interview tips from Dani, the questioning itself had gone smoothly. Piper had always found it easy to talk to people, having been an extrovert for as long as she could remember. But formal interviews in which Piper whipped out her phone or a pad and pen seemed to make some people clam up. As an investigative reporter, Dani had far more experience than Piper, so she wasn't surprised that Dani's tactics were more skillful.

King had also instructed her not to focus too hard on the people themselves. That pounding a footpath like this was also good for churning up details that would help solidify their case.

He'd instructed Piper to note everything she could about Samantha's life. From the features of her apartment building —she was on the top floor of three levels and one of four units to a floor; the stone exterior probably couldn't be scaled —to the kind of people who hung out in the area.

By almost seven that evening, Piper knew how long it took Samantha to walk to her classes and the route she took. She'd even discovered that Samantha used to work as a lab assistant in one of the campus laboratories up until two semesters ago. So Piper went *back* to the campus and interviewed everyone in the lab and department she could find.

Was that why her back was hurting? When was the last

time she'd sat down for two minutes? She checked her watch. She'd been at this for almost six hours.

What she wouldn't give to have Lou's gift once in a while, to just pop in and out wherever she wanted.

Speaking of Lou, where the hell was she? She'd been stalking that New York murderer for a few days, and she hadn't heard from her since.

Piper made a mental note to check on Lou later, after she was done with this interviewing mess. And definitely after she had a shower.

And something to eat.

Maybe also a nap.

That was another thing Lou could help her with, identifying the stalker. All King had managed to grab was a fuzzy photo of a man shape in a hoodie and jean jacket. It could've been literally anyone of medium build in the city. She couldn't even guess a height based on it.

King had given her some crap about how it was probably a man because most stalkers were, but Piper had chalked this up to a bit of sexism. She'd had plenty of her own exes with stalkerish tendencies and knew firsthand that women were just as capable of getting too possessive as men. Of course, none of her exes had left her a creepy note made of cut-out magazine letters informing her that *You Belong To Me*, which was what had brought Samantha to the police station in the first place and why she'd been referred to King.

She knocked on the last door in Samantha's apartment building for five minutes before accepting that either no one was home or no one planned to answer the door for a stranger. Piper wrote her reason for visiting and phone number on a piece of paper and shoved it under the door.

As her side began to cramp, Piper thought, *This is the real reason why he gave me this case. Because he didn't want to walk all over this freaking city.*

"That's not why he gave the case to me," she reassured herself. "He gave it to me because he knows I'm smart and capable and I can build an amazing case that will hold up well in court."

Outside, she sank onto a bench beneath the live oak tree to catch her breath.

She had two missed texts from Dani, who said she was just leaving the office and would put the enchiladas she'd prepped that morning in the oven when she got home if Piper could just let her know when she'd be arriving.

Twenty or thirty minutes? Depends on the bus.

The truth was it depended on how long she needed to rest on this park bench and catch her breath. The ache in her side was no joke. If she was going to start chasing down criminals, maybe she needed to take up jogging or something.

She looked at the collection of shops and restaurants around her and wondered if she should go into each and ask the workers if they'd seen anyone suspicious lurking around in a black hoodie and jean jacket.

Later, her body begged. *I'll come back later.*

She was about to get up when a strange feeling made Piper look to the left suddenly, as if someone was watching her.

Someone *was* watching her.

On the other side of the large oak, under a curtain of Spanish moss, stood a figure.

Jean jacket over a black hoodie. The hood was pulled up to hide the person's face and the hands were in the pockets. She tried to note the shoes—white sneakers—and the pants—basic black sweats—but there wasn't anything defining about the person or the clothes.

Piper rose from the bench. "Hey. Sir, can I ask you a few questions?"

Don't be creepy, she warned herself. *Don't make it weird.*

She tried to brighten her smile and force some bubbliness into her voice.

I just want a closer look at you.

"Are you a student at UNO? Do you have a minute to talk about the university's cafeteria menu?"

He bolted.

"Wait!" Piper called out. "This is important! Food allergies are to be taken seriously, sir!"

He didn't stop or turn back to look at her.

"Damn," she murmured. She'd thought she'd chosen a pretty non-threatening line of inquiry.

Who doesn't like to talk about food?

King chose that moment to text her for an update. *How's the case shaping up? Anything to help us identify our guy?*

Only that our stalker might not like food or surveys, she thought. Instead she wrote, *I covered a lot of ground today. Literally.*

Piper scanned the area one last time, but it was too dark.

Whoever had been watching her was gone.

10

Lou woke with a splitting headache. She'd agreed to take the disgusting medicine that Konstantine had procured for her from the corner pharmacy, and had even washed the foul liquid down with a large glass of water. This had been a horrible experience, but he'd been pleased. He'd said it was Isadora who had prescribed it and that the syrup had a sedative in it that was meant to help her sleep off whatever was making her sick.

Lou hoped the medicine might help quell the restlessness within her, but now her limbs were heavy and disobedient. She felt like she was trying to move underwater.

This was terrible because her compass was very much alive and well. It was pulling, tugging, demanding that Lou get the hell out of bed and on her feet. Her vision swam. The world was lurching one way, then the other.

She clasped her head as if trying to keep it on her neck.

"What's wrong?" Konstantine said. His hands were on her back. "Lay down."

"What the hell was in that medicine?" she asked.

"Codeine, I believe," he said. "You need to lay down."

"Someone's in trouble."

"You can't go like this. How will you fight?"

Lou didn't have an answer to that. But her compass was insistent, the urgent feeling unmistakable.

"Let's find out," she said.

She managed to get on her feet and take one step, then two. The world tilted, but Lou found her center of gravity intact. She remained on her feet.

"*Amore mio, please*," Konstantine said. "If you insist on going, take me with you."

He was already pulling his spare gun out of the sock drawer as if it'd been decided.

"You'll just be one more person for me to try and keep safe," she said.

His look hardened. "I ask that you not underestimate me any more than I underestimate you."

"If you get shot or stabbed, it's your own fault."

The compass thrummed at a fever pitch now. There was no more time. Lou wrapped one hand around Konstantine's waist and pulled—or rather fell—through the dark.

THE GIRL WAS CRYING. THAT DIDN'T BOTHER RIKU MUCH. He liked the pitiful mewling sound.

"Get up," he said.

When she didn't, he yanked her up by the arm.

"Get up, I said!"

Her scream increased in pitch, her eyes squeezed shut as twin streams ran down her cheeks.

He looked at her torn dress and the red handprint on her cheek, another where he'd gripped her thigh. The limb had been small enough for him to wrap his whole hand around.

Unable to contain his rage any longer, he lifted her and threw her onto his bed. Her dress flew up, revealing that she wore no underwear beneath. Someone hadn't cared enough to dress her properly, or perhaps his assistant Yui had removed it on Riku's behalf before handing the girl over to his care.

He was undoing the button on his pants without a thought in his head. There was no room for thoughts when he was consumed only by a desperate need for release.

Finally. Finally. Finally. Finally.

He barely noted his bedroom, the shift of its shadows, as he reached across the bed and yanked the girl to its edge where he stood, her legs on either side of him.

He'd only just unzipped his pants when someone grabbed his shoulder and spun him.

Riku fell against the bedroom wall. His pants began to slip, making it harder for him to right himself.

What the fuck is this?

His eyes tried to comprehend the sight of a woman, dark-haired, lifting the child from the bed.

Yui?

No. This woman wasn't even Japanese.

The girl—his girl—was desperately twining her arms around the woman's neck without question as she smoothed her dress down and into place.

Riku forgot about the zipper, but he did button his pants in order to keep them in place. Then he pushed himself off the wall. He reached out to grab the woman by the hair but never made it.

A gun pressed into his face, shoving his head sharply to the left.

Riku froze, seeing the long black snout of the pistol digging into his cheekbone. He tried to turn his head, but the gun pressed into his bone so hard it hurt.

"Don't," a man said in English.

Riku struggled to place the voice. It was low, almost a

growl. It was hard to tell what accent he was hearing or who was barking the command.

Riku's eyes went to the woman cooing reassurances into the girl's ears.

"Let's go," the woman said. She was also speaking in English, but she hadn't bothered to keep her voice low or guarded.

American, he knew. The woman was American. He had that much at least.

"Where—" Riku began. He'd wanted to ask, *Where do you think you're going?* There was nowhere they could go that he would not find them.

Riku never finished his sentence.

The butt of the gun slammed into Riku's jaw, knocking him to the floor. His world was a world of pain as his head throbbed and ears rang.

But even from his hands and knees, he managed to look up at the last minute.

He saw the man's face.

He saw him, and knew *exactly* who he was.

KONSTANTINE'S EARS FELT LIKE THEY MIGHT BLEED. Stefano hadn't stopped yelling since Konstantine had agreed to meet him at the church. When Stefano heard the news that they'd made a move against Yamamoto, he'd been so angry that he'd burst into Konstantine's apartment without knocking.

"*Che cazzo hai fatto?*" he'd cried, throwing his hands up in the air.

Konstantine had shushed him, telling him that Lou was ill and sleeping upstairs. That whatever problem they needed to deal with they could address in the sanctity of his private office at the church.

What had followed was a very tense walk from Konstantine's apartment as Stefano strode ahead of him as if they were not even acquaintances.

He'd hoped the other man would tire some of his rage before they reached the church, but there had been no such luck.

Still, Konstantine waved to Matteo and the other boys kicking a soccer ball across the stone portico outside the church's door. He offered them chocolates from his pockets. He carried on as if nothing whatsoever was wrong.

This attempt at normalcy ended when Konstantine shut the door to his office, sealing himself inside with Stefano.

"He saw you," Stefano growled. "Riku Yamamoto is now telling everyone who will listen that Paolo Konstantine wants war. That you broke into his apartment and attacked him in the dead of night. He's demanding retribution."

"He won't get it," Konstantine said calmly. Even if Konstantine had been willing to make amends with the clan, he couldn't now. Not after what he'd seen.

Stefano sank into the chair opposite Konstantine's desk and took a deep, steadying breath. "You can't possibly *want* to go to war with him."

"I don't want to go to war. *Ever.* You know that," he said. He began moving wood from its waiting rack into the fireplace.

He hadn't planned to come into the office today. He'd wanted to remain with Lou, but Stefano was right. What happened with Yamamoto changed things.

Konstantine wasn't mad. He was thankful that Lou's intuition was so accurate, and that as sick as she was, she was still willing to save that little girl from a horrible attack. And the way the mother had cried when the little girl had been returned to her arms.

Konstantine wasn't sure the sound of it would ever leave his ears.

He could forgive Lou's stubbornness for such a thing. At least now she was sleeping again, or she *had* been when he'd kissed her goodbye before leaving with Stefano.

That had been their bargain. She'd promised to go back to sleep after they returned the girl to her family. All he could do was trust that she would do as she'd promised.

"If you refuse to give him retribution, nor do you want to go to war, then what will you do?" Stefano asked. His reason was returning to him, though the ends of his words remained sharp. "Will you send *La Strega* to finish him?"

"That will have complications of its own, and you know it," Konstantine said.

He wasn't a fool.

He knew that many mobs, including those far richer than his own, had grown their wealth by selling humans. Children and women. Sometimes men too. It didn't matter. They were still property to be sold to the highest bidder. Riku Yamamoto might have slaves working his opium farms. Or he might have even given them to other crime families as gifts. And it wasn't always sex or hard labor they were used for. They could be working in any of the thousands of businesses that Yamamoto owned throughout Tokyo and the rest of Japan.

Konstantine was grateful that Padre Leo had never allowed enslavement in the Ravengers.

I am in the business of freeing those confined by their poverty, he had said on many occasions. *Not exploiting them for it.*

When Konstantine took over as head of their gang, he had been insistent in weeding out the last of their connections to the clans who profited from enslavement. He'd demanded compliance from all of those who'd sworn allegiance to him, no matter how casual the business connection.

"He lied to us," Konstantine said.

Stefano stilled. "What do you mean?"

"The Yamamoto clan claimed that they'd stopped all trafficking. But we know now that's not true."

"We can't take down every organization with prostitutes," Stefano cried.

"Prostitution is one thing, if the women are willing," Konstantine conceded. "But stealing children like Busaba—"

Like the child Lou held in her arms tonight.

"—he has broken his good faith with us," Konstantine finished.

Stefano was rubbing his brow as if it would smooth his skull back into place.

"There are stories that his men are unhappy with him for other reasons," Stefano said.

Konstantine looked up. "What reasons?"

"He does not lead well. He follows his own interests ahead of those he promises to protect. He is careless with their lives."

Konstantine considered this as he lit the fire and stoked it to a full burn. "Then there might be an opportunity to eliminate Yamamoto and make an alliance with a new leader within the group."

"That is not our most pressing problem. He said you went into his home. Did you?"

"Yes."

Stefano swore. "Was it worth it?"

"*Yes,*" Konstantine said without hesitation. He couldn't stop thinking of the way the girl had wrapped her arms around Lou's neck.

But Stefano was right. This still left them with the mess he'd made by letting Riku see his face.

Stefano rubbed his jaw and sighed. "We have to cast doubt on his story. It will be your word against his."

"Find out who we have planted in Tokyo," Konstantine said. "I want to start rumors. Sow unrest and distrust. If we hope to remove Riku from power without war, then we need to give them good reason to break rank with him. Identify his most likely replacement, someone their clan already prefers, and let us throw our support behind them, too."

"And what about his direct challenge? He wants your head."

"Given what that man does in his bedroom, I don't believe he will have proof I was there." Konstantine clenched and unclenched his fist. "No cameras, no video. Though I'll do a search to be sure."

A child. She was only a child.

"Do they believe in the *strega* rumors?" Konstantine asked.

Stefano waved a hand. "After Nico and Petrov, and especially Erjon, there isn't a clan on this planet who has not heard of her."

Konstantine forced his hand to relax. "Feed that rumor too. Tell them that it wasn't me that Yamamoto saw. It was *La Strega*. She has noted his *misdeeds*, and plans to punish him."

"His misdeeds?"

"His affection for children."

"*Santa Madonna*." Stefano's green eyes filled with disgust. "Sick bastard. It helps that when she attacks she usually kills everyone with rank. Those closest to him will be afraid for their own lives."

"Yes, and it will leave them with no reason to stand behind Yamamoto. I will step in with an attractive counteroffer in exchange for Yamamoto when the time is right. Now, let me work for a few hours. I can't stay for long. I need to get back to her."

Stefano rose.

"One more thing," Konstantine called out just as he'd

reached the door. "See if Yamamoto has any family. In or out of the business."

"A wife? Or someone like Vittoria?"

"*Sì*," Konstantine said, turning his attention to the documents on his desk and powering on the computer waiting there. "Someone who may be able to shed more light on Yamamoto's secrets."

11

———

Lou had woken briefly to the heated argument between Konstantine and Stefano, before dropping off to sleep not long after the apartment door had clicked shut. Hadn't Konstantine kissed her goodbye? Didn't he say something in her ear about Stefano before he'd left?

It was a haze now as she climbed from the bed, sliding past the sleeping Octavia on her way downstairs. The apartment was empty. There were water bottles and cans of soup and a bag of bread rolls on the counter, but no coffee.

What she wanted was coffee.

She tried to take measure of her body and gain a sense of how much time had passed since they'd taken the child—Riku Yamamoto's captive—back to her family.

That medicine was no joke.

Isadora hadn't been playing around when she'd told Lou to rest. As if sensing that Lou wouldn't have rested without intervention, she'd given her something that would *keep* her in bed.

Except now the medicine's effects had worn off and Lou

was left with a sluggish, unfinished feeling, as if she were caught somewhere between awake and asleep.

Her legs were shaky, her stomach raw, and her mind unfocused at its edges.

Lou grabbed the pen off of Konstantine's desk and scribbled a note on the blank pad there.

I'll be back.

That's all he was getting from her. He'd better be happy that she'd left a note at all.

Lou let the shadows overtake her where she stood and slipped through this side of the world, to the other.

For the first time in her life, Lou was dizzy when the world reformed around her, and she stepped into her apartment with her head swimming.

The day was still bright in St. Louis, the Mississippi River shining beyond her big picture window. The shimmering sunlight reflecting off the water hurt Lou's eyes, and she turned away from the window. She kept her eyes at a squint until she made it to the bathroom and shut herself inside.

This room didn't have any windows, so Lou was able to shower with only the dim bulb of the overhead light. She didn't run the water as hot as she could have, for fear the heat would make her dizziness worse.

She dressed in a fresh black sweater and cargo pants and took the time to dry her hair before pulling on her leather jacket and shades.

At least drink a glass of water. It was Konstantine's voice.

Are you going to be a voice in my head now too? she thought bitterly.

Grudgingly, she pulled a glass down from the cabinet and filled it at the sink. She drank it all despite her stomach's protest.

She felt a little stronger, a little more like herself, when she stepped into the closet again.

When she stepped into the Crescent City Detective Agency, she wasn't entirely sure what time it was in New Orleans.

She guessed it was in the late afternoon, given the slant of light beyond the windows and the fact that both King and Piper were at their desks.

Piper did a double take when she saw her. "Hey, Lou-blue. I was just about to page you. Where the heck—"

Her words broke off as Lou walked past them and straight to the coffee pot. She grabbed a mug from the table beside the maker and emptied the glass carafe into it.

King snorted.

"O-*kay*. A little desperate for the magic bean juice, are we?" Piper asked.

Lou didn't reply.

"*Anyway*," Piper went on. "As I was saying, where've you been?"

"Working." Lou wasn't about to tell them she was sick. She just kept a polite distance to make sure she didn't spread her germs.

"Yeah, how's the NYC case going?"

"He's dead."

"You know we can't prosecute when they're dead," King said, lifting his coffee mug to his lips. After a look from Lou, he added, "It's fine. We can still do recovery for the families."

"Do you need help digging up the bodies?" Piper asked.

Lou didn't think she was in any shape to dig up the bodies.

"Because I won't lie," Piper went on, misunderstanding her hesitation. "I walked about fifty miles yesterday doing all these interviews and I'm *still* tired."

"The bodies can wait," Lou said.

Piper sighed contentedly. "Thank heavens for that. I have other stuff I need your help on anyway."

Lou sank down into the chair opposite Piper's desk as the girl prattled on.

"Are you okay?" King asked.

Lou turned to him. "What do you mean?"

She was pretty sure that she looked fine. Her eyes would give her away. They were glassy just like Konstantine had said. She'd seen that for herself after her shower. But she was wearing her mirrored shades now. King couldn't see her eyes.

"I'm sorry," he said, mistaking her silence for offense. "You just sort of *plopped* into the chair. I thought maybe you were tired."

Piper laughed. "It's Louie we're talking about. She doesn't get tired. She's indestructible."

Lou had absolutely nothing to say to this, so Piper reclaimed the reins of the conversation. King, however, was still watching Lou too closely.

"So if I could just get you to do your slippy-slip thing so we can nab this guy—"

"Who are you talking about?" King asked, going to the coffee pot for his own refill.

"The stalker. We've had zero luck identifying him, but if Lou uses her compass, she could find him like *that*." Piper snapped her fingers. "Then we would know who to gather the info on."

"Knowing who he is might be helpful, but you can't cut any corners building the case." King pointed his mug at her. "You don't have to prove his identity, you have to prove he did the *crime*."

"I'm still building the case!" Piper said. "I just think it would help if I knew who I was building it against."

"That seems like cheating," King said.

Piper stuck out her bottom lip. "You never said that when you were using Lou to solve one of your cases."

Lou's head was swimming. She wondered if she could stand without stumbling.

"Fine," Piper groaned. "I won't ask Lou to find that guy for me *yet*. But I'm sure that Mel wants her to find Zoey. She can do that, right? Or is it also cheating?"

"Zoey?" Lou asked.

"Yeah, so Mel had this dream that a girl was going to die, and King was like, 'She's not even real,' but he was wrong, and she *is* real, and she's been missing for two weeks. Now Mel is freaked out that she's absolutely going to get murdered or something, so we have to scoop her up before something bad happens. That's no problem, though—you can just do your thing and we'll find her in less than a hop, skip, and jump. Right?"

Piper looked to her expectantly.

"Yeah, I just—" *I'm just going to be sick.* "Excuse me."

Lou was out of her seat and in the closet faster than she'd thought possible.

She didn't make it all the way to the bathroom before she threw up. She'd only managed to push open her linen closet door before she puked all over her living room floor.

She heaved up the coffee until her clenching stomach wasn't able to expel any more.

"Shit," she whispered, before pinching her eyes closed and wiping her mouth with the back of her hand. "At least there's no carpet."

By the time Lou had dumped the mop bucket for the second time and rinsed it clean, she was very aware of the sagging ache in her shoulders and back. She'd used the last bit of her strength to strip off all her clothes, wash up, and change *again*.

When she returned to Konstantine's apartment, he was

there, one leg crossed casually over the other as he sat behind his desk, his laptop open in front of him. At first glance, Lou could have made the mistake of thinking he was at ease.

It wasn't until she realized how tight his jaw was that she knew he was pissed.

"Did you go home for fresh clothes?" he asked.

His voice was steady, no hint of fury in it.

"I also checked in with Piper and King," she said. "They were wondering where I was."

"I could have sent them a message for you."

"I don't want them to know I'm sick." It wasn't until she'd said it that she realized there was some embarrassment attached to it. As if she'd done something wrong by getting sick. "Why are you pissed?"

"Because you should be resting," he said. "Perhaps you truly do not know how this works, blessed as you are to have never been ill. So let me tell you. You have to *rest* in order to get better."

There was more than a little bitterness in his voice.

"If I'm bothering you, I'll go back to my apartment."

"No." The anger broke. His face softened. "I'm sorry. I don't mean to be angry at you."

"But you are."

"Because I want you to be well and you refuse—" He pressed his mouth closed. "Please lay down. You look like hell."

If she was any other woman in the world, she might take offense at such a comment. But Lou *felt* like hell. She doubted he was saying anything but the truth.

"Can we strike a bargain? If you promise to rest, *in bed*, for the rest of the day, I will help you work a few hours tomorrow."

"How many hours?" she asked, something inside her uncoiling.

"How long have you been up now?"

Her head was too fuzzy to do the math. "Two hours? Maybe three."

"Fine. Two or three hours," he said. "Until you get tired again."

"I need to find people. Both Piper and Mel are looking for people."

"I can go with you. I am not some iron-fisted ruler who refuses to let anyone run the show but him," he said. "There is Stefano, and below him, Andrea. I will not be missed."

"What about Riku?" she asked. "I still want to kill him."

She said this defiantly, as if daring him to try and stop her.

"All the more reason for you to get better quickly," he said. "What do I have to say to you to get you back into bed?"

She considered making a face here. Some kind of come-hither sex joke, but her body wasn't willing. She hadn't even realized she'd closed her eyes until Konstantine had wrapped his arms around her.

"*Amore mio, please*," he whispered into her hair.

She leaned her weight against him, and he stumbled back but held her.

"You cannot go on like this," he said. "I haven't seen you this unwell since you faced Petrov."

Because Lou had been unwell then. It hadn't been her body, really. It had been her mind.

There had been something about murdering the mob boss's son that had tormented her. She hadn't slept for weeks because when she did, in her dreams the son would turn into Lou's father, looking up at her from the flat of his back and always a second too late before she could stop herself from pulling the trigger.

"You have to take better care of yourself, and until you learn how, let me take care of you."

Everything coming out of his mouth annoyed her, but she was too tired to fight him.

"Just please stop talking," she said.

The dark shifted around them and the living room fell away. In its place was Konstantine's bedroom. Octavia meowed when she saw them but didn't get up from where she lay stretched on the bed.

Lou fell back against it, all the energy leaving her as soon as she hit the soft mattress. Her aching back and shoulders surrendered immediately.

Konstantine placed his hands on her thighs.

"Do you realize you aren't wearing shoes? Where are your boots? Did King and the others see you like this?"

They did. Was that the real reason why King had asked if she was okay?

"I didn't go outside," she said, and hoped this would hide the fact that she'd simply forgotten to put them back on.

"*Amore mio*," Konstantine chided, straightening her out in the bed and covering her with the thick blankets. He pushed the hair back from her head. "What am I going to do with you?"

"Hold me," she said.

He crawled into the bed behind her and wrapped his arms around her.

"You know," he said, "you will hate me for this, but I like you a little pitiful."

She jabbed him in the ribs with her elbow and he grunted a laugh.

Even my strikes are weak, she thought grumpily.

"There is no shame in wanting to be cared for once in a while," he said. "I like it too, you know. To be cared for when I don't feel well. My mother was the best at it."

Lou turned toward him, snuggling up closer to his chest,

enjoying the warmth of him against her face and the heavy, reassuring arm across her shoulder. He kept her close.

"Rest," he said, kissing her forehead again. "I'll be here."

As Konstantine watched her sleep, he felt the weight of his guilt. He had lied to her. He had lied to her, and worried that it might cause a rift between them should she discover the truth. When Isadora had called with the lab results, she told Konstantine that she was sure Lou was exhausted. Run down because she did not eat well, sleep well, or even seem to understand the basic necessities that one's health required.

But she'd also told him that the microbes they'd found in Lou's blood had in fact diminished. The original count and saturation point were nearly twice as high as they were now.

Did Konstantine think that Lou's illness had anything to do with the test result? No.

He agreed with Isadora that the illness was the result of Lou's lack of care for her own well-being. He also felt that the diminished count confirmed his theory—that the microbes entered Lou's body through open wounds. Knife wounds. Bullet wounds. Perhaps a small number could be introduced through the nose, ears, mouth, or eyes, but Lou had admitted herself that she tried not to swallow that water because she knew just how many bodies—and strange creatures—lived in that lake.

What would have happened if Konstantine had told her that the blood count had changed?

He was convinced that she would have used it as an excuse to go hunting, to justify getting stabbed—or, heaven forbid, *shot*—for the sake of boosting the numbers of those foreign microbes seemingly responsible for her rapid healing.

That she would have used the test result as an excuse to hunt instead of taking the time to rest.

No.

He wanted her to get well. More than that, he wanted her to value taking care of herself above putting herself in danger. He didn't want to say or do anything to cultivate that devil-may-care attitude she had toward her own life.

So he had lied. And now he felt terrible about it.

Forgive me, he thought as he regarded the dark lashes resting on her pale cheeks. *It is better this way.*

She slept deeply even without the help of the medicine that Isadora had prescribed to sedate her. He pushed the hair back from her face and she didn't even stir.

He hated the dark circles under her eyes, though the extra color in her cheeks was cute. It gave her a girlish look that reminded him of the first time he'd seen her.

In fact, watching her sleep beside him was very much like those early days when she'd appeared in his bed in the dead of night, her brow furrowed against bad dreams.

They were closer now than they'd been all those years ago as children.

Then, they were not yet killers.

"You can do this," he whispered, pulling the cover up to her shoulder and smoothing it over her back.

You excel at everything. You will learn how to do this too.

12

___

King was nearly asleep beside Beth when he got the phone call. He'd been dozing, his hand laid loosely over Beth's hip, when his phone began to buzz and spin on the side table. He sat up, pressing his hands to his eyes to clear the sleep away.

"Don't take all the cover with you," Beth chided, shivering.

"I'm sorry." King adjusted the sheets to cover her naked body beside him. He hadn't meant to strip her of protection as he'd grabbed for the phone.

"King," he barked once he finally managed the phone to his ear.

"Robbie, I know it's late, but you'd better come down here."

It was Detective White. His slow-as-molasses voice was recognizable anywhere.

"What's happened?" King said. His first thought went to Piper.

"We've pulled a body out of the river, and we think it might be the girl you're looking for."

The girl he was looking for.

He sat on the side of Beth's bed, his mind frantically trying to run through his list of open and pending cases, but no one stuck out. Then he remembered Mel's dream. "Zoey Peterson?"

"We think we've got her here. You should come down and take a look."

King glanced at the clock on the bedside table. It was almost midnight.

"I'll hurry."

"We're still interviewing the guy who found her," White said. "If HR starts crying about mistreatment of witnesses, we'll have to move it down to the station."

"I'll find you either way." King ended the call.

When he turned back, Beth's dark, wet eyes were watching him. Her cool hand touched his bare back. He shivered.

"Duty calls?" she asked.

"They pulled a body out of the river. White wants me to come identify her and see if she's the one Mel is looking for."

Beth sat up on her elbow, slipping on her eyeglasses from the side table. "I hope for both your sakes it's not."

"Me too."

"Go on then," she said.

He leaned across the shadowed bed and kissed her lightly on the mouth. "Will you forgive me for leaving early?"

She smiled and pushed her fingers through his hair. "I was looking forward to the breakfast you promised, but yes. You're excused."

He kissed her again and then rose to pull on the clothes he'd thrown over the plush armchair in the corner.

"I'll make breakfast up to you," he said.

"Of course you will." She smiled, her head resting in her cupped hand.

Her face turned serious.

"Let me know about the girl once you find out," she said. "I'll pray for you both."

"Thank you." Religious or not, King always accepted prayers.

It took him twenty minutes to reach the crime scene. It was further east than he'd expected it to be. From what Melandra had described about her dream, he'd expected the girl to be found in almost the exact same place on the river-walk, between the French Market and the cluster of Colon-nade shops and praline boutiques beyond it.

However, the part of the road they'd taped off was almost half a mile from there. The flashing lights and uniforms had been visible from several blocks away, as well as the cluster of looky-loos clogging up the street where he needed to park.

He put his Buick between White's Escalade and a black-and-white. The officer who spotted him, Davies, must have known he was coming. He lifted the tape and waved King through before King even had to ask where the detective was.

"Robbie!" White called out. He was little more than a smudge against the backdrop of the river and the illuminated barges clogging the water, but King followed his voice.

White, tall, and broad-shouldered, he came into focus. He wore a wrinkled dress shirt under his NOPD jacket.

"Thanks for coming," he said once King was in ear shot.

"Thanks for calling me." King clasped the man's hand. "Not everyone would've had the courtesy."

White gestured at the body bag lying on the sidewalk at their feet. "Here she is."

King pulled on the latex gloves that White offered and bent down to move the bag off of her face.

It was hard to tell if it was Zoey Peterson, given how blue and bloated the body was. Swollen corpses were clearly human, but it wasn't so easy to tell exactly *which* human.

The hair color was correct, as well as approximate age and height. Beyond that, King couldn't say for sure.

"Did you already notify her family?" he asked.

"We've asked them to ID the body and to agree to a DNA test if they can't recognize her. I suspect that's the problem you're having now."

"It is," he admitted. "The features are similar, but it's hard to say."

"I've seen worse," White said.

King had no doubt this was true. "Do we have a cause of death?"

"They won't know until the full autopsy is completed, but there are ligature marks across her throat. She was definitely strangled, and some of her hair was cut."

"Any idea as to who might have done this?" King asked.

"Not a clue."

King took in the scene. The officers in their NOPD jackets crawling over the walkway, combing the water. Someone stood at the river's edge in scuba gear, obviously about to dive in and look for more evidence. That would be nearly impossible unless the evidence had been tied down by the killer or serendipitously got caught on something. A river like the Mississippi had one job, to carry everything out to sea. For better or worse, it was very good at that job.

The night had a surreal quality to it, with the lights, the low voices. The breath fogging in front of their faces.

King's hands were cold. "Once you talk to the parents, will you let me know what they say?"

"I didn't call you down here just to cut you out later," White said.

"Until you do, don't mention this to Mel, if you don't mind. I don't want her to worry for nothing."

White frowned. "Was the girl a relative?"

King hesitated. "A friend."

If White could sense the lie in this, he was kind enough to say nothing.

"She'll be heartbroken if it's her," he added. This, at least, he knew to be true.

"I think we're too late for that." White blew hot air into his cupped hands.

King's heart kicked. "What do you mean?"

White nodded in the direction of the parked cars and the cluster of people watching.

King turned, scanning the scene. That's when he saw her.

Melandra stood just beyond the yellow tape, mixed in with the bystanders. However, unlike the other looky-loos, who were obviously gawking at the morbidity of the moment, relishing the excitement of something new and unexpected, Mel looked ill.

Her face was grave, her eyes wide and unblinking.

"Excuse me," King said, and left White where he stood.

"Of course," White said, bending to zip the body bag up again.

King stopped just short of the yellow tape.

"You're up late," he said by way of greeting.

"Is it her?" Mel asked.

"How did you know there was a body down here?"

"I had a feeling."

King didn't want to challenge this. "That's a very specific feeling. A body in a river feeling."

"Is it her?" she asked again.

"We don't know. The body is too—"

He searched for a polite word. Disfigured? Unrecognizable?

"It's swollen from the water," he said. *Swollen* wasn't too bad, right?

He thought *swollen* was a better word choice than the others that had come to his mind. If he had been less specific, she might think the girl had been beaten or stabbed beyond recognition or something equally horrifying.

She still pinched her eyes shut. "I was too late."

"You don't know that," King said. "That body could've come from anywhere upstream."

Mel twisted the bangles on her wrist, forcing them to chime musically. This seemed to make her more stressed rather than calm. Hadn't she once told King that she wore them to calm herself down?

Time for a new trigger, he thought.

"How did you get here?"

"I walked," she said.

King lifted the tape, crossing over to her side. "Let me take you home."

"What if they—"

"There's nothing else we can do tonight," King told her. "Maybe the divers will find something, but the body is going to the morgue. White promised to call me when they know more."

King took her elbow gently and moved her away from the crowd toward his parked Buick. Reluctantly, Mel let herself be led to the car and eased into the passenger seat.

Once she was safely inside, King shut the door and jogged around to the driver's side.

He turned on the car and mashed the buttons to get the heat going. "Unfortunately, this beauty is so old we won't feel the heat before I've already got her parked back at the shop."

Mel pulled her jacket closer around her. "I don't mind the cold."

"I do," King said, looking over his shoulder to make sure no one was behind him.

The sullen mood continued as he drove them through the French Quarter streets—all quiet except for Bourbon, of course—and pulled into the alley beside the shop.

"Let's get inside," he said. He removed the keys from the ignition. "We'll be warmer."

Mel didn't move.

Then King saw the tears on her cheeks.

"Hey," he said. "Don't cry."

I shouldn't have said that. She can cry if she wants to.

He tried again. "We don't know that it's her. You might be upset for no reason."

"They just pulled a girl out of the river. No matter what, they just pulled somebody's baby out of a river, Robert. I'd say that's a very good reason to cry."

Shit. "You're right. I'm sorry."

He rummaged in his glove compartment for tissues and found a few scratchy paper napkins.

He tried to straighten them into a less crumpled version of themselves and pressed them into her hand.

She used them to dab at her eyes and wipe at her nose.

"I just don't want you to feel like you've failed when we don't even know if it's her yet," he said.

"How can I not feel like I've failed? We weren't quick enough. We—"

King's phone buzzed again. It was a text message from White.

Peterson's little sister doesn't think it's her. Girl was by two days ago to borrow money. If true, the timeline doesn't match. Preliminary forensics thinks Jane's been in the water for at least a week.

King read the text to Mel.

Mel held the napkin against her runny nose. "She was alive two days ago? Where does the sister live?"

King asked White via text. He answered.

"Biloxi, according to White."

Mel's shoulders relaxed. "So it might not be her."

"It's probably *not* her," King insisted. He was trying to remember what he'd learned about crime scenes where the body had been recovered from water. He didn't think it was possible to pinpoint exactly how long a corpse had been in a wet environment, but yes, there was quite a difference between a corpse that had been submerged for weeks or months and one that had taken barely more than a long bath.

He did not convey these morbid details to Mel.

Mel pressed the heels of her hands into her eyes. "I really thought I'd messed this up."

"You haven't. The case is still open. Don't give up yet," King said. "Come here."

He pulled Melandra into a hug.

"It's going to be all right," he said. He stopped short of promising that the girl would live, because he'd been at this too long to make such fake reassurances.

Mel straightened the scarf on her head and took a big breath. "We should go inside. I can't feel my fingers."

"Now you're talking sense," he said, and threw open his heavy door.

It was too cold of a night to keep sitting in the car like this. He used his own key to open Fortunes and Fixes and ushered her inside. He let her take the stairs first as he locked up the shop behind them.

She stopped at the top, turning back.

"What is it?" he asked, standing a few steps below her.

"If it's not too much to ask, will you sit up with me for a little while? I don't want to go back to bed yet."

King checked his own energy levels and found that he was pretty awake himself. The cold air was partially responsible, but also the excitement of getting a call in the dead of night and the bustle of the crime scene. While he wouldn't wish this sort of night on anyone, he'd forgotten how thrilling it could be.

"Sure," he said. "Do we need coffee?"

"No," she said. "I *am* trying to go back to bed, just not right away."

"Bad dreams?"

Her nod was barely noticeable as she turned away from him and slid the key into the lock of her apartment door. When she pushed it open, Lady was there, tail thumping against the linoleum.

"*Ma grande*," Mel said, scratching the pup behind her ears.

Lady pushed her cool nose into King's palm in turn. "Thanks for holding down the fort. Good girl."

Lady's tail wagged harder.

"I'm thinking QVC," Melandra said, crossing to the television and turning it on. "If I don't get sleepy looking at jewelry and crockery, I don't know what else will do it."

King settled down onto the sofa beside her. "I bought the most amazing vacuum from this channel once."

"You can't be talking about that old thing you have in your apartment." She pulled the blanket off the arm of the couch and threw it over King's lap. Then she grabbed a second for herself from the adjacent chair.

"No, this one was from a long time ago. I still regret letting my wife take it in the divorce."

The woman on the television was all smiles. "For just six payments of thirty-nine ninety-nine, you can own this beautiful crystal tea set. It comes with the delicate hand-painted tray and—"

He turned to Mel. Her head was against the cushion, her eyes closed.

Well that was quick, he thought, and wondered if he should slip out now and go back to his apartment.

No, he'd better wait. She may have dozed off, but there was no way she was in a deep sleep two minutes in. He might wake her if he tried to leave now.

King grabbed the remote and turned the volume down

before using it to channel surf. He settled on a movie about Bundy, played by a hot young kid with all the charisma but none of the crazy in his eyes.

They'd just gotten to the part about how he'd met the girl that would become his wife when King's eyes began to flutter closed. He was asleep before the first body was even found.

13

———

Riku smashed the shot glass against the table and it shattered, bursting open against his hand. He turned it over, exposing the ring of blood forming in his palm. The deep gashes filled red as he inspected the damage in the light. The glass still stuck to his skin glittered.

Yui placed a bowl under his hand and Watanabe put a large glass of water beside the bowl so he could wash the wound clean.

Neither said, *Be more careful, sir*, or *What happened, sir.* He didn't even get an *Are you all right, sir?*

They'd stopped after the first few attempts, when their care had only made his fury worse.

He'd been irritable like this for days, since that Italian bastard had the audacity to enter his home—*his home.*

His bodyguards had insisted that it wasn't possible. They did a sweep of his quarters while he'd been away, as they were always instructed to do, and again before he was due back home, to make sure there were no would-be assassins hoping to catch Riku unaware.

Once Riku began insisting that Konstantine had come

with the witch, that he had popped in and out of his dark bedroom just as the rumors had said La Strega could do, they'd stopped asking questions.

"Why don't you believe me?" Riku said now. There was no whininess or pitifulness in his voice. Only the anger remained.

"You misunderstand, sir," Watanabe said, pushing the clean water toward his hand, urging him to use it.

When he didn't, Yui took his hand in hers and opened the palm. Riku allowed this. He held still while she poured the cold water over his cut. The water washed the palm clean, carrying the glass shards into the bowl.

"What do I misunderstand?" Riku looked to Watanabe, who lowered his gaze. "Are you telling me that you *don't* think I'm crazy? That you *don't* think I'm lying about the Italian being in my bedroom? Or that he had a woman with him?"

"We believe you that the woman was in your bedroom," Watanabe said, keeping his gaze down, fixed somewhere on the countertop beneath Riku's resting arms.

Yui continued to work without comment.

Pain through Riku's hand and he snatched it away. Yui didn't flinch. He liked that about her. He could backhand her now and she wouldn't move from the spot where she stood. Perhaps that was the reason why she was the only woman in his personal entourage.

Once he lowered his hand, she pressed a clean towel to it.

"If you believe me then why isn't anyone doing what I say? I *want* his *head*."

"There is no definite proof that the woman works for Konstantine. She has killed as many of his men as from any other group. We can't retaliate against him without proof. His connections in Europe and North America are so strong that—"

"We are the third-largest economy in the world!" Riku

slammed his injured hand on the tabletop. "We own half of Japan. I will *not* bow to him."

"No one is asking you to, sir," Watanabe said. His face was red now. "We are trying to make contact now. You will be the first to know when we reach him."

It wasn't enough. It wasn't fast enough and it wasn't brutal enough. How could they ask him to sit here and wait like this?

Riku twisted the cloth Yui had left in his palm until his fingers were nearly purple.

"For fifteen years I have been looking for her. Fifteen years! And I am close, *so* close. I will not have that witch or Konstantine—not *anyone*—stop me now."

Yui and Watanabe exchanged a look. It was Watanabe who asked, "Who are you looking for, sir?"

Mai.

His precious Mai. He knew that she was here, somewhere in this world. Because she'd killed herself, she would have been reborn in terrible circumstances. But no matter where she was, he would find her. They would be together again.

He had begun to feel like the little girl he'd found might be her—she was the first one to call forth those feelings in him again—but they'd taken her away before he could be sure.

So close. He'd been *so* close.

"Both of you. Get out of here," Riku said with a wave of his hand.

"But about the Song clan—" Watanabe began.

"Forget the Song clan! Get out! *Get out!*" Riku grabbed another glass and threw it. Watanabe moved at the last moment, and it shattered against the refrigerator behind him.

Yui was out of the apartment first. Watanabe closed the door just behind them.

Riku was left alone with the throbbing in his hand and the pounding in his head.

They don't understand. I know what I saw. I know, and that bastard has to pay for this violation.

He squeezed his hand until blood seeped out from between his fingers.

Why did they think he should fear them? *He?* Riku Yamamoto? One of the most powerful men in the world? He didn't believe the rumors that Petrov had been destroyed by the witch. Nor did he believe that she could open fire on a hundred men and be the only one to walk out of the room alive.

That she'd been shot and stabbed but always survived. That she was, in other words, immortal.

Did he believe that she could move through the darkness?

Now he did. But rumors were almost always blown out of proportion. Perhaps she was part kitsune or jorōgumo, but even those creatures could be brought down by someone clever.

Whatever she was or wasn't, he knew that just because she had one ability, it did not mean she was capable of all the great and terrible things that Riku had heard about her.

That she knew a man's secret thoughts.

That she could find her prey anywhere, anytime, no matter where he hid himself.

That if she chose to take a man, he would never be seen again.

It was ridiculous.

She was no god.

A fierce woman at best.

He knew fierce women. He'd nearly been killed when he'd challenged Saeko for ownership of this very organization. Yet despite her best efforts, he had still twisted his blade in her stomach and spilt her guts on the floor for all those gathered to see.

Sato Song was another fierce woman. She led the Song clan and controlled much of the Southern Asian territories. Riku avoided upsetting her, but only for the sake of simplicity. Not because he feared her.

He feared nothing.

He would find Mai again. Even if he had to move heaven and earth to make it happen.

He poured himself another shot of sake and tipped it back.

Let them think what they wanted of him. It didn't matter. They would obey his commands all the same.

A rough knock on the door reawakened the irritation he'd almost managed to quell.

"What is it?" Riku called out.

"We have the one you asked for, sir."

Riku brightened. "Come in."

Kenchi pushed open the door and held it for the others who followed. Shibu and a slender young man entered.

The young man couldn't be more than seventeen or eighteen. He had no facial hair to speak of.

"Who is this?" he asked in Japanese.

Shibu nudged the boy and said in English, "Tell him your name."

"My name is Riccardo."

Riku smiled. "What accent do I hear? Where do you come from?"

The boy licked his lips nervously. "Italy, sir."

"Italy? Really? Which part of the country?"

"Florence, sir."

"Then you must know a man named Konstantine."

It wasn't a question, so the young man made no response.

Riku twisted the towel still wrapped around his hand and gritted his teeth. "Do you know him?"

"Yes, sir."

"Good. I want you to give him a message for me."

Riku's eyes cut to Kenchi.

Kenchi pulled the switch blade from his pocket and pressed steel to the boy's cheek, just below his eye. He pressed hard, until the boy gasped and blood began spilling down his cheek.

"I-I'm sorry! I don't know anything!" the boy cried.

"That's all right," Riku said. "You don't need to know anything to deliver this message."

By following the routine Isadora recommended, Lou's strength slowly returned.

On the third evening, she stood in Konstantine's apartment, stretching her neck from one side to the other, trying to gauge how her body felt.

Her limbs were shaky but held well enough. Her stomach and throat still felt raw. Her mind soft at its edges.

"And?" he asked.

"I feel better," she told him.

He regarded her with skepticism from the bed, where he was scratching Octavia's head.

"Would you lie to me just so you can get back to work?" he said.

"I'm not your prisoner."

"You're not my prisoner," he repeated with a tone of mockery. "But may I ask what task is so pressing?"

Lou thought of the girl Melandra wanted to find and the stalker Piper had yet to identify. A third possibility was the NYC killer's bodies hidden in upstate New York. Dani had told her there was no rush. If the killer was dead, and so were the victims he'd left behind, then they could be uncovered at any time.

"I want to find the girl Mel is looking for. And the stalker Piper is trying to ID."

Konstantine relaxed.

"What?" she asked. "What did you think I was going to say?"

When he didn't answer, she arched a brow.

"I thought you were going to do what Busaba asked of you."

Busaba.

After what Lou saw in Yamamoto's bedroom, Lou had little doubt what happened to girls in Riku's care.

"When I tried to take Busaba, it wasn't clean," Lou admitted.

Konstantine's lip twitched in a smile.

"I *am* going to destroy him."

"I have no doubt," he said.

"But I might need another day or two for that," she added.

"Or five," Konstantine countered.

She shifted her weight. "Are you coming or not?"

"I am." He lifted Octavia from his lap and touched his nose to hers.

It took him five minutes to change his shirt despite Lou's protests that no one they would be seeing gave a damn if he had cat hair on his clothes.

Konstantine wouldn't let it go. He wanted a new shirt, a new sweater, and a leather jacket of his own before he declared that he was ready to go.

"No, wait." He put a pistol in the waistband of his pants at the small of his back. "Okay, now I'm ready."

"I hope we won't need that."

"You can never be too sure," he said, and smiled down

at her.

Lou slid her arms around his waist, enjoying the feel of her cheek against his throat the moment before his bedroom fell away.

When the world reformed around them, they were in a closet. The smell of cardboard boxes hung in the air. Lou groped for a handle and found it.

The door swung open on Fortunes and Fixes. Melandra wore a ruby-red hair scarf today and a long purple skirt that cut across her brown boots. She was on the telephone, scribbling something down on the notepad by the register.

"Yes, I understand," Mel said, glancing up.

She held up one finger when she saw them.

"Yes, I'll hold again," she said with a sigh. Then she put her palm over the receiver.

"What are you two doing here?" she asked, her dark eyes flitting from Lou's face to Konstantine's and back. She frowned as she took in Lou's appearance.

"Are you okay?" she asked. "You look pale. I mean, paler than usual."

Lou ignored this. "Do you still want me to find the girl you're looking for?"

"Yes, hello. I'm still here." Mel held up a finger again. She nodded, listening to the voice on the other end of the line. "Three weeks? I guess that's better than the eight weeks the other one quoted me. All right. I'll take both cases. Yes. Yes, that's correct. Just put it all on that card, please."

Mel jotted two rows of numbers down on the pad while the other person spoke.

"Yes, thank you. Have a nice day."

"Distribution," Mel complained. "It just ain't what it used to be."

"The girl," Lou gently reminded her. She didn't want to

waste time. She didn't expect her stamina to be at a hundred percent this soon.

Mel sighed. "She's probably dead. The police just pulled a girl out of the river. We're waiting to see what the parents say, and I ain't had a dream since."

"What was her name again?"

"Zoey Peterson," Mel said, tugging at the scarf on her head while she flashed Konstantine a tight smile.

Is the girl she's looking for alive?

Lou reached for her inner knowing, to the compass always whirling and clicking within her. She waited, eyes closed, getting a feel for the directional pull.

"She's around," Lou said. "Or at least the compass is pulling toward something."

Melandra bit her lip. "If it's not too much trouble, could you—"

"It's not any trouble." Lou stepped into the storage closet and waited for Konstantine to join her.

Konstantine must've seen her smile before she pulled the door closed and sealed them up in the dark.

"What's so funny?" he asked.

"Do you know how many girls Piper has made out with in here?"

His hands were on either side of her face, bending in for the kiss. "Will she be upset if we—"

"I can hear you," Melandra called. "And Piper knows I hate it when anybody's kissing in the storage closet. This is a *business* establishment."

Konstantine was still holding Lou's face when Fortunes and Fixes disappeared and a new room rose up to replace it.

A door creaked open and light spilled over them.

"I'm so sorry," a woman cried, and swung the door shut. "I knocked but didn't hear you."

Lou attuned her ears to the world outside the room.

The smell of coffee was strong and the sound of fingers flying across keyboards was nonstop. Plates clattered and someone called out an order.

A diner? A café?

Konstantine released her. "Where are we?"

"Let's find out." Lou pushed open the door.

The woman was still standing outside the door when Lou stepped out into the café.

"I'm sorry," she murmured again, her eyes sliding from Lou to Konstantine. At the sight of Konstantine, her face turned redder.

"It's not a problem," Konstantine said, and flashed a charming grin.

The woman looked ready to burst.

I can't take him anywhere.

Lou stepped out of the way of a man balancing two coffees on a tray.

Her gaze slid over the tables and their occupants, trying to figure out why the compass had brought her here. Because it wasn't for the redhead hovering in the bathroom doorway, shamelessly checking out Konstantine.

She wondered if they were near a university. The crowd was younger, and many of the tables had two or three occupants with laptops open in front of them.

Only one table had a girl sitting alone, earbuds in her ears.

Lou's navel snagged.

"That's her," Lou said.

Konstantine followed her gaze. "You're sure?"

She was. "What are the chances we can get her to step into the bathroom with us?"

"I would be willing to do that," a voice said behind them. "Just so you know."

Lou turned to find the woman who'd opened the bathroom door on them. One look sent her scurrying.

"You can't blame her, *amore mio*," Konstantine said gently. "If I saw you, I wouldn't be able to pass up the opportunity either."

Lou snorted. "It's not me she wants."

"Are you going to order or what?"

Konstantine turned to find a young man wearing a beanie gesturing at the counter.

They were blocking the line.

"Excuse us," Konstantine said, pulling Lou to one side.

By the time she turned back, the table was empty.

Lou spotted Zoey moving toward the exit, a gray backpack tossed over one shoulder. She tugged on Konstantine's arm as she passed, moving to catch her before she got too far.

The girl was halfway across the parking lot before Lou managed to get one hand on her shoulder.

"What's your problem?" She whirled, her hands coming up in fists before her eyes even found Lou's.

Her navel snagged again, and that was all Lou needed to know this was Zoey.

Zoey's gaze slid past Lou to Konstantine. Then back to Lou again.

Her eyes went wide. She had none of the enamored longing in her gaze that the other woman in the café had. "Are you guys going to hurt me?"

"No," Lou said. "But my friend is looking for you."

The girl stepped backward into the shadow of a willow tree, and Lou entered the darkness with her. Konstantine, probably sensing the imminent departure, placed one hand on her hip.

"There are people, *amore mio*."

"They won't know what they saw," she said, and wrapped her hand around the girl's arm.

Zoey opened her mouth, but the scream forming on her

lips never materialized. It was swallowed by the shifting space between them.

When the world became solid again, Lou opened the storage closet as quickly as she could. She didn't want the girl to start swinging in the dark.

Lou and Konstantine stood in the shop, waiting for Zoey to come out of the closet. If Lou hadn't been sure she'd brought the girl over, she'd start to wonder if the closet was empty, given the silence.

"Did you find her?" Mel came around the register and peered into the dark. "Zoey?"

Nothing.

"Zoey, honey, are you in there?"

Slowly, the girl inched into the light. She looked Mel over from head to toe, then at the shop around them.

Cradling her elbow, she asked, "What the hell just happened?"

14

———

Melandra's heart raced. Here she was. In the flesh, the girl she'd been dreaming about for nights on end. She even wore the same green coat. Blessedly, there was no blood smeared on the front of her clothes, but that wouldn't be enough to ease the dread Melandra had been carrying in her heart since the first night the dream had come.

"Who the hell are you and what do you want from me?" Zoey demanded again. Then she turned on the storage closet light and searched the small room. "Where did they go?"

Think of something. Anything. Give her a reason to stay.

"My name is Melandra Durand," Mel said finally, because she had no idea where else to start. *I've been dreaming about you* seemed too forward. Lord, she wished Grandmamie had given her more instruction on what to do once someone found the person they'd been looking for.

"I own this store," she went on. "Melandra's Fortune and Fixes. We're in the French Quarter of New Orleans."

"The French Quarter," the girl said. "I made it all the way to Biloxi. How the hell am I back in Louisiana?"

She went to the door, and Mel thought, *This is it. This is where she runs away and never comes back.*

Only she didn't run away. She stood in the street outside of Fortunes and Fixes and stared in disbelief.

Slowly, she came back into the shop and dropped her backpack on the floor by the register.

"What's happening? Is this magic or something? Are you a witch? Are those friends of yours vampires or demons or what?"

So she was a superstitious one.

"I can't tell you what they are because I don't know," Mel said, standing a little straighter. She lowered her voice to the one she used for readings. It had taken her many years to cultivate that mystical air and ominous tone. If that was what she had to do to keep this girl here and safe, she wasn't above using such tricks.

"I asked my...servants to find you because you are in *grave* danger."

Zoey Peterson's eyes widened. "How did you know?"

"I had a—" *Don't say dream.* "—vision about you, and the spirits asked me to keep you safe."

Zoey gripped the side of the glass case. Melandra tried not to scowl at the fingerprints she was leaving behind.

It's fine, it's fine. They'll come off.

"Are you being serious right now?" Zoey asked. "You had a vision about me? Some voodoo occult lady had a vision *about me?*"

Melandra resisted the urge to correct her. This wasn't voodoo and she shouldn't talk about something she didn't understand so casually. Instead, she let it go. It was important to pick one's battles.

"Yes, a powerful vision. So I asked that you be brought here so I can keep you safe."

Of course, she'd considered telling her the truth, but Mel

knew that dreams weren't that reliable. They could convey that the girl was in trouble and that something was going to happen, maybe even that the riverwalk really was involved. But the other details weren't to be counted on. Would she be shot? Stabbed? Hit by a car?

Mel wouldn't know until the moment of truth arrived.

"What's going to happen to me?"

"It's not clear," Mel said. "Visions change. Will you stay close to me until the danger passes? Can you do that?"

The girl looked around the shop.

"What do you mean, stay close to you? Like, in this shop or something?"

"I understand that you ran away from home," Mel said.

The girl took a step back, and Mel felt certain she was going to turn and bolt from the store.

"I don't care about that," Mel said. "I'm not going to turn you in or tell your parents. I only ask because that means you're not from here. Do you have a safe place to stay?"

"No, not really."

"I have an apartment upstairs, and the cutest dog you've ever seen. Do you want to stay with me?"

When the girl looked uncertain, Mel called Lady around the counter.

"*Ma grande.*" Lady came to attention at her side. To Zoey, Mel said, "Do you want to pet her?"

She was placing her bet on the girl being an animal lover. Some people hated or feared dogs, and Mel really hoped this girl wasn't one of them, or the idea of staying in Mel's apartment with one might be a dealbreaker for her.

Zoey's eyes rounded and she dropped to a crouch in front of Lady, immediately adopting the voice that most people used with their dog. "Oh my goodness. You're so cute. Look at these ears."

She gave the softest *bop* to the top of each of Lady's erect ears.

"You look like a police dog," Zoey said. "So regal."

She straightened and puffed out her own chest in imitation.

Lady's tail thumped against the floor.

"I'm sure it's weird having an old woman make such an offer, but I just want to keep an eye on you until the danger passes. I'm not usually wrong about these things."

The girl had an expression on her face that Mel couldn't quite place. The sadness was clear enough, but there was something else mixed in.

"Why would you help me?" the girl asked.

"I told you. I had a vision."

The girl frowned. "Yeah, but you could've had a vision about anybody. Why would you have a vision about *me?*"

That was an excellent question and one Mel did not have an answer to. There was only one way to handle this. In her best fortune teller voice, she said, "I don't question the source of my gifts. I only do what the source asks of me, when asked."

The girl's eyes were as wide as saucers. "Okay. I'll stay, but only for a little while."

Zoey's stomach rumbled, and her embarrassment shone on her face.

Mel relaxed. "How about we get you a hot meal?"

Piper was trying to find her gloves. Her favorite pair with the fingers cut off had been in the pocket of her winter coat, but now they weren't. Had Dani washed them?

"Just one second," she said. "I know they're here somewhere."

Lou stood in her living room in her leather jacket and

mirrored shades. Her hair hung loose around her face, and Piper thought her cheeks were a little more flushed than usual.

The Italian stallion was with her, so that might have something to do with it. The fact she'd brought him along was unusual, but Piper wasn't going to ask what was up with the boyfriend standing right there.

"Do you want me to help you?" Konstantine asked.

"No, it'll just be a second," Piper said, waving him away. "Maybe they fell out of my pocket."

Geez, why did he have to sound like that? With his large, pouty lips and big doe eyes.

That freaking jaw, man. She sort of wanted to hit it with something to see what would take more damage. The jaw or the object.

Why am I thinking about how pretty he is?

Because I'm still trying to figure out if my friend deserves better, she assured herself.

Her mind began counting the number of times Konstantine had run to Lou's aid. When he'd cared for her and had dropped everything to make sure she was safe.

Fine, she thought. *I guess he's good enough. Even if he is king of the underworld or whatever.*

She opened her coat closet by her apartment door and turned on the light.

There they were. The two black gloves *had* fallen from her pockets. One was on the floor of the closet, but the other had landed on the tall cuff of Dani's boot and hung there as if impaled.

Piper pulled them on, wiggling the tips of her exposed fingers. "Okay. I'm ready."

Adjusting her coat across her back and shoulders, she stood in front of Konstantine and Lou.

Lou put one hand on Piper's arm and the other on Konstantine's.

How cute. It's bring your boyfriend to work day, she thought grumpily. She didn't realize until that moment that she'd been missing some alone time with Lou. They hadn't hung out for weeks. She'd have to ask Lou to take them somewhere fun soon so they could chat and catch up on each other's lives.

Well, Piper would chat. Lou would listen intensely and stare in that direct way of hers, but hey. Heavy eye contact was a love language in its own right.

"We're looking for the guy who is stalking Samantha Brown."

"There are probably a thousand Samantha Browns in the world," Lou said.

Where was this attitude coming from?

Piper pulled her phone from her coat pocket and scrolled for a picture. She found one of Samantha and turned the screen toward Lou so she could see. "This Samantha Brown. We're looking for the guy stalking *this* girl."

She tapped her nails against the screen.

There was a beat of silence, and Piper had a chance to look at Konstantine in profile, given that all of his attention was on Lou.

"Are you okay, *amore mio*?" he asked softly.

Lou scowled. "I'm fine."

Before Piper could ask why Lou wouldn't be okay, the world twisted in on itself. Like a hand reaching into a bag, grabbing the bottom, and pulling it inside out.

Piper's hand went up instinctively to grab ahold of Lou, but there was nothing in the darkness. It wasn't like traveling through a space with her. Piper had done this enough to know that inside the *in between*, as she'd come to think of it, there was nothing. The idea that Lou was even holding on to her was an illusion.

The world reformed and Piper bent her knees to steady herself. It was a habit she'd picked up so that she didn't lose her balance. Konstantine also, irritatingly, stood perfectly still beside Lou.

Show off.

The sound of water running caught Piper's ears.

"He's in the bathroom," Lou said softly.

Piper saw the light seeping from beneath the closed door.

They stood ten feet away at the top of a staircase. There were three other doors, but they were all closed except one, which appeared to be some sort of office.

"This looks like a nice house," Piper whispered.

"Brock, do you want potatoes or no?" a woman called from somewhere below. That's when Piper fully realized they were standing on a landing upstairs.

"Brock?" the woman called again.

The three of them froze.

Oh shit. Don't come up here, don't come up here, don't—

"I think he's in the shower, honey," a man said.

Sounds of kitchen cabinets opening and closing. A burner being turned off.

Piper strained to hear the barest hint of footfall.

Nothing.

"They're not coming," Konstantine whispered.

Lou had already put one arm on Piper's in preparation of a quick exit. Now she relaxed it.

Must be his parents, Piper thought. *Brock* lived at home with his parents. Or maybe grandparents? But the voices hadn't sounded very old.

She listened to the shower run for a moment longer, and convinced that he wasn't getting out yet, went to the office. She slid past the neat desk and bookcase to the open window. Outside, there were quiet little houses lining the opposite side of the street. She tried to get a good look at this house but saw only the blue siding and a few bricks. No mailbox with a number on it or a helpful green sign indicating the name of the street.

She went back to Lou and whispered, "I don't know where we are."

Lou turned her wrist, illuminating its face, and pushed a few buttons. "I've dropped a pin."

Piper's phone vibrated in her pocket, and she opened the text from Lou showing where she was.

Man, was she glad King had made Lou update her communications. Before, the best she got was when Lou would return her page.

Her page. What era was that?

This was way more useful.

"We're in Seabrook," she whispered. "What the hell?"

Seabrook wasn't even in New Orleans proper. What did this guy do, drive into town to terrorize college girls?

The shower turned off, and Piper lifted her phone and turned on the camera. She aimed it at the bathroom door.

Lou's grip on her shoulder tightened.

"Not yet," Piper whispered. "I want a picture of his face."

"That means he will also see *your* face," Konstantine whispered.

No one asked you, buddy, she thought. She just pulled up her hood and held her phone in front of her to block as much of her face as possible.

"He won't be sure what he sees. As soon as I get the—"

The bathroom door swung open and there was a bare-chested young man with a towel wrapped around his waist.

Piper snapped the photo, and the young man turned toward her, drawn by the recognizable *click*.

Before she could check to make sure the photo had worked, Lou was pulling them through the shadows.

Piper's apartment formed around them, and this time

Piper did stumble, as she hadn't had time to prepare for the slip.

"Did you get what you needed?" Lou asked.

Her voice sounded hoarse.

Piper used her fingers to zoom in on the picture she'd taken.

"*Boom*. Got you." There he was, looking very much like a *Brock*. Athletic and entitled.

She turned the phone so Lou could see the picture. "Yeah. With this and his parents' address I should be able to ID him —*Whoa*. Are you okay?"

Lou swayed on her feet. Actually *swayed*, as if falling into a swoon.

When she did, her sunglasses slipped, and Konstantine caught them and removed them from her face. He slipped them into a pocket somehow without ever releasing her.

"Okay, so you've got some moves," Piper said.

Konstantine didn't even spare her a smile. All of his attention was on Lou. "We should go."

"You can't just leave," Piper said. "What was that? What just happened?"

When Lou didn't answer, Piper cocked a brow at Konstantine.

"She's sick."

A hand went to Piper's chest reflexively. "Oh my god—like *cancer?*"

"No. A cold."

"Geez. You scared the hell out of me." Piper loosed a breath. Then she frowned and took a step back. "Wait, you have a *cold?*"

The very idea was bizarre. Piper's mind dilated as if trying to make room for this impossibility.

"*You*," she said, taking in Lou's glassy eyes and red cheeks. "*You* have a cold?"

Lou scowled at her.

"You need to lay down. You've been on your feet too long," Konstantine said.

Piper didn't think they'd been gone that long.

"You found two people. You helped your friends. That's enough for today," he chided her.

Two people. Your friends. So she got Mel's girl too. Or maybe someone else, but Piper doubted it. Lou didn't have many friends.

"We'll talk about cold etiquette later. Just go lie down," Piper said.

"Cold etiquette?" Lou frowned.

"Yeah, like the fact you don't go around other people *at all* when you have one."

"I don't think you'll catch this," Konstantine said reassuringly.

"Thanks." Piper rolled her eyes at him. *I'm sorry I missed the MD at the end of your name.*

To Lou, she said, "Please go lay down. There's nothing happening that can't wait a week. I'll tell Mel and King to leave you alone too."

Piper blinked and they were gone. She stood in her dark apartment alone with Lou's expression burned into her mind. Had that been embarrassment?

Was Lou embarrassed to be sick?

If so, Piper needed to convince her that everyone got sick once in a while. A fever wasn't some sort of personal failing.

"I'll add it to the list of birthday things I want to do," she said, and made a note on her cell phone. *Pep talk about getting sick.*

Lou's birthday.

Piper checked the date.

She still had time. Hopefully Lou would feel better before her big day rolled around.

15

Someone was knocking on Konstantine's apartment door. Lou rose up on her forearms, squinting into the dark.

"It's only Stefano, come to talk business with me," Konstantine said, pressing a hand to her forehead. "Rest, *amore mio.*"

Her eyes fluttered closed, and Konstantine hoped the medicine would be strong enough to send her off to sleep for several hours. She'd overdone it with the two hunts. Granted, they might not have been as physically demanding as those that ended in a kill, but she'd still been on her feet and had still used her gifts, which he suspected required more energy than Lou herself even realized.

When Konstantine reached the bottom of the stairs, Stefano was sitting on his sofa with one leg crossed over the other.

"Why knock if you were going to let yourself in?" Konstantine asked.

"I didn't want to interrupt anything," he said.

Konstantine expected to see a teasing look in Stefano's eyes, but they were dark. Even gloomier than usual.

"What's happened?" Konstantine asked.

"Someone overnighted a box to us."

"What was in it?"

"One of our men," Stefano said. "He'd been tortured. *Fatto a pezzi.*"

Konstantine suddenly didn't want to sit. His stomach twisted. "Who?"

"Riccardo."

Riccardo. He was barely a man. He'd been in Tokyo for six months. They were supposed to bring him home weeks ago but had decided to leave him at the last minute.

"Don't blame yourself," Stefano said.

Konstantine cared about his people. Stefano's soft green eyes said he knew this.

Despite his disappointment with the outcome of the situation, there was no disdain in Stefano's voice. No accusations. Only regret.

Stefano knew as well as anyone that sometimes even the best decisions led to bad results.

"Forgive me for overstepping your command, but I already told all of our people to leave Japan at once. Not just Tokyo. I didn't want to waste time asking you," Stefano said.

Konstantine nodded. "A good choice. Did they all make it out?"

"Yes. I've sent Diablo and his team to bring them home."

"Good." Konstantine crossed to the kitchen and pulled the coffee beans out of the cabinet. He plugged in the grinder, then checked the time. "Would you like a cappuccino or an espresso?"

"A cappuccino."

"*Sembra che hai visto un fantasma,*" Konstantine said, and he spoke honestly.

Stefano was as white as a ghost.

"It was a fucking mess," he said. "They made a mess of him."

Stefano rubbed his brow.

"*Mi dispiace che non sono potuto andare.*" If Konstantine had been the one there, then he could have spared Stefano the horror.

Stefano waved him away.

But even before Konstantine could pour the coffee from the moka and offer the steaming cup to Stefano, his eyes were turning dark again.

"This is getting bad." His eyes had flicked past Konstantine's shoulders to the ceiling above. "You will have to ask her to save us, if it comes to it."

"We will save ourselves," Konstantine assured him, taking a seat at his desk and sipping his own cappuccino. He hoped the caffeine would not keep him awake when he wanted to return to bed with Lou soon. The truth was that she wasn't the only one benefiting from the extra sleep. "*Dubiti di me?*"

"No, I don't doubt you," Stefano said. "But we could use the help. She will owe it to us if she provokes war with him. How many of his women has she taken?"

"Only Busaba," he said. *And the little girl.*

Stefano arched a brow.

"She will help us when she can," Konstantine assured him. "In the meantime, we will hold our own. Unless you no longer believe I can do such a thing."

Stefano didn't dignify this with a reply. "I have complete faith in you, *fratello*. But you must admit she makes things much easier. We lose fewer people, we spend fewer resources."

His words trailed off as if he were looking for more reasons.

"Fear," he said finally. "Her greatest weapon is fear."

That reminded Konstantine of something he should have thought of sooner.

I'd better not get this cold, he thought, pushing away the haze of his mind. Perhaps he was only tired too.

"Did you start the rumors before calling our people home?" Konstantine asked.

"*Sì*. And I found Yamamoto's family. His parents are dead, but he had a brother and a sister. His brother, Hinato Yamamoto, lives in Kyoto. He's a schoolteacher. It seems he never became involved in—" He waved his hand, searching for the word he wanted. "This business. His brother's business. Their sister, Mai Yamamoto, died about twenty years ago. She was younger than both of her brothers by quite a bit. Riku was seventeen when she was born."

"How did she die?" Konstantine asked.

"Suicide—or at least, someone made it *look* like a suicide." Stefano shrugged. "It will be an easy thing for *La Strega* to find and question the brother."

Konstantine thought of the way Louie had swayed on her feet today in Piper's apartment. Once they'd returned to his place, he'd confirmed his fear. Lou's fever had spiked again.

It was his fault for not keeping her on a strict schedule with the medicine.

I have to do better.

"It will have to wait," Konstantine said, rising with his empty cup and going to the sink. "For now."

KING THANKED THE OFFICER WHO'D CALLED HIM AND slipped his cell phone back into the pocket of his sweats. He stared down at the ground beef in the pan on his stove without really seeing it. His emotions were mixed. On one hand, a family was going to get terrible news tonight. It was hard to feel relief and excitement knowing that someone would be hit with the worst news a person can receive. Their daughter was dead and had most certainly experienced horrible torment and violence before the killer threw her into the river like trash.

Even with this in the forefront of his mind, the relief was palpable. The girl hadn't been the one Mel was looking for. This meant Mel couldn't assume responsibility for this tragedy just yet.

He scraped the ground beef out of the pan and into the tortilla wrap waiting on a plate. He would add guacamole, cheese, sour cream, and lettuce to it before sitting down to watch the news, but the full plating would have to wait.

In only his socked feet, King stepped out of his apartment and padded down the hallway to Melandra's front door. He knocked on it, calling out, "It's just me, Mel."

The door swung open and Melandra appeared in her own version of night clothes. Silk pajamas with a gold *M* stamped into the maroon pocket. They were a gift he'd given her for Christmas two years ago.

"Mr. King," she said. Lady stood behind her in the center of the kitchen, her tail wagging gently from side to side, now that she knew it was only her co-master and not some threat that she needed to alert her mistress to.

Mel didn't invite him in. That was the first thing King noticed.

The second was the girl who appeared behind her, a towel in her hand.

"Miss Mel, can I use this to—" Her voice cut off when she saw King standing in the doorway.

King blinked twice, but he was not mistaken. There she was, just as Melandra had described her. Zoey Peterson. Strawberry blond, round face, and dark eyes.

"Hello," he said cautiously. "I'm sorry if I'm interrupting."

Melandra turned and looked to see what the girl wanted.

"Yes, that's fine, honey. You can use it." When she didn't immediately leave to take a shower, Mel added, "This is my friend, Robert King. He lives just across the hallway, in the other apartment."

"Nice to meet you," the girl said shyly.

To King, Mel said, "Let's step over to your apartment if you've got something to tell me."

"I do," he said.

"I'll be right back," Melandra said, speaking as much to Lady as to the girl, who was finally turning away, presumably to return to the bathroom.

King waited until he was back inside his apartment and Mel had closed the door before he said, "You found her."

"With Louie's help," she said. "But she's as skittish as a mouse in a serpent den. That's why I didn't tell her you were a cop."

King had noticed that. "I'm not a cop."

"I don't want her to think I even know a cop," Mel added.

"Why? Now that you've found her, we can get her back to her family. They must be worried sick." He glanced at his unfinished burrito cooling on the counter but forgot it almost as quickly. "You said the bad thing happens in New Orleans. Her family isn't in New Orleans. We should send her back."

"Robert," she said, and that stopped him.

She never used his first name.

"Please," she said. "I want to keep her close until I know the danger is past. So please. *Please* do this for me."

King thought of the girl they'd pulled out of the water. Of the weeping parents who wouldn't sleep tonight, or any night, possibly for a long time to come.

"They identified the body from the river," he said. "Rebecca Reed. She was a UNO student. Her remains show signs of peri-mortem trauma. They think she was probably kept somewhere, kept for a few days before he killed her and dumped the body."

Melandra's hand went to her throat. "How long was she missing before they found her?"

"Two months."

"Two months. Dear Lord." Mel crossed herself. "Where is her family?"

"They're local. Detective White will have talked to them by now."

Am I really going to let this go? King wondered. *We've got someone killing girls that look just like Zoey in the area and Mel's intuition saying she's in danger...Am I really going to not call it in?*

If he did, Mel would feel like it was a question of her intuition, or at the very least, a question of her ability to keep the girl safe.

"I know what you're thinking," she said. "All I ask for is a little more time."

"I trust you," he said. "Do what you need to do."

The unease didn't release completely, but it had felt like the right thing to say.

Mel visibly relaxed, at least. "Thank you. I promise to keep you in the loop."

"Please do," he said, turning back toward the burrito. There wasn't any steam rising from the ground beef anymore. He tested it with his finger and found it cold.

Oh well. Nothing thirty seconds in the microwave won't fix.

"Mel," he said as she turned to leave.

"What is it?" she asked.

"You'll have to keep her out of sight of White and the others. They're duty bound by law to report her whereabouts if they see her. And it could damage my relationship with them if they think I'm the kind of private investigator that'll keep case details to myself."

"I'll be careful," she said, before pulling his apartment door shut.

King stared at the closed door for a moment and hoped that was true.

"Ha! Found you, Brock *Adkins*. Look at him." Piper turned her computer so that Dani could see. They were both on the sofa in the apartment, their backs against opposite arms and their feet meeting beneath the shared blanket at its center.

Dani pulled her glasses down on her nose. "He looks..."

"The word that came to my mind was 'aggressive.'" Piper turned the screen back to face herself.

Adkins did have one of those bad-guy faces. Piper wasn't sure if it was the sallow cheeks or the hollow look to his dark eyes. If she had to bet money, she'd probably go with the malicious ghost of a smirk that tugged at his lips. "But here he is. I've IDed my bad guy."

Dani pressed her foot against the bottom of Piper's. "I'm really proud of you, baby."

Piper bit her lip. "It's not cheating though, right?"

"What?"

"Getting Lou to find the guy for me. Is that cheating? This still counts as my win, doesn't it?"

Dani met her gaze over the top of her laptop, frowning. "How could it be cheating?"

"I don't know, because King was an agent for decades before Lou came around, and he managed to solve his cases without someone who can drop GPS pins and stuff. And there are so many people out there doing crime work, and they can't just, you know, *poof*, 'Oh, here's my guy.'"

Dani reached for her tea on the coffee table. "I see where you're going with this."

"It just feels like cheating." She closed her laptop. "Like maybe if I didn't have Lou I would be a shit detective."

Dani lifted the mug to her lips and took a sip. "With that logic, then I cheat doing investigative work as a journalist because I have the internet and they didn't have that in the sixties and seventies."

"Are you comparing Lou to the internet? Or a shiny new smart phone? I'm going to tell her you said that."

Dani closed her computer. "*Don't.*"

Piper launched herself across the sofa. Dani just had enough time to put the mug down and the laptop on the floor before Piper was on top of her.

"I'm going to go up to her and say, 'Where do you keep the battery, man?'"

Dani covered her face. "Stop it. I was trying to comfort you, and now you're picking on me."

"You're right. I'm sorry." Piper slid onto her side so that she and Dani could lie facing each other. "What are you working on?"

"Nothing. I have a beautiful girl on me."

Piper smiled. "What *were* you working on?"

"I'm trying to figure out who I know in upstate New York."

"Is this about Lou's latest hunt?"

Dani didn't seem to hear her. "Evangeline is going to try and find me a contact, but it's taking her longer than I thought it would."

"Evangeline, huh? Sounds like another rich girl."

Dani gave her a warning look.

"I don't *hate* rich people as a rule," Piper said, forcing an extra dose of amiability into her voice. "But if you tell me something happened between the two of you then I'll have a reason not to like her."

Dani tilted her head. "Well..."

"Well *what*?"

"There was that time we practiced kissing at the equestrian camp."

Piper pretended to crack her knuckles. "That's it. I want her number."

Dani laughed and pulled her into a kiss. "The only one I'll be kissing from now on is you. Though I like to see you jealous. If I get another dirty look from one of your exes—"

"They're not exes," Piper interjected.

"Fine. One of your *previous paramours*, or whatever you'd like to call them, I'm going to lose it. Especially that one with the curls."

"Scarlet." Piper hissed through her teeth. "Yeah, she's a bit much."

"She needs to get a new girl to be possessive over. She shoulder-checked me coming out of Café du Monde last week. If I hadn't moved my coffee arm at the last second, I would've been wearing it."

"If I see her, I'll talk to her," Piper said. "I promise."

"I'm not sure that will help," Dani said. "Maybe just leave it for now."

"Wait. How did we get distracted? We were talking about you kissing Evangeline."

"You have nothing to worry about, my love. She lives in NYC and she has a fiancé."

"Man or woman?" Piper asked.

"Theodore is a man."

Piper squinted her eyes. "That doesn't mean anything. I've gotten pretty far with women who've had boyfriends."

"I think that says more about you than about straight women in general."

Piper wanted to argue that Dani was the enticing one.

All day she'd been thinking of how beautiful Dani was, naked and astride her, one thick thigh on either side of

Piper's hips. The way she'd tilted her head back to reveal a slender throat just before she climaxed.

Piper pursed her lips. "I find it hard to believe Evangeline would turn you down."

Dani kissed her. The moment their lips touched, Piper's stomach twisted in on itself, flopping in that delicious, hopelessly in love way.

She's really here, her mind marveled for the hundredth time that week. *This beautiful woman is here. In this apartment, my apartment.*

Her mind began to slide toward her mother. Toward the drugs, and violence and constant state of unease. As always, her old fears crept in with these thoughts and began spinning new horrifying possibilities.

Maybe one day Dani would change her mind and realize Piper really wasn't what she wanted. Or maybe she'd get hit by a car, or shot, or murdered. Or that Piper would wake from a coma and find this had all been a dream. This beautiful apartment, this beautiful girlfriend, having two jobs she really liked and studying what she wanted.

Dani's hands seized her cheeks, forcing Piper to look at her. "I'm right here."

"Sorry," Piper said. "I didn't mean to go away."

"I know." Dani kissed her on the nose. "I also know sometimes it can't be helped."

They were lucky that Dani hadn't awakened screaming in the night for a while now. The panic attacks caused by her PTSD were becoming few and far between. Sometimes they still sprang up, usually for reasons they didn't see coming, and Dani would go back to believing that Dmitri Petrov was somehow back to hurt her again.

That's why Dani still saw a therapist for an hour every week.

Dani slid her hand down to the side of Piper's neck. "We're here and we're happy and we're safe."

Dani's stomach rumbled.

"And we're hungry!" Piper called before rolling Dani onto her back and blowing a raspberry on her stomach. "I hear you in there. Don't worry. I'm on it."

Dani laughed. "You're ridiculous."

"Babe, the stomach gremlins have spoken. If you don't feed them, something bad will happen." She checked her imaginary watch. "It's not midnight yet. We still have time."

"One day I will watch this movie and understand all of your references to it," Dani said, pushing her fingers through Piper's hair.

"If I had any proof that your childhood was terrible despite the kissing camps and money, it's that you haven't seen *any* of the good movies from the eighties and nineties. A real shame. As for dinner—"

"We have plenty of leftovers," Dani said. "Let's just throw everything together."

"Mix and match," Piper said. "Got it."

She went to the kitchen, pulled two plates from the cabinet, and fished out the week's takeout boxes from the fridge. They had leftover creole and Mexican and even spring rolls from that sushi place.

As Piper put the spring rolls, red beans and rice, and cheesy potato empanadas on a plate, Dani came up behind her and wrapped her arms around her stomach. She kissed the back of Piper's neck.

"I love you," she whispered.

"I love you," Piper said, and her voice was strong. Certain.

But she was glad Dani couldn't see her face.

She hated this unsteady feeling inside her. A feeling that said things were too good.

That something—any minute now—was going to break.

16

―――

Lou woke to thin sunlight pouring across the covers. The window was still shuttered against winter, but the day had found the cracks in the wooden barricade. She pushed herself up onto her elbows and found the bed empty, except for Octavia, who sat at the end of the bed, watching her with an unflinching golden stare.

"Good morning," Lou said with an arched brow.

That stare said she would like to murder Lou if she could.

You're not the only one who'd like to see me dead, Lou thought with amusement. That was her first indication that things had turned for the better. She tried to remember what had happened after they'd helped Melandra and Piper the day before. Wait. Had it been the day before or two days before?

She had vague recollections of Konstantine appearing with soup and medicine and water at different intervals. For a while there it had felt like as soon as her eyes had closed and she'd managed to drift off to sleep, he'd been back with something else.

Time to eat, amore mio.

You must drink more water, amore mio.

Your medicine, amore mio.

Amore mio, amore mio, amore mio.

It had been like a chant in the darkness.

But where was Konstantine now? She strained to hear movement in the apartment. The shower was silent, no water dripping into the drain. She heard no fingers flying across a keyboard. No movement in the kitchen either.

She threw back the covers and stood. As her weight settled into her heels, she assessed her body.

She felt weak in her arms and legs, a little shaky. Yet the terrible weight had been lifted. It no longer felt like a hand was pressing down on her shoulders and arms, trying to force her to collapse.

She splashed cold water on her face first and regarded herself in the mirror. She needed a shower, that was for sure, and her mouth felt like Octavia had shat in it. But her eyes were clear and the excess of color had faded from her cheeks.

She was standing in the empty living room when the front door opened and Konstantine walked in with a small brown bag.

"You're awake," he said when he saw her. There was a hint of panic in the way he tore his key from the door and swung it shut behind him. "How do you feel?"

"Fine," she said.

When he made no effort to hide his skepticism, she added, "Not *great,* but fine."

That was the truth.

Still, after putting the sack on the kitchen counter, he insisted on taking her temperature. Lou allowed this, sitting down on the sofa as he knelt in front of her.

She admired the black shirt tight across his chest and upper arms. It made him look very...touchable.

He caught her looking at him and rolled his green eyes up to meet hers. "What is it?"

She didn't answer until the thermometer beeped and he removed it from her mouth. "You're nice to look at."

He laughed. "Thank you."

"But you're getting dark circles under your eyes. Did I make you sick?"

"No," he said. "I'm not sick."

She wanted to kiss him but was still very aware that she wasn't sure of the last time she'd brushed her teeth. "Well?"

"Your fever is gone," he conceded, taking the device to the sink and washing it before returning it to its case. "I am glad of it. Are you hungry?"

"I need a shower more." *And a toothbrush.*

She saw his eyes slide away from the paper sack and knew she'd disappointed him.

"The shower can wait until after I have breakfast with you," she said.

He didn't try to hide his smile as he plated the warm bread and made fresh coffee. They sat at his desk together. Lou was in his seat behind it, and he'd pulled up another chair from the wall to sit cattycorner from her at the edge of the desk.

She ate her breakfast, enjoying the look of him there and the smell of him. She laughed.

"What is it?" He looked up from his coffee.

"I was thinking of how pleasant you are as company. You smell nice, you look *clean.*"

Konstantine frowned. "You've said that twice this morning. You're making me self-conscious. Am I not usually *clean?*"

"You are. I'm not," she said. "Especially not right now."

He was out of his seat then, leaning across the desk to kiss her. She let him despite the fact her mouth was full of warm baked bread.

"Every moment with you is divine," he said.

"Divine?" she said. "Wow. And here I was fairly certain I

can smell myself and have been wearing the same clothes for two days. I was way off."

Konstantine only smiled as he settled back into his chair, a satisfied grin on his face.

"You forget that you come to me covered in the blood and brains of other men and smelling of the underworld, *amore mio*. A little sweat and bad breath is nothing."

There. He'd said it. She did have bad breath.

She rose from her seat then, brushing breadcrumbs from her fingers.

"Where are you going?"

"Home," she said. "I'll be back later."

He grabbed her hand just before she was out of his reach. "Promise me you will take it easy. No fighting yet."

"As long as no one starts a fight with *me*," she said, and brushed a kiss across his lips.

LOU UNDERSTOOD INTELLECTUALLY THAT THERE WAS NO medical evidence to suggest that she would get sick if she went outside with her hair wet, and yet, she still took the extra time to dry her hair completely after her shower. The heat and steam had intensified her shakiness, and for the first time in her life, her system was clear enough to notice that the coffee made her jittery. Her fingers trembled with the excess stimulation, something she hadn't experienced in a *very* long time.

But overstimulation aside, she felt better—so much better—in a fresh pair of thick cargo pants and her leather jacket.

Konstantine had been right to warn her against fighting, because almost as soon as Lou tasted this hint of recovery, she wanted to go. She wanted to pull a gun on someone, pull someone's hair, *something*. Anything more exciting than lying in bed for days had been.

But she remembered the way she'd swayed on her feet after just two little searches for Piper and Mel. The way the doctor had looked at her when she'd said *esausta*.

She stood in front of her large apartment window and looked out over the river. There were no boats on the water today. Of course, there were fewer in the winter. She could still see people, little clusters of ant-like shapes moving around on the boardwalk. Tourists or workers or maybe even locals out to enjoy the day despite the icy wind. Because no doubt the wind rolling off the water would be cold and unforgiving.

Slowly, she told herself. *I can work a little. I'll just pick something easy.*

She thought of the way Busaba had run into her family's arms. The way the tears had streamed down her face.

Yes. She could do that. She could save as many girls as her body would allow.

She just had to be careful about who she targeted.

No guns and running down alleyways, she thought. *Someone I can take that won't be immediately missed.*

The compass sparked to life inside her as she turned away from the beautiful view of the shining river and stepped inside her linen closet.

She closed the door behind her, listening to her breath in the dark space.

Someone I can save, and where I won't be noticed, she thought.

The darkness softened around her, embracing her as if it had missed her even though their time apart had been brief.

Any one of Riku's girls will do, she thought. *Surely there has to be at least one or two.*

She was right about that.

·   ·   ·

Lou stepped from the shade of the pond-side pagoda. In the pond, a fountain sprang from its center, pouring water prettily down on its stone surface. Koi fish flicked their tails back and forth in the current, a flash of gold and white, even red, as Lou stepped out onto the garden path. A pair of ducks swam close together while a blue heron fished, its long yellow beak spearing the water.

Some of the trees off the park's path were labeled.

Himalayan cedar. Cypress. Tulip tree. Weeping cherry.

She noted these names at a glance, but her attention was fixated on the girls ahead of her. They seemed ordinary at first. Two girls walking together, arm in arm, with a male escort at each end, hanging a foot or so behind them. As they walked the manicured path, the wind blew their hair back from their faces and smoothed their curls like a lover's hand.

Then the four of them went to the bathrooms at the end of the path, beside the café. The young women went into the bathroom while the two men stood outside the doors, waiting.

Lou sidestepped beneath the shade of a large tree, just off the footpath, and into one of the bathroom stalls before they could spot her.

The bathroom had the two women in it, but also a mother trying to hold her toddler up high enough to wash her hands in the sink.

The girls took their time reapplying their lipstick, speaking softly to each other.

Lou waited until the mother left before reaching out and turning off the light. The girls she'd been following let out squeals of surprise, but they were cut short. Lou had pulled them through the shadows before either of the men managed to turn the lights back on.

. . .

SHE FOUND THREE MORE GIRLS WORKING IN A MAID CAFÉ near Shinjuku Station. Lou had been surprised when she stepped from the single-person bathroom into the brightly lit café. Several of the maids were bouncing up and down on a platform, singing along to a cute song that Lou didn't know. One looked like she was pretending to be a cat, washing her ears.

Other maids were placing ice cream sundaes made to look like floppy-eared rabbits and grinning pandas on the table in front of a group of American tourists. Lou relied on her compass to identify which of the girls were in Riku's clutches.

Her compass zinged into place when the song ended and three new girls climbed up onto the karaoke platform.

Them, she knew. Though she wasn't sure how to get close enough to take all three at once.

They saw her watching and began to wave excitedly to her.

"Karaoke! Karaoke!" they cried, hauling her up to the platform.

They knew the song and the choreography and weren't shy trying to teach Lou how to move as they did. She managed only to move left when they moved left and right when they moved right.

At the end of the song, the lights died. The karaoke prompters switched off and waited for the next command.

The girls clapped wildly at Lou. "Good job!"

I'm sure it was the worst dancing you've ever seen, she thought.

"Picture," Lou said, hoping to capitalize on this momentary darkness.

"Picture, picture!" they agreed, and huddled in close.

Their smiles were still bright when Lou placed herself at the center and slid her arms around them. She managed to pull them through the dark before the flash went off.

. . .

THE ARCADE WAS BRIGHT AND NOISY, AND YET STILL HELD enough shadows to slip in and out of between the machines and press of bodies. It was the chaotic nature of the place—the blaring music, the loud rumble of laughter from the teenagers trying to speak over each other—that made Lou less noticeable. She would be difficult to spot in a crowd already thick with people and enough noise and light to distract even the most focused players.

A tug in Lou's navel drew her attention to the girl standing beside her. She looked like she should be there. Her glossy black hair was rolled into twin buns on the top of her head, and her slender throat was covered by a red ribbon, tied at the back.

Her clothes were scant, especially when one considered the season, and the robe she wore was a sheer gossamer sheath with white feathers lining its cuffs and trim.

If the girl was cold or uncomfortable, she ignored it, giving her full attention to the young man who bounced and danced on the machine. He was trying to mimic the moves of the cartoon players on the screen and match them perfectly. He was doing well, so her encouragement seemed natural, except that it didn't reach her eyes.

Lou didn't miss that.

As the challenge increased, the game's prompts coming faster and faster, the young man's concentration intensified. Others crowded in around the platform, heckling or cheering in turn.

It was easy for Lou to slip up beside the girl and hook one arm around her waist. She was so small and thin, it took almost no effort at all to pull her into the dark between the dancing machine and the wall it stood against.

The girl only managed to open her mouth in surprise before they slipped.

· · ·

THE ALLEY BESIDE THE MATCHA CAFÉ SMELLED LIKE TRASH. Usually, Lou associated the smell of hot garbage with summer, a time when the relentless sun baked the plastic bags without mercy or exception. Yet here in Tokyo's winter, for whatever reason, bags of trash had been lined along the street, as if there was a pickup scheduled for later that day.

Where are all the trash cans? Lou marveled as she followed the pull of her compass to the café's door. She didn't see a large dumpster like the ones she so often found beside residential or commercial buildings in the United States.

The café itself was cheerful and bright, and smelled like spun sugar. It was absurdly sweet and inviting compared to the stench of trash outside.

The decor was white and minimalist, as if to emphasize the enticing green desserts and drinks on display. The menu was in Japanese, English, Korean, and Chinese. Lou suspected she must still be in the touristy part of Tokyo, given how many of the patrons were not Asian.

A woman asked Lou if she wanted anything. Lou held up her hand, pretending to read the menu. In truth, behind the reflection of her mirrored sunglasses, she was scanning the café for her target.

Click.

It was the two young girls by the front window with a matcha sundae between them. The ice cream was green with little slivers of yellow cake resting beneath the whipped cream. Each girl had a spoon which they dipped into the dessert delicately, as if afraid of taking too much for themselves.

The one on the left covered her mouth and laughed, but it was the other one that had Lou's attention.

She hadn't missed the way she'd looked at her companion regretfully, as if she were about to tell her some terrible secret. Something like, *Sorry, but my parents won't let me be your friend anymore.*

Lou had a feeling it was something more along the lines of entrapment. Had Riku—or someone beneath him—ordered the girl to recruit others for him? Lou wouldn't be surprised.

The girl was young. Very young. No more than twelve or thirteen years old, which meant that she must have eyes on her.

Lou scanned the shop and spotted him two tables away. He was pretending to read the newspaper. She knew he was pretending because the only thing on that page was an advertisement for a new Toyota, and as beautiful as the truck was, he'd been looking at it for a long time.

Either you're waiting for your chance to grab that girl or you're really in the market for a new truck.

Let's find out which.

Lou got a matcha latte for herself and sat down at the table behind the man so that she could watch all three of them. She wished she had a paper or computer of her own to hide the fact that she was simply sitting there.

She'd made it halfway through her drink when the two girls rose and gathered up their Hello Kitty backpacks. One looked back toward the man, confirming Lou's suspicions about what she was seeing. Then they were out on the street, walking past the large glass storefront and out of sight.

The man folded his paper, laid it on the table, and then went out after them.

Lou abandoned her latte.

On the street, she was almost a block behind them.

No matter. It was easy for her to step into one shadowed alleyway and appear in another, ahead of the trio.

When the girls passed her, she grabbed them both by their backpacks and hauled them into the alley.

They squealed like the girls in the bathroom had. Getting

dragged into the dark will do that to a person. Yet Lou couldn't afford to be subtle in bright daylight with little room to maneuver.

And it didn't matter anyway.

The man following them could do nothing about it now.

THE PARTY WAS A SURPRISE. AFTER DROPPING OFF THE CAFÉ girls—one to a grandmother and another to two older brothers, who her compass had assured Lou were safe—she'd found herself in a lavish high-rise apartment. When she stepped out of the quiet coat closet and into the room full of drinking and laughter, she was worried it might be Riku's apartment, given its impressive view of Tokyo and the posh people crowding the space.

Then she realized it wasn't. The skyline was different. Riku's apartment had been near Shinjuku, within walking distance of Takeshita Street.

She remembered the view of giant billboards flashing neon with commercials or clips of anime—sometimes Lou couldn't tell the difference. And she was fairly certain that she'd caught a glimpse of Godzilla's head peeking out above a cluster of buildings before she'd disappeared with the crying child in her arms.

In contrast, this apartment had a clear view of Tokyo Tower, a sort of red Eiffel Tower in the Shiba-koen district.

Not to say that Riku couldn't have more than one apartment in Tokyo, but she trusted her compass.

She wandered the room, letting that tug in her guts pull her through the shifting crowd.

Click.

The crowd parted and Lou's eyes fixed on her mark.

It was a young woman in her twenties, painted prettily with her long legs showcased by the cut of her skirt. She drank a beer and looked out over the city. She didn't look happy despite her lavish dress and the friendly faces around her.

Lou put a hand on her arm. It was dark enough from the low light used to create intimacy for Lou to disappear where she stood. So she took her, leaving the girl on the steps of a house in some tropical clime far warmer than the Japanese winter night they'd left behind.

One more, Lou thought, and found she was back in the apartment she'd just left.

There was the Tokyo Tower.

Okay. Clearly there's someone else here.

"Oh, you're American," a man said.

A Japanese man stopped in front of her, his face red and eyes bleary. Lou could only guess how many drinks he'd had.

"I think American women are so fun."

"I think you should go fuck yourself," she said, and stepped around him.

A little harsh, her inner critic said. He might not even know the girls were sent here as entertainment from Riku.

He's still profiting, Lou thought. She'd put a bullet in someone's head for less.

At the very least, she wouldn't let herself be deterred from finishing the job she was spending her precious energy on.

Lou found a second girl, then a third.

The fourth time she returned to the apartment, she thought, *Seriously, this is the last one. I'm drawing too much attention.*

Her compass made no reply. It only fixated on the girl dancing in the center of the room with several men standing around her.

"How is that subtle?" she muttered.

Her compass insisted, tugging Lou toward the crowd. Once she got closer, she understood why.

Lou could feel the men's fever pitch of desire. The way they stood close to the shiny, glittering creature at their center. Their smiles weren't good-natured. They were hungry.

Ravenous.

This better not come to guns.

Because Lou hadn't brought one. She had only the darkness as her ally now.

Lou slid through the thick line of men in suits to the woman in the silver dress and hooked one arm around her waist.

Someone said something in a low, suggestive voice.

Lou forced her best grin and led the girl away.

The coat closet by the front door was only a few feet away. If she could just get there, she could shut them inside and leave the drunks to puzzle over what had happened.

Lou did manage to get the closet open and push the girl inside, but in the dark, the girl let out a little cry of surprise, her glitter nails going up to grab the arms of the jackets pressing against her face.

Either she was very drunk or very high. Possibly both.

"Wait," someone said. Two of the men had followed them.

The closest wrapped his hand around Lou's arm.

"Come with me," he said.

Without thinking, she trapped his hand and rotated her wrist until the bone snapped. A satisfying crunch made her skin shiver.

His mouth opened to release the scream forming there, but before a sound came out, Lou pulled the closet door shut between them and was gone.

AFTER THE PARTY, LOU WAS EXHAUSTED. SHE'D GOTTEN the last girl to Malaysia, recognizing at once the Petronas Tower in the distance as Kuala Lumpur. The house where the compass had led Lou was humble, but friendly-looking with its bright turquoise door and red shutters. The girl seemed to be in shock to see it.

Lou had to knock on the door for five minutes before a woman opened up. She'd frowned at Lou—not an uncommon response to the mirrored shades and leather jacket—but when she saw the girl in the silver dress, her buzz clearly waning, she screamed.

Screamed.

"She was kidnapped and taken to Japan. I'm just bringing her back," Lou said in English, having little to no expectation that the woman would understand. "She might be—"*Addicted to who knows what.* "—sick for a while."

The woman surprised Lou. "Kidnapped. *Kidnapped!*"

She just kept repeating it.

No more today, Lou thought. This one made twelve.

Just as she had with each of the girls before, Lou asked her compass, *Is she safe here?*

Her compass tugged reassuringly, promising in its way that this choice of destination was not a mistake.

That would have to be enough for Lou. The weight of her exhaustion was returning as well as the dull throb in her head.

She had no choice but to slip away before the reunion was over, becoming one with the darkness beyond the house lights again.

17

———

"Gotcha," Piper whispered, and ducked behind the dumpster outside of Samantha's apartment. With her back against the cold metal, she scrolled through her phone, reviewing the photos she'd just snapped.

They were good. Mostly. Several were just of Brock's back, the black hoodie pulled up over his head to hide his hair and obscure most of his face. In others, his face was clear, and Samantha's building identifiable in the frame.

"Here you are looking right at her window, Mr. Adkins," Piper whispered.

And unlike with the photo she'd snapped of Adkins coming out of his bathroom, King couldn't wax poetic about how only *lawfully* obtained evidence can be *lawfully* used in court.

A hand clamped down over her arm.

"*Jesus!*"

It was Lou, crouching down in front of Piper.

"For fuck's sake. Between you and Mel I've got no years left in my life."

"Are you hurt?" Lou asked.

"Wait, what? No, I'm doing reconnaissance on the stalker case. Why?"

"I had a feeling."

"Oh." Piper slipped her phone into her pocket. "Like a bad feeling?"

Lou didn't answer.

Piper glanced around the dumpster, but Adkins was gone. The street outside of Samantha's apartment building was clear. There was no danger from what Piper could tell. Maybe Lou's cold was sending her compass haywire?

She turned back to Lou. "How do you feel?"

"Better," Lou said. She was also searching the area as if looking for someone. Finally, she said, "Do you want to eat ramen with me?"

"Only if we can go somewhere that has those little rice pockets," Piper said. "I love those."

"Inari." Lou offered her a hand and pulled her to standing.

"But seriously, do you feel okay?" Piper asked. "You're resting, right? I'm only saying yes because ramen is like a soup. Sick people gotta eat soup."

"Should we get Dani?" Lou asked.

How could Piper say that she'd missed Lou and wanted her all to herself? The hesitation must've been answer enough.

Lou looked at her watch. "She's working."

"Yes," Piper said, relieved. "Yes, she is."

When New Orleans fell away and the world reshaped itself around her, Piper expected to find herself in Japan. That was where Lou usually ate her ramen, after all. But one look around told her that this was clearly Lincoln Park. Chicago.

The honk of the yellow taxis. There was the guy with the hot dog cart. A woman walking two white poodles up the wide street. Lou pointed at a lit sign with a bowl of ramen and two chopsticks on it.

"That's it," she said.

"Why Chicago?" Piper asked.

"I wanted a break from Japan."

Piper opened the door for her. "Have you been spending a lot of time in Japan?"

"Yes."

It was moments like this that Piper wished Lou was a *tad* chattier. She liked the strong and silent vibe, but it made getting information more difficult than it had to be. "You've been spending a lot of time there because...?"

Lou put her sunglasses in the front pocket of her leather jacket. "I want to destroy Riku Yamamoto."

"Cool, I hate that guy." Piper leaned her weight against the vacant hostess stand. "Remind me again who Riku Yama-what's-it is?"

At last Piper got the string of words she'd been hoping for as Lou explained what was going on, starting with some girl named Busaba and ending with a skeezy-sounding party that she'd just left less than an hour before. As she spoke, the hostess came and seated them in a booth by the electric fireplace and gave them menus printed in English with vegetarian options clearly labeled.

Yeah, definitely not in Japan.

The menu promised garlic tonkatsu, light yuzu shio ramen, and even dipping noodles. She spotted the inari pockets beside some pork dumplings.

"Are you ready to order?" the waitress asked upon returning.

Piper ordered for both of them and waited until they were alone again before she turned her attention back to Lou. "If you ask me, it sounds like Riku's got it coming. I've gotten comfortable with a lot of shady shit, but I can't get on board with a guy who rapes kids."

Lou was silent, watching the restaurant around them in that intense way of hers.

"You're about the only woman I'd say this to, but you look tired," Piper said, before taking a drink of water.

"I am."

"Twelve girls might have been pushing it for your first night." Piper was aiming for casual, conversational. She didn't want Lou to feel like she was ragging on her. It was just so good to see her and have a minute to themselves.

"It was."

"Wow. It's really going around, huh?" Piper whistled, earning a mean look from the woman at the table beside her. "First Dani admitted it, then me, and now *you're* saying that you're overworking. That's—that's like a pig flying or Hell freezing over or whatever the kids say these days. What's wrong with us? Are we getting"—Piper placed a hand dramatically over her heart—"*old?*"

"Possibly." Lou smiled. "How's the case coming?"

The waitress put the dumplings and rice ball pockets on the tabletop. Piper placed a few on her plate and pushed the dish toward Lou. Lou took a dumpling but ignored the inari.

"I've got witnesses and photographic evidence that Brock Adkins has been hanging around outside of Samantha's apartment. The night that he broke into her place, a neighbor saw him running down the fire escape at the back of the building as the police were going in to investigate. I've got all the paperwork and details together for the DA, I just want a shot of him following her on the street, with them both in the same frame."

"When does he follow her?"

"To and from her classes. I just wish I knew what his motive is."

"You don't have one?"

"There's not a clear connection between him and Samantha."

"It might be random," Lou said.

"Sure. He could've just spotted her on the street or seen her going into her apartment, but juries like *reasons*. Or so King tells me. I gotta find out why *her* out of any girl he could pick."

"Maybe he has a type," Lou offered.

The waitress placed a steaming bowl of tonkatsu ramen in front of Lou and the shoyu ramen in front of Piper.

"Can I get you ladies anything else?" she asked.

"Hot sauce," Piper said.

Lou stirred the ramen. "Be careful with Adkins."

"Oh *no*. Don't tell me you're gonna give me a lecture like King."

Lou leveled Piper with a stare. "When I came to get you tonight, it was because my compass told me to."

"That doesn't sound nearly as sweet as I think you mean it to."

Lou ignored her light tone. "Did Adkins know you were there? Was he watching you?"

Piper accepted the hot sauce bottle from the waitress and sent her away with her thanks. "I don't think so."

If he knows you're following him, he might hurt you. Guys like that don't like to think they've been caught."

"I'm being careful." Piper reached across the table and squeezed Lou's hand. It was cold. "I promise."

This earned her a weak smile.

"And now I will be washing my hands because I'm not convinced you aren't still a walking germ factory. Excuse me."

. . .

Konstantine was almost asleep when he felt the mattress shift and a cool body slide in beside his. She smelled like food. Something warm and spicy.

Good. That was all he wanted, for her to show herself more care.

"How do you feel?" he asked.

"Tired."

He kissed her cheeks and pulled her close. "Then sleep with me."

Her grin turned sly. "What do you think I'm here for?"

A laugh escaped him. "*No.*"

But her arms were already wrapping around his waist in a hungry way, her leg going over the side of his hip and hooking him to her.

"*No,*" he said. "You need sleep."

"We can sleep after."

"We can sleep first and sex after," he said. He wasn't going to be responsible for some lapse in her condition. Isadora had been firm that any excessive physical exertion would only exacerbate her exhaustion. And while his desire for Lou was always a deep and throbbing need, he was very aware that what they did when they removed the clothes between them *definitely* qualified as excessive physical exertion.

She exhaled, nuzzling into the crook of his neck. "You'll have to make it up to me."

"I will." He kissed her and tasted salt and something hot. "What did you eat?"

"I brushed my teeth *three times* today."

He laughed again. "It's not bad. I'm just wondering what it is. It's savory."

"Tonkatsu ramen."

It was a good choice for her current condition.

"It's unhealthy to eat alone. I would have gone with you."

"I was with Piper." She kissed his throat again. "When was the last time you did some digging?"

He considered this. "With you. When we found my mother."

When his father's enemies had his mother executed and thrown into an unmarked grave, Konstantine hadn't known where her body was. He'd remembered everything about that night. The feel of the air on his skin, the smell of his mother's fear and sweat. The way she'd begged the men for Konstantine's life. The way her eyes had widened as the bullet passed through her skull and she was pitched forward into the grave as if she were nothing more than a bag of trash, or some dirty secret to be buried.

He remembered it all—*everything*—except where they'd been. They'd had their heads covered on the way to the gravesite, and Konstantine had lost himself to grief when he was taken back.

One of his greatest hopes in finding Lou and winning her to his side was the promise that she would be able to do what he hadn't been able to—find his mother and give her a proper burial.

And she had.

"It won't be sentimental this time," Lou said, one hand on his bicep, her fingers tracing the thick lines of his tattoo. "Piper will be with us."

"When do you want to uncover the graves?"

"When we wake up," she said. "I told Piper to be ready at midnight. We'll need to dress warm for the woods."

"The woods? Your killer didn't hide the bodies somewhere in the city?"

"No. He took them upstate," she said. "I was hoping that the graves were already disturbed, but they aren't. Hence the digging."

It was his turn to run a hand along her arm, enjoying the

feel of them lying in bed together, even if their topic of conversation could be more pleasant. "What do you mean about the graves being disturbed?"

"From what King tells me, serial killers usually go back to their victims' graves in order to relive the excitement of the experience. They do what Jeffery Fish had done."

Konstantine did not want to envision the man masturbating into the open grave. He pushed back against the rising image.

"I was hoping he'd gone back and there would be evidence on the surface."

"Why does it need to be on the surface?"

"You can't break the story without evidence. Dani could say she got an anonymous tip that there were bodies buried in a certain location, but the people who own the property could refuse to let the police dig without a warrant, which you can't get based on a tip alone. That's why you have to be able to see something with the naked eye. Then a court could force a full excavation. Or so King tells me."

"Because the earth is undisturbed, you want us to dig up the graves and expose the evidence."

"Yes," she said, and moved in closer. Her face fit perfectly in the hollow of his throat beneath his chin. "It shouldn't take more than a few hours. It'll be faster if I help you."

"No," he said into her hair. "I'll do it. You can watch from under a thick blanket. I'll even let you take a hot coffee with you."

She snorted.

"What?" he asked.

"*Let* me," she said.

Konstantine woke at six in the morning out of habit. He left Lou dozing in the bed while he made their morning coffee and procured breakfast from the shop across the street from his apartment. By the time he got back at 6:20, she was awake, and they ate together. Lou reminded him that she couldn't be carrying a coffee while trying to shepherd them around the world, so they drank while watching sunlight fill up the Arno River.

"Ready?" Lou asked.

"Yes." He enjoyed the delicious, if momentary, pleasure of her leaning her weight against him in the dark.

Then reality warped around him.

He'd asked her once what it felt like for her to move through the world in this way, and she'd said she felt nothing. It was as natural as taking a step, lifting her foot from one place and putting it down in another. That was when he knew she must be the only creature in this world—especially since her aunt Lucy's death—who was meant to move like this.

Piper's apartment opened up around him. Despite the hour, a horn honked outside and Konstantine noted the distant rumble of music.

"What is that?" he asked.

"Bourbon Street," Piper said.

She was sitting on the sofa beside the other girl, Daniella. They looked half asleep, both holding warm cups of something between them.

"Do you want coffee?" Piper asked them, lifting her own cup.

"We already had some." Lou released Konstantine and stepped into the living room. "Why are you sitting in the dark?"

"First of all, it's midnight," Piper said. "Secondly, it's soothing."

"It'll also help our night vision," Daniella said from the sofa.

Lou fixed her eyes on her. "You're coming too?"

"And King," Piper said. "I told them you were sick and needed backup, and they volunteered. Mel said she can't because she's working on something. I think it has to do with the dream girl."

"Four of you is more than enough," Lou said.

A bell rang out downstairs.

"That'll be King," Piper said.

This seemed to be confirmed by the heavy footfall on the stairs, followed by a rap at the door.

Daniella was up and opening it before the knocking ended.

"Hey, Dani," he said cheerfully. Then he saw everyone standing in the room. Standing, with the exception of Piper, who was still holding her warm coffee cup the way the ship-wrecked cling to a life raft.

"It's a regular party in here," he said, nodding toward Konstantine, who returned it.

To Lou, he said, "Is it true you have a cold?"

"I'm over it," Lou said.

"Almost," Konstantine said.

This earned him a menacing look.

King lifted his brows. "You might be more like the rest of us than I thought. Oh, before I forget."

He reached into his pockets and pulled out a handful of little flags, triangles of bright yellow plastic wrapped around thin metal shafts. He handed them to Lou.

"What are these for?" she asked.

"To mark where we should dig."

Lou was relieved to find it was easy to move all of them from Piper's apartment to the snowy forest, even with the beach chair and thick blanket that Piper had insisted on bringing for Lou. Konstantine had been so impressed with the idea, he'd offered to carry the chair.

But none of them, except for Lou, had been prepared for the temperature shift.

Neither New Orleans nor Florence had temperatures half as cold as a winter night in upstate New York.

They'd stood beneath the large moon and waited silently as Lou let her instincts lead her from one grave to the next. The snow crunched beneath her boots as her compass steered her through the night. Every time it pulled her to a stop, drawing her gaze down to the packed earth beneath her feet, Lou bent and stuck one of the yellow flags King had given her into the dirt. The frozen earth was reluctant to yield to this intrusion, but with a forceful push, the metal managed to pierce the thin layer of ice.

Lou had already placed three shovels against a tree before going to Piper's apartment—just on the off chance that she could get away with digging too, without a full rebellion from Konstantine and Piper. But now with Dani and King here, she'd gone back to the farm from where she usually *borrowed* shovels and found there was only one more.

She gave the fourth to Dani. Piper, Konstantine, and King had already started on the marked graves.

Lou found eight graves in all before feeling her compass go still inside her.

"That's it," she said, holding out the remaining yellow flags to King.

He plucked them from her fingers and slipped them back into the pocket of his coat.

Piper counted them out, pointing at each flag in turn. "So we've got eight graves. That's two each. Okay, okay." Then she pointed at the large evergreen covered in snow at Lou's back. "Now you sit over there on the chair, Lou-blue, and use that blanket I brought you."

"You don't have to stay out here," Konstantine countered. "You could wait somewhere warm."

Lou noted that he had not used the customary *amore mio* at the end of his sentence, as if he didn't want to embarrass her in front of her friends.

"If I get too cold, I'll leave," she said. They all knew she was lying.

The truth was Lou had no intention of stranding them out here.

With her back toward the tree and the thick blanket over her lap, Lou watched their progress from the beach chair, wrestling with a vacillating sense of amusement and annoyance.

Dani finished her grave first.

"I'm impressed," Konstantine said, seeing her progress.

"You ever mucked a horse barn?" Dani wiped her wet brow on the cuff of her sweater.

Konstantine shook his head.

"Let's just say that dirt isn't much heavier than horse shit," Dani said. "And when you're shoveling horse shit, you learn to work fast."

"And here I thought you were just a rich girl who did tea parties and fancy dinners," Piper called from her hole. She was about halfway through her own grave, only her upper torso and head showing aboveground.

Dani started on a second grave and was a third of the way through it when Konstantine pulled himself out of his hole and brushed the dirt from his knees. King finished after him.

For a long time, all Lou heard was their panting breath and the sound of shovels striking the earth.

"I'm starting to smell something," Piper said once she'd dug deep enough to be out of sight.

"It probably means that yours is fresh," Dani said.

"Oh man, why do I have to get the juicy one?" Piper

groaned. "You know, some friends bond in bars or hang out doing putt-putt golf."

Piper's voice was muffled by the dirt walls on all sides of her.

"But no. We have to get together to dig up corpses and —*oh shit*."

"What?" Lou and King asked in unison.

Lou stood, leaving the blanket across her shoulders as she went to the edge of Piper's grave.

"Someone get me out before I puke on the evidence."

Lou dropped the blanket and slipped from the snowy world above, into the grave where Piper stood, one hand over her mouth.

Lou had only a moment to register the hot, wet stench of the body before she grabbed ahold of Piper and pulled them both out of the grave. Before disappearing, she saw the clear outline of the corpse in the moonlight.

As soon as their feet hit the concrete, Piper vomited onto the alley's pavement.

Lou waited, letting the girl finish before she said, "Is the smell of trash making it worse?"

"It's okay," Piper said, heaving again. "I'm glad you didn't take me back to my apartment. If I'd hurled there, I would've had to clean it up. This is bet—"

She heaved for a third time.

Lou took a step back, easing her boots out of the splash zone.

"Are you sure it's the corpse that made you sick?" Lou asked.

Piper wiped her mouth on her sleeve and turned to look up at Lou. "Why? Were you throwing up?"

"I did. Once."

Piper considered this. "No, it's got to be the corpse. I felt fine until I saw the hand."

18

———

Konstantine rotated his shoulder in its socket, trying to ease some of the soreness that it had held since they'd dug up the bodies in the woods. In the end, Konstantine and King had each dug two, Piper one, and Daniella *three*. She had not looked like she could be built for hard labor, as curvy and feminine as that one was, but he'd clearly been wrong. She might not have Lou's leanness or hardness, but she had the stamina.

Stefano rolled a coin across his knuckles. "What will you do about him?"

Konstantine pulled his mind back to the present. To his office and the warm fire at his back. It was the crackling fire that made his mind tired. He always struggled like this in winter, when his body felt the cold more and his desire to sleep the months away was heavy across his chest.

"Lou can speak to Yamamoto's brother," he said. "He might find one of us to be too intimidating. Or he might think Riku sent me. No one would look at Lou and believe she works for anyone but herself."

"Do you think he'll answer her questions honestly?" Stefano asked.

"It depends on what you want me to ask," Lou said.

Konstantine had not felt her enter the room. The usual pop and squeeze of pressure from his ears must have been overlooked given the strain in his shoulders and back. *Especially* his back.

Stefano looked into the darkness, watching Lou separate from the thick shadows and ease into the ring of light thrown by the blazing fire.

He inclined his head toward her.

A snake of jealousy coiled in Konstantine, and he couldn't help but consider the similarities between them. The same hazel-green eyes, the same dark hair, though he wore his shorter than Stefano's, above the ears, while Stefano's cut across his cheeks.

Given that Konstantine and Stefano could pass for brothers, did that mean she found Stefano just as handsome?

Konstantine pushed these thoughts down. "I want to know more about Riku. I'm hoping you will interview his brother and find out what you can."

Lou rested one hip against the edge of Konstantine's desk, looking down on him. "Can you be more specific? I doubt his favorite color or vacation getaway is what you're after."

Stefano snorted.

"Does he speak English?" she asked.

"Hinato teaches at an English-language school," Stefano said, cleaning his nails.

"And you want me to ask what?" she pressed.

"I want to know more about Riku's past. His fears. His vulnerabilities. Is there something he wants badly enough that he would forgo war with us in order to have it?"

Lou's jaw was clenched when she said, "There's no point in finding out what he wants. I'm going to kill him."

"I need it to look as if I am making the effort to broker peace, *amore mio*. The number of casualties in this game will come down to how well we convince those who serve Riku that they no longer *want* to serve him. This is not like Erjon's clan. They are truly a formidable economic force in the East. It will take time to dismantle him."

"I do not think she cares about the politics of it," Stefano said. "She sees a man she wants dead, am I right, *Strega?*"

Don't pretend to know her better than I, he thought bitterly, wrestling again with the snake coiling within him.

But Lou's eyes never left Konstantine's face. "If you think there is a way to save innocent people, fine. I can wait. As long as you're clear that he isn't going to make it through this alive."

Konstantine took her hand and brushed a kiss across her knuckles. He did this more for himself than for her.

"I cannot stop you," he promised, rolling his eyes up to meet hers. "I only beg for your patience."

She pulled her hand away. "I'll speak to the brother then. What will you do?"

"We will continue what we've already started," Konstantine said. "Undermine his position and the faith his people have in him."

"Are you a king or are you a mob boss?" she asked with a smirk. "Sometimes it's hard to tell."

"Political intrigue is present wherever there is power," Konstantine said. "No throne is required. The brother, Hinato, he's in Kyoto."

"I know," she said, and disappeared.

Lou stood outside the orange temple and marveled at its entrance. It reminded her a little of the π symbol, the way the top bar rested across its parallel pillars. The crowds were thick even in January. Lou noted the tourists of all ethnicities and nationalities, making their way up the stone steps toward the temple's entrance. Outside were food stalls. Some sizzled meat and tofu on griddles. Others dipped fruit like oranges and strawberries into a candy coating that hardened into a shiny, attractive glaze.

A line had formed outside a café, where two girls walked out holding large scoops of green-and-white ice cream cradled in waffle cones, despite the chill of the day.

At the top of the stairs, stone foxes sat elevated on pedestals, each pressing a great paw against a sphere. What the sphere represented or what was its purpose, Lou couldn't say.

Girls dressed like geisha in elegant robes, flowers and ornate combs dangling in their hair, scurried past her, laughing.

The combs caught the soft winter sunlight and sparkled. One girl opened a paper umbrella and lifted her hem enough to show the strange wooden slippers she wore. Part platform, part sandal, with a thick red cord affixing the socked foot to its shoe.

Lou passed the people writing their wishes on prayer strips before throwing them—and a donation—into a well beneath a bell. She followed the footpath, listening to that inner pull that drew her deeper and deeper into the sunlit temple compound in search of Hinato.

She'd come to the edge of a tranquil pond when the muscles below her navel twinged. She stopped.

A balding man in a uniform stood in front of a group of little children. The children also wore matching school uniforms and watched their guide obediently as he pointed out something on the building off to his right.

She could tell by his voice that he was excited about the building—its significance, architecture, and importance—and wanted the children to be excited, too. He seemed to be achieving his goal with about half of them.

Lou followed the group through the compound at a distance. She pretended to watch the black swans swim on the water and to consider the temple souvenirs that could be bought from kiosks every few feet. There was also all the picture-taking. Several couples posed themselves in front of the stone statues and buildings. Lou saw more foreign women in kimonos and wondered if there was some sort of shop outside the temple gates that rented the clothes and combs by the day.

It had been almost an hour before the man finally handed the children over to a woman. She wore the same uniform as the man, their navy blue and red colors matching, but with a long pencil skirt instead of pants.

As soon as the woman led the children away, he turned and headed back toward the café near the entrance. He'd just sat down at a table with his drink when Lou slid into the seat across from him.

"Hinato Yamamoto?" she asked. He looked up and frowned.

Lou wasn't sure if it was her mirrored shades, her leather jacket, or maybe simply her unexpected presence that displeased him.

"I need to talk to you about your brother, Riku," she said.

He tensed, and his eyes swept the café around them.

"I'm here alone," she added.

This was confirmed by the fact that the only other person present was making drinks and running the register. Still, he twisted all the way around in his seat.

"You can speak and understand English?" she asked, hoping to ease him into the conversation.

"Of course," he said with a small dip of his head. "But I don't know what you want me to tell you about him."

"His weaknesses, his goals, his obsessions," she said plainly. There was no point in pretending that she was a friend or an ally. More importantly, she sensed a very different personality—an energy, Aunt Lucy would've called it—from Hinato. He wasn't like Riku.

Riku was clearly predatory, but Hinato had been very kind, very tender, with the little ones in his care.

"He's hurting people," Lou said. "Girls and children."

The brother nodded. "I know."

"Don't you want him stopped?"

"*Yes!*" The response was so vehement and impassioned Lou would have worried about drawing attention to themselves if they'd been in a more public place.

Hinato, too, seemed to realize he was cracking at the edges. More quietly, he said, "Yes. Of course I want to stop him."

"And I want to stop him, too, so what can you tell me?"

Hinato looked into his drink as if he could divine the answers written there. Lou noted that he hadn't asked her name or where she was from. Perhaps when it came to his brother, he knew it was best not to ask questions.

"Riku has always been this way," Hinato said finally. "When we were little, my parents let him do a lot. He was the oldest."

"Is he your only sibling?"

"Yes." He shook his head. "No."

Lou waited for an elaboration.

"Our sister is the youngest by many years. A surprise gift to our mother and father. I was twelve when she was born, and Riku was seventeen."

"Where is she now?"

"Dead," he said.

Lou asked her compass if that was true. She waited to see

if it would whirl and click inside her as it cast its net across the world, searching, trying to find the sister.

But Lou felt something. A snag, a pull.

If the girl was alive, why would Hinato lie to protect her? Or maybe he didn't know she was alive. "What was her name?"

"Mai," he said. "She was a sweet girl. As she grew up, she —she became unhappy. Later she told me why."

A man and a woman with cameras hanging around their necks and dust on their white sneakers entered the café. They tried to order coffee in English, but the girl behind the counter informed them there was no coffee. Only tea, bottled drinks, and ice cream.

Hinato had also turned at the first hint of sound and movement. Satisfied that the tourists weren't there for him, he said, "Riku hurt her. He was very bad to her."

Hinato's eyes pinched shut.

"She told me he had been hurting her ever since she was small but that she didn't understand what was happening. He'd made it seem like a game. Something they did together. In secret."

Lou's blood ran hot. "How did she die?"

"She killed herself," Hinato said. "I should have——"

He didn't seem to know how to finish. He finally looked up from his drink and into Lou's face. Lou lifted her glasses so he could see her eyes. It was enough to make the man burst into tears.

"I should've helped her more. I should have told our parents and made them do more for her. I should've known something was going on. Ever since she was born, Riku had been obsessed with her. He wanted to know always where she was, what she was doing, who was with her. He should've been interested in his friends, work, going out, but he would always volunteer to stay with her, to take care of her and be with her. My parents thought he was devoted, but if we'd known—if we'd *known*—"

He covered his face with his hands.

"It's my fault I did not protect her. I am her older brother. It was my job to keep her safe."

"Riku is to blame," she said simply.

She gave him some time to himself, feeling no need to rush the conversation. Outside the café was a beautiful ravine with trees and a perfectly manicured slope. Even despite the winter, someone was taking good care of the temple grounds. A crane snapped open its white wings and lifted from the creek into the winter sky.

As Hinato began to quiet down, Lou said, "He has always been interested in children."

Hinato started. "There have been other children?"

"Yes."

His mouth hung open as his dark eyes searched her face uncomprehendingly.

"Is that why you want to stop him?"

"Yes." She didn't feel like she needed to elaborate on the complicated nature of his entanglement in the world of enslavement and drugs.

"I did not have the courage to stop my brother. I don't even know how I could now. He is well protected."

"I don't care," Lou said.

Hinato made that head movement again, something between a nod and a bow. "If you can stop him, please do. *Please.* I don't want anyone else to be harmed like Mai was harmed."

Lou leaned across the table. "Then tell me everything you can about him, and I will take care of the rest."

.   .   .

After returning Hinato's bow on the temple steps, Lou walked the streets of Kyoto for two reasons. One, to consider all that he'd said. Secondly, she wanted to see how strong she was. Her head wasn't perfectly clear, but slowly her strength was returning to her.

Across from the temple was a large shopping center. At least ten stories of crystalline glass rose into the sky, pictures of beautiful models plastered to its exterior, showcasing perfume and clothing, the typical emblems of wealth and success.

If Lou could walk from one end of the shopping center to the other, then she would allow herself to go to La Loon.

That was what she really wanted. To emerge from Blood Lake and see Jabbers waiting for her, alive and well. Then she would know everything was ready for Riku. Everything was prepared for that bastard's justice to be swiftly delivered.

Lou followed the flow of foot traffic past the row of waiting buses and through the clear doors sliding open, inviting her into the shopping center.

There were no defined stores inside as Lou was used to in the US malls, but rather an endless parade of kiosks. A chocolatier counter turned into a patisserie, then into a cheese, wine, and alcohol boutique with breads and bottled drinks. Lou couldn't get over how many things purported to be made of matcha. Matcha cakes. Matcha powder. Matcha chocolates.

There was a circular sponge cake with a green exterior and butter-yellow interior that was appealing, and Lou considered buying it. She would have if she hadn't wanted to go straight from the mall to La Loon. She didn't want to chance leaving the cake—no matter how well it might be wrapped—on the shores of her Alaskan lake while she crossed over. Any manner of creature could find it and tear into it and have themselves a feast before she made it back.

The cake could wait. Perhaps she'd eat it to celebrate the end of Riku Yamamoto's reign.

Lou found herself amongst the racks of clothing. Rows of boots and black leather shoes.

When stores ended and the doors finally opened onto a park, Lou admitted to herself that she was a little winded and her arms were beginning to feel heavy again. She sat down on the stone bench beside the fountain to catch her breath.

I'll make it a quick trip to La Loon, she said to herself. *Then I'll wash the lake out of my hair and go straight to bed. Konstantine will love that.*

She did the math and realized it was still morning in Florence. He wouldn't even notice she wasn't back yet.

When Lou's breath had fully returned to her, she rose from the bench and walked in the direction of the bathroom she'd seen just before the clothing racks.

Lou turned off the light, much to the annoyance of the woman who'd been alone in the last stall.

19

———

Lou stood on the edge of the Alaskan lake, enjoying the sight of the water in the moonlight. The end of her nose was beginning to turn cold, feeling icy to the touch. She shrugged out of her leather jacket and stepped into the frigid water. It rose past her knees, her thighs, and stomach. When it reached her breasts, a movement from the corner of her eye made her turn just in time to see a coyote backing away from the water's edge.

She hadn't seen it. It had remained perfectly still, perfectly quiet, no doubt watching to see what she would do. Lou was extra glad she'd decided to wait on the cake.

"Don't piss on my coat," she said, and dipped her head beneath the water's surface.

The cold water was refreshing against her face and the back of her neck. The darkness was complete. She let herself sink, the weight of water in her boots helping to carry her down toward the bottom of the lake.

Only she never reached the bottom. The waters began to turn red, warming around her, and she opened her eyes, propelling herself toward the surface with the thrust of her arms and legs.

As she found her footing on the gentle slope leading up the embankment of Blood Lake, the smell of sulfur hit her, clogging her nose like a soaked rag.

On the shore, she squeezed the excess water from her hair and waited.

A group of fins, reminding Lou of the orcas they had in her world, cut the surface of the lake twenty meters from the shore. It occurred to her for the first time that those strange pod-dwelling beasts must be freshwater creatures, because Blood Lake was not salty.

Lou could move into it from salt water or fresh water— from a bathtub or the ocean—but the lake itself held no sting of salt when she opened her eyes underwater. She should know, as many times as she'd dunked herself in it.

The shore and the valley surrounding the lake were empty. Silent.

"Hello?" she called out. "I'm here."

She resisted the urge to say, *Honey, I'm home.*

There was something about the stillness in the air. About the way her words hung around her rather than echoing out in all directions.

Her stomach twisted again.

She walked away from the shore toward the gray cliff face in the distance. She wasn't sure she had the strength to climb up to Jabbers's rock lair, but she would ask herself that once she reached the rocks.

Oil-black leaves and something that could be mistaken for tall grasses brushed at Lou's legs as she traversed the wide-open field. By her estimation, it took her twenty minutes to make it from the shallows of the lake to the base of the cliff face.

She hadn't been to the cave since her first night with

Konstantine. She smiled, remembering the expression of terror he'd tried to hide as he warred with the twin desires of not being naked in this bizarre place but also wanting to have sex with her.

She held on to this image as she reached out for the closest jagged rock and began to haul herself up onto the next ledge.

Her arms shook, but she found her footing and pushed herself up to the hand hold. Her boots dug into the cliff face well, and yet her whole body was trembling by the time she found the mouth of Jabbers's cave and hauled herself up to the ledge abutting its entrance.

She peered into the lair.

At first, she didn't understand what she was looking at. Her eyes couldn't comprehend much more than a mass of serpentine coiling, twisting, throbbing.

She thought, *Is Jabbers sick?*

Then, *Maybe she's shedding her skin.* Because it looked as if she were transforming somehow. There was a weird excess of limbs and scales to this new, grotesque form.

Then a great eye opened and saw her. Only it wasn't one of the yellow eyes Lou knew so well. This one was blood red. The same color as a Cooper's hawk, like the one her father had pointed out in the sky above their house when she was a child.

Then Lou realized what she was seeing.

There wasn't one monstrous body in the cave.

There were two.

"Fuck."

The strange new beast roared. Its large body slammed into one side of the cave and rubble rained down from the ceiling onto the black plates along its spine.

A second ear-splitting scream set Lou in motion. The panicked chanting in her mind obliterated all thought.

Not Jabbers. Not jabbers.

It doesn't know me. It doesn't know me. It doesn't know me.

The beast she saw now was like the one she met all those years ago, when at ten years old, she'd slipped from her bathtub to this strange place and a beast twice her size had leapt onto her, sinking its rows of teeth into her shoulder. It would have killed her if she hadn't fallen back into the water, saving herself.

Lou's elbow connected hard with a jagged rock, splitting open the skin on the back of her arm. She was pitched forward by the force of it, and her knee connected with another rock. She screamed, managing to roll herself at the last moment onto her left hip and slide down the side of the mountain. Her arms and clothes absorbed the brunt of her descent, leaving Lou free to look up just in time to see not one but two black tails whipping and writhing from the open mouth of the cave.

When she hit the bottom of the mountain, she shoved herself up to standing.

She ran, busted knee and all. She didn't stop.

Another ear-splitting scream tore through the air, and the cliff face began to tremble. Rocks tumbled out of the cave and down the front of the cliff.

Lou looked over her shoulder in time to see a black body erupt from the lair, its cotton-white mouth exposed and teeth bared. It tore down the side of the mountain, its enormous claws carving new trenches in the rockface.

Claws sharp enough to open her body easily.

When it hit the ground, the earth quaked. Lou lost her balance against the tremor and was pitched forward onto her hands and knees.

She righted herself again and kept running. It didn't matter that her arms and legs were on fire and her lungs burned as if they were full of acid.

She ran and ran and ran.

And *ran*.

As she reached Blood Lake, a cry echoed through the air. It was mournful, like the one from Lou's dream.

Lou turned to find two beasts locked in terrible battle. One was slightly larger than the other. The one with yellow eyes.

Yellow eyes.

Lou's heart leapt. Jabbers was alive.

Jabbers held her own against the other of her kind.

That one—the red-eyed one—was trying to get to Lou, she realized. Those red eyes held none of the discernment that Jabbers's did.

This new beast broke free of Jabbers's hold on its limb and lunged in Lou's direction.

Jabbers knocked it back with one thrash of her tail, sending it skidding across the field, a tumble of serpentine grace.

She's protecting me.

The red-eyed beast broke free again, and Jabbers grabbed the back of its neck, pinning it down against the ground.

She's trying to keep it from reaching me.

Lou dove into the water and sank beneath the depths with the sounds of reptilian screaming still ringing in her ears.

Lou's body shook with adrenaline and fatigue as she stepped from the cold Alaskan night into her apartment. Trembling, she shoved open the linen closet door. The shift in temperature was welcome, the warmth reaching out to envelop her, as she shed her clothes and padded sopping wet down the hallway to her bathroom.

As she washed the other world from her hair and her body, she hissed.

She'd been all but skinned on one side of her body. And that said nothing of the gashes on her knee and above her elbow.

"Shit." She held the towel away from her body as she turned one way in the mirror, then the other, to note the extent of the damage.

"I'm never going to hear the end of this," she told herself.

At the very least, Konstantine would pout or give her the silent treatment while grinding his teeth.

Lou dressed in black sweats and one of her father's soft green flannels. Then she fetched her kit, a tin box the size of a laundry basket, and took a seat at the edge of her bed.

She rummaged through the plastic shelves and organizers, trying to decide what she needed. Tweezers, pliers, iodine? Rubbing alcohol, antibiotic ointment, gauze?

She fingered the wounds, determining their severity and clearing them of debris.

By the light of the soft lamp in the corner, with the moon as her witness, she stitched her knee and arm and placed clean bandages over the scrapes on the side of her body. Fortunately, there had been nothing that required surgical scissors, clamps, or the cauterizing iron.

She had just put the roll of surgical tape back in her box when a small tug in her stomach stole her attention. Someone wanted her. Someone in New Orleans, by the feel of it. It wasn't the panicked, urgent pull of someone in danger, but it was a request for her presence nonetheless.

Satisfied with her work, Lou packed up the first aid box and pulled on a thick hoodie before answering the call.

She found herself in the Crescent City Detective Agency. Dani and Piper were sharing one desk and King was behind the other.

"There she is," King called out, squeezing a stress ball in his right hand.

Only, Lou realized once she got closer that it wasn't a stress ball. It was a stress... *penguin?*

He saw her looking at it. "Beth got this for me. She said she thought it was cute."

Lou watched as its eyes bulged and contracted, bulged and contracted, in an almost frantic rhythm. The word *cute* didn't immediately come to mind.

Tortured, maybe.

"What do you need?" she asked.

"A massage," Piper whined. "My back is *killing* me."

Dani shot her a look.

Piper quickly changed her tune. "I regret nothing. If a sick friend needs you to dig up some bodies in the middle of the night in January, you do it. It's the bro code."

Dani's look didn't soften. "You need to start going to the gym with me."

King asked, "How do you feel now?"

"Better," Lou lied. Because while it *had* been true that she'd woken feeling almost like herself, she most certainly didn't *now*. Falling down the side of a cliff had changed things.

King's smile was gone. "Where did you get that bruise on your cheek? It looks fresh."

Shit. Lou had seen the red mark on her face when she'd gotten out of the shower, but she'd hoped it was from exertion, or the hot shower.

"I fell," she said.

King arched his brows.

"From a considerable height," she added.

All three of them exchanged looks.

"You're having a hell of a week," King said. "It reminds me of this time where I got shot, broke my arm, and twisted my ankle all over the same weekend."

"No one likes a one-upper, man," Piper said.

King didn't seem to hear this.

"I was only a couple of years older than you. That was about the time I realized my body wasn't indestructible. Maybe you're getting the same message. Lucy would say the universe is speaking loud and clear."

At the mention of his dead wife's name, sadness flitted through his eyes. But the shadows passed and he leaned forward, putting the penguin on the desktop as if it was a delicate thing, not something he'd been assaulting relentlessly for the entire five minutes she'd been standing there.

"Who called me?" Lou asked.

"It was me." Dani got up and pulled a chair over for Lou. "I wanted to give you an update on the New York case."

Lou sat down, hoping she did a decent job of hiding how relieved she was to be off her feet.

"My friend Evangeline—"

"*Evangeline*," Piper mimicked.

They all looked to her.

She wrinkled her nose. "Sorry. Go on."

Dani took a breath and began again. "*Evangeline* was able to get someone from the local office to go out onto the Simpsons' property with her dog and *accidentally* discover the remains."

Dani had used air quotes.

"I'd always thought it was suspicious that dogs were always finding the bodies," Piper said. "Now I know that sometimes they're fake dog walkers."

Dani gave her an unfriendly look. "Are you going to let me finish? I think Lou would like to know if we're going to keep her here all afternoon or not."

"Carry on." Piper pressed her lips closed and pretended to lock them.

"The Simpsons have no idea who could have been out there burying bodies on their land, but they do have two nephews in New York City, and so I suspect we'll find out which one of them is your guy."

"What are the nephews' names?" Lou asked.

"Christopher and Elliot."

"I'm betting on Christopher. What kind of murderer is named Elliot?" Piper asked.

Dani let this comment slide.

"It's Elliot," Lou said, remembering the name he'd spoken the night she killed him.

"How do you know?" Piper asked.

"He told me."

"Mystery solved," King said. "What do we know about the aunt and uncle? Do they hold any responsibility for the murders? Were they accomplices?"

"So far Tina and Dave—the property owners—are cooperating with local law enforcement. Nothing stands out about them. She's a nurse and he used to be a firefighter before he retired. Their financials are fine. They have no kids themselves but seem to be attentive to the two nephews."

"Are the nephews brothers or cousins?" King asked.

"Cousins. Both are only children. Christopher was born to the husband's sister and Elliot was born to the wife's brother." Dani looked to Lou. "Do you think the aunt and uncle helped him hide the bodies on their property?"

Lou shrugged. "I got the impression he was working alone, but it's possible they saw something suspicious and let it go."

"'Why is Elly driving his car out into the woods, honey?'" Piper asked in a high falsetto, then immediately answered herself in a lower voice. "'Oh, you know, honey. Kids these days. They don't camp, they *glamp*.'"

Dani twirled her pen. "Hopefully when the story breaks, they'll start identifying the bodies and notifying the families."

"Any chance we can deliver his body so the grievers know the man responsible is dead?" King asked.

Lou realized that she hadn't seen Elliot's body on the shore of La Loon when she'd visited this afternoon. She'd been so focused on finding Jabbers, she'd forgotten that she'd left it there last time.

"Something ate him," Lou said.

"That's a negative on the body retrieval," Piper said.

King considered this. "Maybe we can set something else up. A badly burned cadaver in a car. Make it look like he was on the run and killed himself."

"Damn, man," Piper said. "I like how you think."

Lou found Konstantine in the church. Stepping away from the shadow cast by one of the cathedral's many old columns, she spotted him sitting in a pew.

He always chose the same one. The first row, closest to the statue of the Virgin Mary. The lights all around the statue illuminated her tilted head and soft, downcast eyes. The delicate way her hand rest over her heart. Those lights made her seem more like a heavenly deity than her position in the cathedral.

She wondered if he was thinking the same thing, or something similar. His eyes were on the Virgin's face, though it was hard to tell if he was really looking at her or if his mind was somewhere else.

Mostly, she just wondered how he could stand the cold of the place. In winter, the draft encouraged by the high ceilings and the lack of insulation blew through this place without restraint.

He turned to look at her then, his back falling against the pew.

"*Buona sera, amore mio.*"

"*Buona sera*," she said, and took a seat beside him.

The open friendliness evaporated when he saw her face.

"Were you fighting?"

He had to mean the bruise on her cheek. She had no makeup to speak of, so trying to hide it from him wasn't a possibility, and in truth, it wasn't Lou's style. She'd never liked the extra work that came with *avoiding* confrontation when the confrontation itself was usually the fastest way to resolution.

"No," she said plainly, and wondered if he could hear her regret. She wished the bruise was from fighting. "I fell."

His brows lifted. "You *fell?*"

She told him of her trip to La Loon. How she'd been met with an empty shore for the second time and how it had driven her to hike to the cave. She described the strange, writhing mass of tangled black limbs and throbbing bodies that had awaited her and how close she'd come to meeting a fate like the one she'd dealt to so many others.

It would have been a karmic end, she thought. Or at least her aunt Lucy might have said so.

Konstantine released her shirt. He'd lifted it while she was talking, taking time to note each bandage and scuff. He was irritated with her. That was evident in his growing scowl.

But he wasn't *pissed*. That was something.

"Some reptiles mate the way you are describing," he said finally. "And they're certainly more aggressive during mating season."

Mating season. Was that what had happened? Had Jabbers simply been missing because she'd been in some sort of heat?

"If she has a mate who doesn't know me, then it won't be safe for me to go there anymore," Lou said, and a stab of disappointment struck her in the heart.

"You said it was smaller than she was," he said. "You could try killing it?"

"I can't kill her boyfriend," Lou said. "Especially since she let you live."

He smiled. "It would seem ungrateful. It's also possible that this is only a temporary arrangement."

"What do you mean?"

He shrugged. "There are large cats who live solitary lives and come together only to mate. Birds too. They come together for the offspring but will separate once this period has passed."

Lou liked this theory. She was ashamed to admit she liked having La Loon—and Jabbers—to herself. The only problem with the theory was that Lou had no idea how long this so-called mating season was to last. In a world where the sky and seasons never changed, Lou had to assume their timeline was much longer than hers. What if a breeding season was years?

What if it spanned the rest of her life?

"I might not be able to go back," she said. Because there was still the matter of babies. Lou couldn't count on the idea that Jabbers's offspring would bond with her the way their mother had.

Konstantine took her hand and squeezed. "I don't need to tell you that there are plenty of places to hide a body in *this* world, do I?"

She knew then that it wasn't just about the convenience of having a dumping ground no one else could reach. It really was about her strange connection to that place, how special it had become to her.

"Be patient," Konstantine said, and pressed a cool hand to her cheek. He was covering her bruise as if he didn't want to see it. "This may resolve itself."

She placed her hand over his, and the last bit of tension relaxed from his shoulders.

"However, we should talk about things you shouldn't do

when ill. Climbing a cliff would be one of those things," he said.

"I wanted to know if I was ready."

"Ready for...?"

"Riku."

"May I ask your verdict?"

"Almost," she said.

His hand fell away from her face. "Yamamoto is very smart, *amore mio*. He will be like Angelo. Well guarded. Always surrounded. He is only alone when he is hurting someone, as you saw. And he will have something the others will not."

"What?" she asked.

"He knows about your gift. Erjon failed because he didn't know what you could do. It will not be the same with Yamamoto. He will not underestimate you. He will see you as he saw Saeko."

Saeko. Did Lou know that name? It sounded very familiar. If so, then it was another high-level crime boss that Lou had crossed paths with at some point in her hunting.

Konstantine must have understood her thoughts because he said, "Saeko was his predecessor. They engaged in ritual combat and he gutted her. Then he assumed power. He didn't just want to kill her and take control, he wanted to make an example of her. Do you understand?"

Did she? Of course.

If power was what Riku was most drawn to, how much would he wield if he was the one to slay *La Strega*? Lou understood how killing her would appeal to such a man. And he would want to do it in the most public way possible.

"Are you just giving me another excuse to buy him more time?" Lou asked.

"No," Konstantine said, and she saw the weariness on his

face. "I hope I don't need to convince you that I worry for you."

"I *am* going to kill him," she said.

"I understand."

"It doesn't matter how many people surround him or how badly he wants to kill me first. Or even if I don't have a place to dump his body"—*Except for maybe the shallows of Blood Lake*—"I'm going to kill him."

He took her hands and pressed them to his face in a silent plea for her to stop.

"I only ask for time, *amore mio*. Just a little more time."

20

———

Melandra awoke from another dreamless night. And yet the fear and worry in her chest wouldn't loosen until she saw the girl, made sure —for the one thousandth time—that she was safe.

Mel rose from her bed, threw back the covers, and went to the living room.

There she was.

Zoey slept soundly on Mel's sofa bed, her strawberry-blond hair spilling over the pillow Mel had given her. She'd been glad she'd kept it. Living in a single-bedroom apartment meant that Mel had to regularly purge things as they built up. For that reason, she'd spent an inordinate amount of time wondering if she should keep the extra pillows she'd stored in the top of her bedroom closet. Her argument had been that she never had guests. She'd bought that very sofa with the built-in full bed on the off chance that one of her many nieces or nephews from back home might want to come to the big city and spend the night with her.

They never had.

Yet here was the girl, using not only the bed but also the pillows. Proving Mel wrong on every front.

Mel moved quietly about the apartment. She cleaned herself up in the bathroom, made herself some coffee and toast. Did her morning prayers.

It was easier to keep her noise to a minimum because Lady was with King. There were no feedings or bathroom breaks that required her attention. Nor did she greet Mel with the usual tail-thumping and friendly barks.

That Belgian Malinois had been the only housemate who'd ever woken at the same time of day as Mel herself. Even as a child, she'd been an early riser, slipping from the house even before the sun itself was fully up.

Zoey had spent three mornings with Mel thus far, and every time, she hadn't woken until after the sun was up, a good two or three hours after Mel's day had begun. She'd eat the eggs and toast that Mel readily gave her and then she'd work in the shop downstairs.

Zoey was a smart girl and had quickly picked up Mel's instructions for cleaning, restocking, running the register, and speaking to customers. Mel thought it was the fifteen dollars an hour that was the real motivator, but she didn't say so.

Piper didn't mind this arrangement because it gave her more time to be with King and put in more hours on the casework she cared about.

More than a few times, Mel had given Zoey a few dollars to go down the road and get them some beignets.

She was definitely not from the city, because every time she returned, she told Mel of some new discovery she'd made. About the buskers playing in the streets and the women who danced with fire. About the man who would lie down on broken glass and ask the crowd for volunteers to step on his head and prove he couldn't be harmed by its sharp corners. Of the jazz bands set up in Jackson Square and the talented artists who could paint beautiful landscapes in what seemed like seconds, with a few furious strokes of their brush.

Mel had only asked that she stay away from the river.

Why had been a fair enough question, and Mel had tried to explain that this area of the Quarter wasn't as safe as the rest of it. This was a bald-faced lie but the best Mel could produce on such short notice.

As she sat at her kitchen table watching the girl sleep, the familiar unease crept in again.

I can't do this forever, she thought.

Zoey wouldn't want to stay in Mel's place forever, no matter how much she might enjoy the job and New Orleans. She would want answers eventually. And when would the danger be over?

The dreams had stopped.

Mel hadn't seen another cardinal in her waking life. She'd even taken the streetcar all the way down St. Charles and hopped off at Audubon just to *look* for one in the park.

But there were no omens. No signs. How was Mel to know when it was over? Had she already averted the danger simply by taking Zoey in? Had she done enough? Or was she going to have to make excuses for prolonging Zoey's stay?

Don't get ahead of yourself now, she told herself. *You got her here and that's what matters.*

She took another sip of her coffee and loosed a slow breath as sunlight began to fill the windows.

You'll know the next step to take when it's time to take it.

You'll know what to do, she assured herself.

She just wasn't sure if it was the truth. Or a prayer.

"Explain it to me," Riku said.

Riku saw the man's nervousness even before he began to speak. He noted the way Kenchi resisted the urge to tug on his hair where it sat bundled at the base of his neck. His hand had gone in that direction twice before pulling itself back mid-motion. The same had been true for the aborted move to get a cigarette.

Riku saw the outline of the pack in the man's breast pocket and the way the hand had wandered toward it compulsively. The twitching muscles in his hand had made the black ink from his tattoos dance like spiders.

It wasn't only Kenchi's habits that Riku had noted. He did this sort of constant review for everyone. It had become such an automatic behavior that Riku now kept a mental list of all the habits of the men around him without thinking about it. After all, if mutiny came, as it had when Riku sought Saeko's position, it would come from the ones closest to him. For that reason alone, it was in Riku's best interest to know everything about them. What they ate, where they slept, who they fucked, *what* they fucked, their fears and vices.

"Tell me the numbers. Again." Riku rose from his desk and went to the window to watch the night overtake Tokyo's downtown.

Kenchi spoke to his back. "There are fourteen missing, but we think two or three of them ran away on their own."

"Which of the fourteen do you think ran?" Riku asked. Bright screens flashed and pulsed in the night, and the street noise could be heard even at this height.

"We know the Filipino girls were taken. Takashi saw a hand grab them and pull them into the alley and—"

"I didn't ask you which ones you knew were taken," Riku interrupted. "I asked which ones ran."

Kenchi swallowed. "We aren't sure."

Riku watched a light turn and a rush of pedestrians blotting out the lines of the crosswalk they swarmed like ants.

"She could have taken all fourteen," Riku said.

Kenchi swallowed. "Yes."

It wasn't the number that upset Riku. He had almost fifteen thousand women and children. Perhaps another two thousand men and boys. What was fourteen when one owned thousands?

It was the principle of the matter.

She had taken from him.

Again.

She went unpunished.

Again.

"This won't do, Kenchi," Riku said, tearing his eyes away from the crowd below. "What kind of message does it send if we allow someone to steal what belongs to us?"

"I think we're lucky it's only fourteen, sir."

"You *think*?"

"No, sir," he said.

How quickly he tries to take back his words, Riku noted.

Riku wanted to kill him suddenly. Or at the very least, hurt him badly. Could he take a blade to that tattoo at his throat, perhaps, and carve it out of the muscles with a few twists of his knife?

That won't do, he counseled himself.

If *La Strega* and that Italian bastard wanted to start a war with him, then now wasn't the time to have petty disagreements over fourteen pieces of cargo. He'd already begun to notice the strain amongst his people. The hardened glares. The subtle shifts in their body language and manner toward him.

And here, now, with Kenchi.

Wasn't he one of Riku's most devoted? Wasn't that how he'd been able to move up the ranks to be Riku's personal bodyguard despite the rigid requirements of the position? True, Riku had also allowed that idiot Shibu to join them, but that was because he was too stupid to pull off a coup. Kenchi, on the other hand, had the power and the intelligence.

Riku could only let a man like that get close because he'd believed in the man's loyalty.

Was that a mistake?

That bitch is making me question everything.

In a lit window across the street, perhaps five or six floors lower than Riku's office, he saw a woman cradling her son. The child's unhappiness was plain, the face screwed in a wail of agony despite the seemingly good care he received. His mother bounced him, smoothed back his hair, dabbed at his eyes. By the twist of her mouth, she looked close to tears herself.

An idea sparked in his mind, like a match struck and hissing in the dark.

"Perhaps I can solve all of my problems at once," Riku said to himself as the mother and son stepped away from the window.

"I'm sorry, sir?" Kenchi called from his seat behind him.

All this time my mind has been wandering and my back has been to him. He could have killed me at any time, but didn't.

I suppose I have use for him yet.

Riku met Kenchi's eyes. "I want to have a party."

The other man's gaze fell. "What kind of party, sir?"

"A large one. We will have it in the ballroom of one of our hotels. Whichever you think can accommodate all of us."

"All of us?"

"Yes, tell everyone in our organization that attendance is required. I mean *everyone*—no matter their position, I want them there. Everyone is to arrive by eight and they will leave only when I tell them to."

"As soon as you decide the date—"

"Tomorrow night," Riku said.

"That isn't much time to prepare a party for thirty thousand people, sir."

"Then it will be the night after tomorrow," Riku said, but he would not wait any longer than that.

Kenchi's hand flexed toward his cigarettes again. "I am not good with parties, sir. Do you want me to send Yui so you can go over the accommodations and the specifications you want?"

"Send her in on your way out."

"What about the fourteen missing?" Kenchi asked. He would look no higher than Riku's chin.

"We will ignore this and consider ourselves lucky, as you suggest."

Was Riku imagining it? Did Kenchi relax at this suggestion? And if so, was it because of the praise Riku included or because he truly feared that woman so much?

Fool, he thought. He would show him—all of them—that *La Strega* was nothing.

Nothing compared to Riku and his tremendous will.

He would destroy her, and he would let every last one of them watch him do it.

Hold on, Mai, hold on, he thought. *We will be together soon.*

Piper was *not* a fan of all this walking. Who knew that private investigation involved so many steps in a given day. Before this gig, Piper had been fairly certain that she was an active person. After all, she walked everywhere, never having owned a car. It was true that she didn't have the best diet and she never did anything resembling formal exercise like Dani. Dani was in the gym three times a week, lifting weights, and went for a four-mile run on the other mornings.

Piper's weightlifting included large boxes of inventory for Fortunes and Fixes and she'd never tried to run unless her life was in actual peril, which unfortunately had been a real thing once or twice.

Yet here she was, following Brock Adkins with a sizable cramp in her side.

At least she was getting good pictures this time. She'd spotted him hiding in the park outside of Samantha's building, and sure enough, he stepped out from behind the hedgerow and fell into step behind her as she walked to class unaware.

Now Piper was following him.

She checked the picture she'd just snapped. *"Boo-yah. That's a good one."*

There was a clear shot of Brock's profile as he was turning the corner after Samantha.

Piper jogged to make up the distance she'd lost.

Only, when she hooked the corner, a knee came out of nowhere, hitting her hard in the gut.

She dropped her phone and it clattered to the pavement. Piper collapsed to her hands.

Then someone was turning her over, pulling back her hood to reveal her face.

"I knew it was you, you bitch," Brock said.

He bent over her, sneering down into Piper's face.

"Why the fuck do you keep following me? Do you really want my attention so badly?" He laughed. "You know you're pretty enough you could've just asked."

"I don't know where you learned to flirt," Piper said, trying to catch the breath he'd knocked out of her, "but usually you don't hit the girl *before* you do it."

He bent and picked up her phone.

"You can give that back now."

"The fuck I will." He hauled her to her feet and threw her against the brick wall with one arm. "What's the passcode?"

"Screw you. All one word."

He hit her then. The punch struck her ear in such a way

that it began ringing. She wasn't sure anyone had ever punched her in the ear before.

Piper opened her mouth to crack a joke about this, but her voice sputtered. Brock held a blade to her throat. It couldn't have been longer than four inches, but it looked sharp, and just that one small press to her skin stung like hell.

He held the phone over her face, but it didn't recognize her.

"Is this even your phone?"

She considered lying.

"Passcode," he said again between gritted teeth.

She told him. It was the date Dani and Piper became an official couple.

He didn't remove the knife from her throat as she looked up and down the small side street. She couldn't look far to the right, but to her left, the lane was empty.

No one. There's no one to see and stop this.

Piper's heart kicked in her chest. The fear was real now.

Lou, she thought. *Lou-blue, I could use a little help.*

"You have a lot of fucking pictures of me," Brock said, his face twisted. "Why?"

Piper opened her mouth to answer, but apparently she wasn't quick enough.

He pressed harder, and something warm flowed down over her collar.

Blood. It had to be blood.

"Why?" He shoved her against the wall again.

That's when the bat came out of nowhere.

Because of Piper's inability to turn her head lest she cut herself more on Brock's knife, the baseball bat looked like a disembodied force, swinging out of thin air and striking Brock in the back of the head.

His eyes rolled up, revealing a flash of white, and then he dropped to the ground at Piper's feet.

"Weird. You've never used a bat before," Piper said, relief overtaking her. She turned toward Lou, ready to throw herself into her savior's arms. Only it wasn't Lou.

It was a girl, no more than sixteen, maybe seventeen years old. She was stick thin with an aluminum baseball bat propped against one shoulder and a lollipop stick hanging out of the corner of her mouth. Her hair was pulled up in a high ponytail, and though her features and eyes were dark, her hair was hot pink.

"Oh, hey." Piper wasn't sure what else to say. By the look of the girl, this could go either way. It was unclear if she was helping her out of the bad situation with Brock or if she was about to rob Piper herself. Her only clue was that the baseball bat was resting against her shoulder rather than in a swing position.

The girl pulled the lollipop from her mouth and raised her chin at Piper. Then she said something Piper would have never guessed.

"How come every time I see you, someone's kickin' your ass?"

21

———————

This was the first time Lou had stolen a corpse from a morgue and wrecked a car with it. It had been difficult to time everything just right. After taking an unclaimed body from a Cleveland morgue, Lou had driven the killer's car into the concrete wall, kicking it up to almost ninety before disappearing and letting it hit the barrier at full speed with the body inside. This had to be done under the cover of night, and not only because she didn't want to draw attention to herself.

King wasn't a forensics specialist, but he'd gone into great detail about how if a body was burned badly enough, it would be impossible to get DNA evidence from the remains. So all they needed to do was leave evidence at the scene tying the body to Elliot Simpson.

In addition to using Elliot's car, Lou had taken his license and personal effects from his apartment and scattered them beside the concrete barrier on the deserted highway.

It didn't matter that Elliot's remains had been taken to La Loon. It only mattered that the families who lost loved ones would believe they'd received justice for the murders of their sons if they *thought* Elliot had gotten what he deserved.

She'd included as much gasoline in the car as Konstantine had said she'd need. He'd asked her the type of car she'd use—Elliot's Honda—and questions about the weight and size of the corpse she'd stolen from the morgue. Then, being the European he was, he'd given her the gasoline number in liters.

As she sat on the floor of the Arizona desert, watching the car burn through the night, she wondered who'd taught him to do calculations like that.

If a car weighing 1,860 kilograms hits a concrete barrier at 145 kilometers per hour, how many liters of gasoline would need to be in the car to burn the seventy-kilogram corpse inside to a crisp?

Lou fell asleep on the desert floor to the heat of the car's flames, thinking that she hated word problems. The sun had just risen over the horizon when her compass tugged her from sleep to full alertness.

She was staring at the smoldering car, but her mind had already cast itself out, searching.

Piper, she thought. Piper wanted her.

Then she tasted the girl's fear in the back of her throat.

No. Not wanted her. *Needed* her.

Lou abandoned the car, walking away from the smoking remains as if she hadn't forsaken a warm bed all night in order to see this through.

When she stepped from the shadows pooling around the concrete barrier into the New Orleans alleyway, two things struck her at once.

First, Piper was bleeding.

Second, there was a girl with a baseball bat propped against one shoulder, and Lou knew her from somewhere.

Lou grabbed the girl by her collar and pulled her up to the tips of her toes.

"Hello, gorgeous," the girl said. She wore a smirk, but her

eyes had widened at the corners, showing more white than they should. "Fancy meeting you here."

"It wasn't her," Piper said, touching the edge of her throat and hissing. "It was Adkins."

Lou released the girl with the bat. "The stalker?"

She nudged the man face down on the alleyway with her boot, rolling him over to show his face to the sky. It was Brock Adkins.

"Did you hit him with the bat?" Lou asked her.

"Like pop goes the weasel. Do you know that game? It's my favorite. There's an arcade where you can pop as many as you can in two minutes. Their little plastic heads that pop in and out of the machine like gophers or something. Best game in the world."

Lou took this chattiness to be nerves. So be it. Sometimes that was the effect she had on people. Or maybe the girl was stoned.

"You smell like weed," Lou said.

"Oh yeah? Well you smell like gasoline and burning metal," she replied. The sucker clinking around between her teeth had stained her lips a dark red from its candy coating. "You been blowing shit up?"

Lou didn't answer her.

"Why is it every time your friend is getting her ass kicked, you show up?" the girl asked.

That's when Lou remembered her.

"Alice," she said.

The girl scowled. "*Bane*, actually. As in, 'the bane of your existence.' But yeah, good memory."

She was one of Konstantine's people then. She'd been the first one on the scene when Diana Dennard had attacked Piper and kidnapped Dani before blowing up her apartment building.

"Are you still a Ravenger?" Lou asked.

"If I say yes, does that get me a prize?" the girl asked, her smile like a fox's now.

For Lou, that was answer enough.

"Wait, is that Konstantine's—" Piper began.

Lou shot her a look and Piper's mouth snapped shut.

Piper turned to Bane. "Do you ever get stopped for carrying a bat around like that?"

Smooth, Lou thought, fighting back a smile.

"Sometimes, but what're they going to do? Even if they arrest me, they can't keep me. Funny how all those would-be charges don't seem to stick to my record." Here Bane turned to Lou and leveled her with a knowing stare. "That ever happen to you?"

Lou said nothing.

Bane shrugged. "Maybe he doesn't need to cover for you like he does the rest of us."

Except Konstantine *did* cover for Lou. When it came to video footage or police reports, he removed everything that made her visible in this world. Anything that could create a pattern or lead the authorities to her.

"Where's your pack?" Lou asked her.

"The boys?" Bane snorted. "They're in school."

"Why aren't you in school?"

"I dropped out and got my GED. Now I take college classes online. That's more my style, you know? I like keeping my own schedule. I'm a free woman."

"We should go," Piper said, holding a paper napkin to her throat and picking her phone up off the pavement.

"What about him?" Lou asked.

"Leave him." Piper started off in the direction of her apartment on Royal Street.

Lou fell into step beside her.

"Hey, wait," Bane called after them. When they didn't turn, she added, "Come on, don't be like that. I was very nice to you today!"

Lou spared her a glance.

Bane jogged to catch up and stopped just short of them. "If you're not going to teach your pet here how to fight, someone's got to. She gets into too much trouble to be a punching bag. And I get the sense that maybe you can't be in all the places all the time. Or at least, she might need enough tricks to buy herself some time, am I right?"

Lou still said nothing. She was trying to decide if she trusted the girl or not.

"I have a solution for you. No. An *opportunity*." Bane reached into the front pocket of her jeans and pulled out a business card. The back was white and the front red and blue.

It was for a boxing gym.

"If you're too busy to teach her, I can do it," Bane said, holding the card out to them. "I won't brag too much, but let's just say I can do more than swing a bat."

It was Piper who took the card. "I've seen this place. It's over by City Park."

"Then you know where to find me," Bane said. She propped the bat against her shoulder one last time, and with a little salute, turned and walked west, away from campus.

They watched her go.

"Questions," Piper said, looking from the girl to the card, then back to Lou. "I've got a few questions."

"Dani is going to freak out," Piper moaned. "Geez. Can't you do any better than this?"

Lou lowered the gauze and inspected her work. "No."

"It looks like someone tried to cut my head off." She pulled at the tape. "It reminds me of this urban legend I heard as a kid about this girl who always wore a ribbon around her neck and never took it off, and the kids were teasing her about it, and one night they pulled the ribbon off when she was sleeping and her head rolled to the floor."

Lou wasn't sure what the point of this story was. She didn't think the gauze she'd wrapped around Piper's throat looked like a ribbon at all, nor did it remotely suggest it was keeping her head on her shoulders.

"Why didn't you call the police and report that he assaulted you?" Lou asked. "Why did you just leave the stalker there?"

She understood that Piper was taking after King when it came to handling criminals. Lou giving Brock Adkins a one-way trip to La Loon in the middle of a case would neither be welcome nor appreciated. They wanted to prosecute him for stalking. She understood this, but if the plan was to follow the letter of the law, why hadn't Piper told the authorities he'd pulled a knife on her? Wouldn't that help their case more than anything? Proving that he was violent and capable of attacking a woman?

"If I report it, King will find out," she said, rubbing her forehead.

"So?" Lou asked, knowing that couldn't be all of it.

"I've wanted to run my own case pretty much from the moment he let me start working at the agency. I've been dying to prove that I have what it takes to be an investigator, and if I screw this up, he might never give me another shot."

"How is getting a knife pulled on you 'screwing this up'?" Lou asked, settling back against Piper's sofa with the first aid supplies still spread in front of them on the coffee table.

"You know how he is. He's going to be like, 'It's too dangerous. I should've never let you work alone.' Yadda yadda. It'll be another century before he trusts me to handle something by myself."

Lou didn't think this was true, but she could tell by the earnestness in Piper's face that she believed it. Was King more protective of Piper than he was of Lou? Possibly. After all, Piper didn't have Lou's skills nor gift. She had a dozen reasons to be more careful.

"This means so much to me. I haven't decided if I want to be an investigator or work some other job in law enforcement, but I want this. Do you understand?"

"I do." *Want* was something Lou was very familiar with. "But he can't stop you."

"He can pull me off the case and never give me another."

"Fuck him."

Piper's mouth fell open. "Louie Thorne. *Language!*"

Lou smiled. She was glad that she had broken through the girl's gloom. "You don't need him."

"He has a lot of connections in a lot of different areas of law enforcement. He'd be a good reference and—"

"It doesn't matter," Lou insisted. "If you want something, you can make it happen with or without him."

"But it would be a lot easier with him, if you know what I'm saying." Piper scrubbed at her forehead again. Lou only saw her do this when she was stressed.

"Ugh, and really, it's more than that," the girl added after a beat of silence.

Lou kept quiet, leaving the space for Piper to speak when she was ready. The apartment's heat kicked on, a click and rattle of the radiator coming to life.

"This is going to sound stupid, but I also sort of want to impress King."

Lou worked to keep her face free from emotion.

Piper puffed her cheeks and exhaled. "He's the first guy in my life since my dad died."

"I thought you were close with Henry."

Piper waved this away. "I mean the first guy with dad vibes. I'm not saying I think of him as my dad. But I'd be lying if I said I didn't want him to be proud of me."

The silence built until Piper looked at her, searching Lou's face for some sort of answer.

"You think I'm stupid, don't you?" Piper asked.

"No," Lou said. "I'm proud of you."

"Aww, Lou-blue." Piper threw her arms around Lou's neck. "Thank you."

Lou held her back. Did Lou understand what it was to lose a father? Yes. But she'd never sought someone else's approval then or since.

"I won't tell him," Lou said into Piper's hair before releasing her. "But he'll want to know why your throat looks like that."

"Dani's got a couple of turtlenecks. I'll have to wear them until the cut heals. You heal a lot of cuts. How long will that take?"

Lou wondered if she should offer to take Piper to La Loon and dunk her in the healing waters of Blood Lake. Probably not. She made her best guess instead. "Two or three weeks?"

Piper fell back against the sofa dramatically. "Man, I want to *kill* that guy."

She must've seen something in Lou's face.

"It's a figure of speech. Please don't kidnap him and take me to a dark forest in the dead of night and give me a gun again."

Lou's smile only deepened. "Let me know if you change your mind."

Piper's face changed. "Oh, tell me about that girl."

Lou's mind went first to the little girl she'd taken from Riku's bedroom.

"She seemed like she knew me. And what the hell was up with that baseball bat?" Piper asked.

Then Lou knew they were talking about Bane.

"She works for Konstantine. Or she's got some connection to him. She was the one who found you the night Diana Dennard blew up Dani's apartment."

Piper's eyes widened. "Oh shit. That's what she meant about me always getting my ass kicked."

"It's why you don't remember meeting her," Lou said. "Diana knocked you out."

Piper frowned at her. "Yeah, I remember. Thanks."

"Maybe I should teach you how to fight," Lou said.

Piper considered this. "No offense, Lou-blue, but I'd be a little terrified to fight you. It's not exactly fair. And the way you fight wouldn't be like how I'd have to fight anyway."

She had a point. And Lou already knew her well enough to know that Piper didn't want to learn how to shoot a gun. She'd had that chance already and had turned it down. Maybe one day she would learn for whatever law enforcement job she wanted to do, but she wasn't ready yet.

"Then will you call her?" Lou asked.

"I might," Piper said, and chewed her lower lip. "I just might."

Lou wanted to check one more thing before she returned to Konstantine's. Already her back was aching for the soft compression of his luxurious mattress and his satin-covered pillows that felt as light as air.

Just one more stop, she thought. *One more stop and I'll turn in for the day.*

It was nighttime in New Orleans, and Lou stood in the chilly air, watching Jackson Square alive and throbbing around her. The church was spotlighted, adding a dramatic air to the large windows and tall arches. Around its front, tables upon tables of fortune tellers had set up for the night. After leaving Piper's she'd taken to walking through the Quarter. She loved doing that, walking through cities, looking at the people and the strange things unique to each place. And there was something special about New Orleans. Lou couldn't deny that. Something in the air that she could feel, electric along her skin, much like the invisible presence of the compass inside her.

A tourist was shoving beignets into her mouth and sucking the powdered sugar off each of her fingers when Lou's compass finally caught and snagged into place, giving her the target she was hoping for.

Lou turned and began walking down the alley adjacent to the church. It felt like she'd taken a step back in time to the seventeen hundreds, and maybe the wooden sign of the bookshop hanging above the uneven stone streets that might have been there forever.

Lou melded into the shadows, feeling New Orleans dropping away around her. When the world took shape again, she wasn't sure where she was. It was still night, the air far colder than what Lou had just left behind. She checked her watch and saw she was only an hour ahead of New Orleans.

Where was she then? The northeast?

Lou let her compass lead her up the street five or ten feet. As she walked, she took in the wide boulevard and traffic.

The compass snagged again, and she stopped in front of a glass storefront. She pulled the handle and stepped inside, welcoming the rush of heat.

The sweet tang of wine stung her nose and she realized immediately that this store was dedicated to it. Bottles of red, white, rosé lined every shelf and display. To her left was a tasting station with a few bottles open and little disposable tasting cups resting within reach.

"Hello, ma'am, can I see your ID?"

Lou turned and found a gray-haired woman with a benevolent smile looking up at her. She couldn't have been more than five feet tall.

"I don't have an ID," Lou said.

"Oh, are you American?" she asked.

This gave Lou pause. "Yes."

"You would've had to cross the border with a passport or a visa now, didn't you, dear?"

The border. Canada then. Because there were only two borders for an American to cross.

"It's in my hotel room," Lou lied. "I'm not trying to buy alcohol. I'm looking for someone I know. We went to school together."

Because Lou was certain she was here. Her compass kept fixing in the direction of a door on the far wall.

"She's older than me by a few years. Japanese," Lou said.

"Oh, you mean Mina," the old woman said. "Such a sweet girl. I'll get her for you."

The woman shuffled away and Lou lingered by the door. While she waited, she shook her GPS watch awake and dropped a pin for the wine shop so that she could look up the name of the place later.

Lou spent the remaining minutes watching a woman taste every single one of the red wines on the tasting bar, wrinkling her nose and sticking out her tongue after each sip.

When she caught Lou watching her, she laughed. "I feel like I *should* like red wine because it's supposed to be better for you, but truly I just like a sweet, chilled white. Do you know what I mean?"

Lou was spared from answering because the woman she was looking for came through the door toward her.

When she saw Lou, she frowned, her steps hesitating.

But Lou's compass was never wrong. It was her.

Mai Yamamoto was alive.

22

K ing only had a second to pick up his coffee cup before Dani slammed her legal pad down on his desk.

"I'm sorry it took me so long to get this," she said. She was out of breath and her hair was windswept from the chilly afternoon. The fact that she'd stopped to talk to King before heading straight up to the girls' apartment meant that she'd finally come through on the Peterson case.

Or at least, that's what he thought she was going to talk about. He couldn't remember if he'd asked her for something else.

Dani was still apologizing. "I've had several deadlines crop up this week and then there was the New York case."

"I've got no complaints. You're the best investigative journalist on the payroll," King said, hoping they could hop to the part where she gave him the information. King had promised to have Beth over for dinner promptly at six thirty. It was already ten after five.

"I'm the only investigative journalist on your payroll, but thanks." She shuffled some papers, trying to get her notes in order. "You wanted to know why Zoey took off in the first place?"

"Correct."

"About a week before she left, two things happened, according to her best friend, Madison. The first is that she'd run out of a house party crying, and the boy she'd been dating, Zach, went after her."

King frowned. "Like chased her down?"

Dani shook her head. "No, not violently or anything. He wanted to catch up to her. Something had happened between them. Maybe Zach kissed someone else at the party and Zoey saw and took off, that kind of thing."

"Sounds like a high school drama," King said, taking the penguin off his desk and squeezing it between his palms again.

"Whatever the reason, she left a party early, visibly upset, and the boyfriend left right after her."

"Okay, what's the second thing?" he said, continuing to pulse the penguin in his fist.

"The boyfriend died."

King stopped squeezing the penguin. "That escalated quickly."

"Seriously. The next night the boyfriend told his parents that he was going over to Zoey's to talk to her, possibly break up, but he would be back."

"And?" King asked.

"He never made it. A drunk driver T-boned him through a red light and Zach never woke up. He died in the hospital from his injuries two days later."

"How long after his death did Zoey take off?" King asked.

"The same day, possibly. The last time anyone remembers seeing her was at the hospital the morning Zach died. It seems like as soon as she heard he was dead, she ran."

"She didn't even want to go to the funeral?" King asked.

"Apparently she wasn't invited. According to Madison, Zach's mom said some horrible things to Zoey at the hospital, and she was uninvited even before the arrangements were made."

"Harsh."

"Yeah," Dani said with a deep sigh. "I feel bad for her."

King switched the penguin to his other fist. "I'm not surprised. Grieving people tend to eject their pain on whatever target they can find. Their targets don't always make sense."

Dani looked at her phone and noted the time. "All right, I need to get started on dinner. Piper gets hella cranky if she doesn't eat."

"I've noticed." King snorted. "I'm on my way out anyway. I've got my own dinner plans."

King rose from his seat, stretched, and put the penguin back on its plastic ice stand facing south. Then he grabbed his duster off the back of his chair and checked his pockets for his keys, phone, and wallet.

Dani turned back at the door leading up to the apartment and gave a little wave. "Good night."

"Hey, good work on Zoey," King said. He couldn't be sure if he'd thanked her. "That was a huge help."

Dani dipped her head. "You're welcome."

Then she was gone.

On the step outside the Crescent City Detective Agency, King fussed with the lock, holding it in place the way it demanded in order to get the deadbolt to slide home.

As soon as he managed it, he turned to find Zoey Peterson standing five feet away, her oversized green coat hanging from her shoulders.

He started, but quickly recovered, hoping that Zoey hadn't seen the shift in his face.

"Hey," he said.

Her eyes went from his face to the Crescent City Detective Agency sign printed on the window and then back to him again.

"You're a cop?" she asked.

"No, I'm not a cop. I'm a private investigator," he said, and thought he sounded suspicious as hell even to himself.

Zoey's lip began to tremble. "Did she send you after me?"

King's heart knocked in his chest. "Who? Mel?"

"She did, didn't she? I'm an idiot. I thought she was helping me but it was just to keep me here until you get the evidence she needs, isn't it?"

"Zoey—"

Zoey didn't let him finish. She turned and ran down Royal Street in the opposite direction of Mel's apartment.

"Zoey, wait! Come back!" King didn't bother to run after her. He could see just fine from where he stood that her speed nearly doubled his.

Someone ran track.

"Shit."

I fucked up.

Then another thought followed closely on its heels.

I have to tell Mel.

MEL'S MIND HAD JUST TURNED TOWARD DINNER WHEN King burst through the door of Fortunes and Fixes, breathless. His hair was blown back from his face. There were two customers in the store, a girl who was shuffling through one of the sample tarot decks, admiring the art with close, squinting eyes, and a young man eyeing Mel's display dedicated to Papa Legba. She'd just been about to go over and ask the white boy what he knew about the lwa before King arrived.

King saw her eyes cut to the customers and he gave her a

subtle nod, acknowledging her concerns. His pace was slow and controlled as he approached the register and stopped just short of her.

Lady rose to greet him, her tail thumping. But it stilled when she saw his face.

"Zoey took off," King said.

"I just sent her down to the café to get us some beignets and coffee," Mel said. "She'll be back in twenty or thirty minutes."

King shook his head. "No, she saw me coming out of the agency and accused me of being a cop. She seemed to think that someone had hired me to track her down. It sounded like she believes you're in on it."

Mel frowned, struggling to keep her voice low. "Why would she think that? Who wants to track her down? Her parents?"

"I don't think so," King said, trying to steady his breath. "I think she's talking about the boyfriend's mom."

Mel didn't hide her confusion, and King did his best to explain what Dani had told him from her investigative work while also keeping his voice low enough as to not bother the customers. Though from the furtive glances made by the girl with the tarot cards, Mel had a feeling she was trying her damnedest to hear everything.

"You might've just spooked her," Mel said. "She'll be back. She's only got the twenty bucks I gave her and I have all her stuff upstairs. She wouldn't run off without her stuff, now, would she?"

Mel was hoping he would reassure her. He knew more about runaways than she did.

"She might, if she's scared enough," he said.

"Where are you going?" Mel asked. King had turned away and started up the stairs.

"Beth is coming over for dinner. I'll be right here if you need me."

Mel let him go and kept her eyes on her two customers until the man gave up and wandered away without asking so much as a price and the girl ended up buying one of the oracle decks.

That's when Mel took a chance to run upstairs and check her apartment.

Lady yipped, staying close on her heels as she went inside and eased the door shut behind them. She saw Zoey's backpack on the sofa beside the neatly folded pillows and blankets. Yet for some reason that sense of unease didn't relax in Mel's chest. She checked her sock drawers for her extra cash and found it untouched. Then there was her jewelry box full of things a troubled girl might want to pawn if she was going to run.

But Mel's valuables were all present and accounted for.

It's okay, she told her disquieted mind. *It's okay. She won't run.*

Then a wild idea struck her. Mel turned and bent down beside her bed, reaching underneath its frame into the darkness.

She pulled the shoebox out into the light and opened it.

That's when she knew it had all gone wrong. It wasn't what she saw there in the cardboard lining of the box. It was what she didn't see.

Her gun was gone.

Mel was on her feet, running through her apartment and out the door with Lady barking at her heels.

"Mr. King! Mr. King!"

King's apartment door flew open. King held a spatula in one hand. "What is it? What's happened?"

Mel stopped just short of him, placing one hand on the frame to catch her breath.

"My gun is gone," she said. "Her clothes and everything be right where she left them, but my gun is gone. I know it was there, and no one's been in but her and me."

King's eyes widened. "She stole your gun."

"Don't say it like that. She's a good kid."

He pulled his cellphone from his pocket and began scrolling through his contacts. "A good kid who stole a gun."

"Who are you calling?"

"White. He's in the Quarter tonight. I'll have him keep an eye out for her."

Mel pulled her shawl tight around her body. "I'm going to go looking for her too."

King frowned. "You're going to go looking for the girl who stole your gun. I'll come with you."

"Why?"

"I don't want you out there alone. What if she hurts —*Hey*, White? Yeah, it's King. What's your night shaping up to look like?"

White's voice rumbled through the speaker. "Quiet. Why do I feel like that's about to change?"

"We found Zoey Peterson. She's not here. She took off before we could talk to her. Can you keep your eyes open?"

Mel's heart hammered in her temples. It felt like her pulse was a living, relentless snake throbbing in her body.

"Just hold her if you find her. There's no drugs or nothing like that. But White, she might have a gun on her if you find her. I don't think she'll hurt anybody, but just tell your people to be cautious."

"Roger that," White said.

"Thanks." King ended the call.

"Why did you have to tell them she had a gun?" Mel hissed. "What if they shoot her?"

"It's more dangerous if they don't know she has one and

scare her into using it. Hopefully this way, if they're aware of it, they'll focus on de-escalation tactics."

Mel didn't bother to point out that this was only true because Zoey was a pretty little white girl. Black children had been shot for less.

"Why would she take the gun?" Mel asked, wringing her hands.

"It depends on how threatened she felt," King said. And by who? Who had made the girl feel like her life was in danger?

King was searching her face.

"She might come back," he told her. "She might realize she wants her stuff and has nowhere else to go. For now, let's just sit tight."

"What if she doesn't come back?" Mel asked, nervously touching the bangles on her wrist and making them sing.

"Then we'll go looking for her. All of us together."

"What is it?" Konstantine asked. "What's wrong?"

He had been standing at the stove, pushing garlic and onions back and forth in a pan, when Lou felt her compass spin to life. She'd half turned, as if listening to a sound at the edge of her hearing.

"*Amore mio?*" he asked.

"What time is it in Tokyo?"

No, she thought. *No, not again.*

"Why?" He pulled his phone from his pocket and checked the time. "It's almost midnight there."

The unease growing inside her morphed, folding into a resounding chord of terror.

"I have to go." Lou pushed herself off the counter where she'd been leaning moments before, enjoying the look of

Konstantine in the kitchen, his easy conversation and company. The smell of the delicious food.

How quickly it had all changed.

Lou grabbed his Beretta off his desk as she passed it.

"Wait!" Konstantine cried, the pan clanking as he tried to simultaneously go after her while also moving it off the burner.

Lou was already in his closet before he could manage it.

She expected to step from the darkness into Riku's bedroom. The compass had been clear that it was Riku who was responsible for someone's terror.

When the world reformed around her, she didn't find his bedroom.

She was in pure darkness. Or nearly.

She tried to adjust to her surroundings, to understand where she was and what was happening.

Despite the absolute pitch, she was sure she was back in the world. The floor beneath her feet was firm. There was a child crying, its wailing loud and inconsolable.

The soft murmur all around her gave her the impression that she was in the middle of a crowded room—and yet when she extended her arms, she touched no one. There was also something about the way the sound carried, making her feel as if the ceiling might be quite high above her.

Where the hell am I?

The lights came on.

A flood of light so bright, and it beat down on her from every direction. Her eyes struggled to adjust to the onslaught.

Too much. Too much light.

Gasps circulated the room. The people surrounding her took a step back.

All around her, in every direction she turned, men and women stood in elegant clothes. The room did have a high ceiling, and the floor was made of marble, which explained the strange way sound had traveled in the dark.

"Are you looking for her?" a voice said.

It was difficult to make out distinct faces through the strong light, but the voice she recognized. Lou turned and found Riku standing in the center of the circle fifteen feet from her. In his arms was a little girl. Her dress was pink, her ankle socks white inside her black, shiny shoes.

She was crying so hard her face was red. Her chest shook with each inhalation.

Riku seemed immune to this. He held her with his left arm, pinned close against him. With his right hand, he pointed a gun at Lou.

"You want her?" Riku asked. "Take her."

Lou gauged the distance between them, measuring it again and again with her eyes, but she did not close the gap.

Why not?

Was he hoping to put a bullet in Lou's brain where she stood? Then why wasn't he pulling the trigger? Why was he beckoning her forward?

Riku pressed the gun to the girl's chin.

Lou froze. "Don't."

"Don't?" He laughed. "Is she really the only reason you've come? I thought you came for *me*."

Murmurs echoed through the crowd. Lou didn't know what they were saying, but she saw no one with a gun. No one except Riku.

Riku puffed his chest. "Should we lay down our guns and handle this like—"

Lou pulled the trigger.

The bullet missed the child but slammed into Riku's thigh. He buckled, and the child tumbled out of his arms.

She hit the marble floor with a sickening crack, and after a moment of heart-pounding silence, the screaming burst forth from her, louder than it had been before.

Not dead, Lou told herself. *If she'd cracked her head open on the floor, she wouldn't be able to cry like that.*

Riku had turned off the lights so Lou could come, but unless she figured out how to cut them again, she was stuck here. Surrounded by people. Her compass spun and searched, but there was no exit.

Too much light. Too much fucking light.

A commotion in the back of the room sounded like trouble headed her way. Men were shouting. The crowd was shuffling.

The people with guns are trying to get to their master, Lou thought.

And Lou needed to get to the girl.

23

———

Konstantine had but a moment to stand in his living room, heart pounding, before one of his cell phones rang. He shoved aside the papers beside his computer and uncovered it.

"Yes?" he said, hating how rattled his voice was. Lou had left too quickly, and she'd taken his gun. Whatever she was doing, it had to be dangerous if she wanted his gun.

She wasn't fully healed yet. He knew this.

"Hello?" he said, his impatience coating his words.

"Mr. Konstantine," the man said. "My name is Watanabe Ren."

Konstantine knew the name. "I'm listening."

Screams echoed through the phone.

"Is this a bad time?" Konstantine asked.

"Your..." Watanabe hesitated. "The woman. The woman is here."

The pounding in Konstantine's ears intensified. He tried to slow it down. He inhaled slowly, and with every ounce of his self-control asked, "Is your master misbehaving again?"

"Yes." This question seemed much easier for him to answer. "He has a child and—"

From what Konstantine could hear, there were many people in the room.

Too many, he worried.

"Where are you right now?" Konstantine asked.

Watanabe rattled off the name and address of the hotel. Konstantine rushed to his laptop and threw it open. He began typing commands into his system furiously, searching for the building's cameras.

"Why are you calling me, Watanabe?" Konstantine fought to keep his voice relaxed, a mask of indifference while his fingers flew across the keys.

"To say we accept your terms!" Watanabe cried. "We will make all of the arrangements. Please ask her to spare our lives in exchange for our cooperation."

"It may be too late for that," Konstantine said. His words were coated with unfeeling menace, but it was the truth. The deal he'd worked on with Stefano ever since Busaba's return was falling to pieces. "You assume I control her. I don't know how many times I must tell everyone that she acts according to her own sense of justice."

Please don't kill Riku. Please. Please, his mind chanted.

He wouldn't be able to manage a peaceful transfer of power if Lou murdered Yamamoto's men.

Konstantine needed this to work. He needed the other organizations to believe a peaceful, conflict-free resolution was possible, or things would never change between their factions.

Then he found them. The cameras showed a ballroom full of people. Thousands of people stood in a circle near the middle of the enormous room. At its center were two smudges.

Was one of them Lou? If so, she couldn't be more than fifteen or twenty feet from Riku.

In his ear, someone screamed, and the unmistakable wail of a child rang through the phone.

"It's too bright there," he cursed. *She can't leave.*

"Yes, he turned on the lights thinking—"

Gun shots rang through the room. *Pop. Pop.*

There was a lag in the video. The flash of the gun going off was a second behind the sound in his ear.

The screaming intensified as well as the sounds of rushing feet. On the video feed, Konstantine could see the stampede. Bodies were pushing for the exit, running away from the fray.

"I can try to broker peace with her on your behalf—" Konstantine began.

"Yes!" Watanabe pleaded. "Yes, please, before she destroys us all!"

Watanabe was shouting in Japanese now, seemingly at the top of his lungs. Konstantine understood none of it.

But he knew the sound of gunfire, even before he saw the white flash-pop of two more shots erupting on the screen. Unless Konstantine could find a way to turn off the lights flooding the room, there was no way she would make it out of there alive.

Konstantine took a deep, steadying breath. "All right. If you want my help—"

"Yes, please!" the man begged.

"Okay. Then listen carefully. This is what you must do."

Lou was already running for the child. She fired once and it hit Riku's arm, ripping open his suit and exposing the flesh beneath. Blood began to well up between the layers and darken the fabric.

What a terrible shot, she lamented. *It's the lights. The fucking lights are too bright.*

She fired again, but now Riku was dropping down into a crouch, raising his gun to shoot. Lou dodged at the last second, now only two paces from the girl.

But a woman was rushing forward, scooping the wailing child into her arms.

Lou let her, noting the tears streaming down her face and the way she kept calling the girl's name over and over again like a prayer.

Riku raised his gun to shoot. With that aim, he was going to blow off the mother's head as well as the child's.

Without thinking, Lou threw the full weight of her body against his, and the bullet went astray.

She slugged him across the face and felt his bones shift under her knuckles. She struck him again and the nose split like fruit, warm blood rushing up to coat her knuckles.

After the fifth or sixth punch, he bucked her, pitching her forward, up and over his head. She hit the marble floor on her hands and knees, the gun sliding a few inches away from her.

Forget the gun, her mind screamed. *Your back is to him.*

A foot connected with her spine and she cried out, hitting the ground on her elbows. She rolled at the last second and missed the second kick. The leather shoes slammed against the marble where she'd been just the moment before.

She swung her leg and struck Riku in the back of his. He went down and his head hit the marble floor with a resounding *crack*. She was on him again before he could get his eyes open. She wrenched the gun from his hand, another shot firing into the air as she did. It bounced off the wall and flew skyward, striking and extinguishing one of the lights.

This didn't help her. Too much light remained.

What she didn't see was the second gun, until it was too late. He got it half raised before she could grab his hand. He pulled the trigger and a bullet went through her hip, just missing her pelvic bone, tearing through the fleshy part of her side.

She screamed, feeling the warm blood gush through her clothes.

A second gunman Lou hadn't seen also fired his pistol. The bullet tore through the flesh of her armpit, striking a bundle of nerves and obliterating her mind with the pain of it. Her hold on Riku slackened and he threw her off.

Lou hit the ground on her back.

That's when the lights went off.

Lou lay in the blessed dark, her blood leaving her body too quickly.

Don't! she cursed herself. *He's right there. Right there and—*

Take him. Just grab him and take him with you.

But Lou knew this cold, tingling feeling in her feet and hands. She was bleeding out. And she was bleeding out *fast*. She needed to make a decision between saving her life or killing Riku.

Live to fight another day, a voice said.

It was her father. And it was probably the only voice she would've listened to in that moment because Jack *hadn't* lived to fight another day. That fact had set her on this very path.

So Lou chose herself and embraced the dark alone.

Konstantine stared at the black screen, heart still hammering in his ears. Had it worked? Had it worked?

"Come on, come on, come on, come on." He spoke the mantra over and over again in panicked repetition.

Then he heard her cough. The sound wasn't coming from his computer.

He stood and found Lou on her hands and knees on his

living room floor. The pool of blood under her body was growing quickly.

"Louie!" He knelt beside her. "You're shot!"

"Yes."

"Where?"

"In the hip and under the arm."

"Take us to Isadora," he said, placing one hand on her back. When she didn't immediately move, he asked, "Can you do it?"

Lou didn't answer.

"Louie?"

"Give me a second," she said, her voice strained.

Konstantine left his hand on her back, and he was still kneeling when the world fell away and the clinic formed around them.

Isadora cried out and raised a hand to her chest. "*Santa Madonna!*"

"She's losing blood."

Isadora shouted commands and her team sprang into action. Three women helped to get Lou onto a gurney. Another got an IV into her arm with a single quick prick. Another set up a tray with blood packs and separate tubing, clearly ready to begin the transfusion at the doctor's order.

"Over there, Konstantine," she said, and nodded to one of the chairs along the wall. "Out of the way."

Konstantine obeyed.

Lou hissed when Isadora touched the wound under her arm. That told Konstantine all he needed to know about how painful it was. He'd seen Lou dig bullets out of her body and sew herself shut without so much as a fluttering of the eyelashes. The fact she was showing pain meant it must be terrible.

They worked quickly. Isadora and her assistants moved around her efficiently, passing tools and supplies with ease. It was the mark of a team who did this often and knew how to communicate with the slightest flourish of a hand.

But Konstantine still saw that Isadora's smock was covered in Lou's blood. So much blood.

After a nerve-racking silence, Isadora finally turned to him.

"She will probably make it," she told him, stripping off her gloves and tossing them into the waste basket. "But you know how we can turn the probably into a certainty, no?"

Konstantine's stomach dropped.

The nurse turned off the harsh fluorescents and said to Lou, "Rest, signora. You will feel better soon."

But Lou wasn't resting. Her eyes were boring into Konstantine's.

He struggled to find a reply. This caused the very thing he'd been avoiding to happen. Now Lou would know he'd lied to her.

"The microbes," Isadora said. "You said there was a way for her to get more."

She looked from Konstantine to Lou.

"You know how, don't you?" she asked. "You are low on the microbes, but you know how to get more, don't you?"

Lou's eyes were cold when she said, "Yeah. I do."

When he looked again, she was gone.

LOU STOOD AT THE EDGE OF HER ALASKAN LAKE, HER BODY throbbing and thoughts unclear. It was difficult to think with the anger ricocheting through her mind.

Konstantine had lied to her. She wasn't sure why, but he'd lied to her when he said her microbial levels had not changed.

Why?

Why would he do that?

Stepping into the icy water and wading deeper eased some

of the pain from her wounds. There were no caribou or coyotes crowding the edge of the lake tonight. Lou thought she had seen something cut across the night sky, but it was too far to be sure if that shape was a large bird or simply a dark cloud.

It didn't matter.

She dunked herself below the moonlit surface and sank, willing herself to move from one world to the other.

As the waters began to warm and lighten from midnight blue to red, her mind turned to Konstantine again.

He lied.

He lied to me.

Her mind wouldn't stop repeating it.

It wasn't that she thought him incapable of the act. He could not be who he was and control all that he had if he wasn't a decent liar. It was only that she hadn't expected him to lie to *her*.

She broke the surface of Blood Lake slowly.

With only her eyes above the water, she made her way slowly to the shore, ensuring she was far enough into the shallows that those strange orca-like creatures would not be able to reach her.

Her eyes scanned the embankment, but she saw nothing. No Jabbers. No secondary beast with blood-red eyes.

She wasn't sure if she was relieved or disappointed.

As she searched for any sign of Jabbers—fresh claw marks in the ground, bent or broken branches, *anything*—she considered what she would do next. After much thought, she hadn't managed more than a tentative plan. There was the matter of Riku, of course. He'd tried to trick her by baiting her with a child.

Then he understood at least what drew her to him.

Therefore, there was no guarantee he wouldn't line up a

hundred children and start shooting them executioner style in order to get her attention again.

If he does that, I'll go, she thought. *Healed or not, I'll go.*

That still left the matter of Konstantine and his minor betrayal. His little white lie. What would she do about that?

Go home and take a shower. Eat something.

That was all she could do until she was ready to confront him. Right now, she didn't trust herself to do it without getting angry. But that also meant sleeping in her own bed, which wasn't half as comfortable as his. This remembered fact made her twice as angry.

Fucking Konstantine.

If she was being honest with herself, she'd run to this very shore in order to protect him from her wrath. She wasn't even sure she needed to be in the water again, having just traveled through it to find Jabbers. Had she gotten enough of a microbial boost then? Or had she really needed to return?

She supposed it didn't matter whether it had been an excuse to leave him or not. Either way, the result was the same.

She sat on the slope of the shore but didn't pull herself entirely out of the water. She let the warm waves lap at her legs, occasionally dipping down so that it could soak her hip as well as the wound beneath her arm.

That one still hurt like a bitch.

She lay in the shallows and did the only thing she could do as she scanned the still waters and silent shore.

She waited.

24

Piper had put about five cups of coffee in her body and it wasn't even ten in the morning. Jitters aside, she felt only triumph when she put the enormous bulging file on King's desk with a grin.

"*Bam*," she said.

King looked up from his computer, his own coffee mug about halfway to his mouth. "What's this?"

"*This* is a rock-solid case against one Brock Adkins, Samantha's stalker. I've got witness testimonies from the police, neighbors, and locksmith guy, photographic evidence as well as an ex-girlfriend of Brock willing to testify that he is a violent, controlling, and abusive partner who will dump you just because you dyed your hair brown."

King arched a brow.

Piper shrugged. "Yeah, I don't know what that was about, but apparently Trish, the ex, had blond hair, and then when she dyed it brown, Brock lost his mind about it. Super weird."

"This was before or after he was violent toward her?"

"After," Piper said. "The violence and controlling part happened during their two-year relationship."

"Did you run into any trouble?" he asked. "Did he see you? Try to talk to you?"

Piper thought about how he'd gotten the drop on her when she'd rounded the alley. She relived the moment where his knee had come up and connected with her guts and the press of his blade to her throat. How the blood had felt, warm and sticky, sliding down the front of her neck before wetting her collar. How badly it had stung when Lou cleaned it up.

Getting the turtleneck from Dani had been the easy part.

"No problems," she said. "I guess I'm just that good."

He snorted. "Don't get too cocky. Cocky gets you killed."

King opened the file and flipped through the paperwork Piper had arranged there as well as each of the sections she'd clipped and labeled for clarity.

Somewhere about halfway through his review, he began to nod. "This is good work. Really good. I don't know if the DA office needs all these color-coded sticky tabs, but your work is very meticulous. Good job."

Piper beamed. "Thank you. Thank you *very* much."

She felt like her body was trying to go in five directions at once.

King stood and pulled his jacket off the back of his chair.

"Where are you going?" she asked. She knew this man's schedule by heart. He didn't have anything today until the late afternoon.

"Where *we're* going," he corrected her. "Let's go get a warrant for Adkins's arrest."

In an overwhelming swell of glee, Piper snatched her own coat off the back of her chair and rushed out into the sunny morning after him.

PIPER FELT LIKE HER HEART WAS GOING TO EXPLODE OUT OF her chest. An hour after she had turned her case in to King, the police issued a warrant to search Brock's car and his parents' house where he lived. Upon searching the house, they found ropes, gags, and locks of blond hair, as well as a *lot* of murder and rape pornography on his laptop.

Piper stood on the curb across the street from the Adkins residence beside King, wondering if she'd ever felt so proud in her life.

She'd done this. *She'd* been the one to protect someone.

"I know it's a lot of standing around," King said, misinterpreting why Piper kept shifting her weight. "It's just part of the job."

"It's not that," she said. "I'm just so pumped. This is *amazing*."

King clasped her shoulder and squeezed. "You did good, kid. I'm proud."

His words were the icing on the cake. Piper was smiling so hard her face hurt.

Adkins was led through the front door of his parents' home out to the black-and-white parked on the curb. The police in navy jackets with the yellow *NOPD* stamped on their backs continued to search the house and property. King had warned her that they should go after Adkins was apprehended, that the police would likely spend several hours going through all of the Adkins' personal effects and they would have long died of frostbite before the team called it quits for the day. So that was the plan, to leave as soon as Adkins was in the car.

Piper would wish they'd left sooner.

Brock locked eyes with her, spotting her over the trunk of the police car.

As soon as he saw her, his face contorted into a mask of rage.

"You!" he screamed. "You did this, you little bitch!"

"Do *not* react to that," King said before Piper could flip

him the bird or compose a clever retort. "Professionalism 101, we do not engage with or provoke a suspect unless you're in an active interrogation and trying to achieve a specific result."

Piper sighed. "Fine."

"I'm going to make you pay for this!" he screamed over the trunk, wrenching himself in the officer's grip, trying to break the hold they had on him or at the very least delay being shoved into the back of the car. "Next time I'll really slit your throat and your bitch friend won't be there to save—"

The officer finally managed to push the writhing Adkins into the back of the police car.

It was too late.

King was looking at her. "What's he talking about?"

"I don't know." Piper's voice shook, her heart pounding in her chest. "It's crazy talk."

But King was already hooking a finger into the collar of her turtleneck and yanking it down to reveal the bandage there.

"You told me nothing happened," King said, his jaw working.

"Nothing *much* happened," Piper said. "I'm fine. Look at me."

"Who was the 'bitch friend'? Lou? Did Lou step in and save you?"

"No," Piper said. "It was someone else."

"Lou didn't even get to you in time?" King's voice rose. He was going to lose it on her right here in front of the police and everyone else.

"She didn't need to," Piper whispered, hoping to bring him down an octave. "I'm totally fine."

"If Adkins was close enough to cut your throat, you're not *fine!*" he yelled.

A few cops glanced their way.

Piper shrank from embarrassment.

"You *lied* to me. How am I supposed to trust you to handle assignments solo if you're going to lie to me?"

Tears welled up in Piper's eyes. "This is why I didn't tell you. I knew you'd use it as an excuse to take the case away from me. I might not be Lou, but I can *do* things. I can handle myself."

"Obviously not," King said, and flicked the collar of her turtleneck. Piper felt like she'd been kicked in the stomach all over again. "Taking you off the cases is the right idea. Effective immediately, you're off everything. And I mean *everything*."

Piper threw up her hands. "Don't do that, man. *Please*."

"I don't want to see you again until Monday." He turned his back on her and walked away.

Lou woke with a stiff neck. From the flat of her back she turned her head left and right, cracking the bones on each side in turn. She sat up and rubbed at her eyes. It was the light shimmering off the Mississippi which had roused her to consciousness. She rotated her watch and checked the time. Still morning.

She stretched, missing the warmth of Konstantine's bed and even the soft purr of Octavia sleeping nearby. Here in St. Louis, she was so high above everything. So sterile and removed. In Florence, she felt like she was on the ground level of life, fully emerged in the smells, sounds, and the bustle of the city.

The fact that she woke up sore and missing it made her all the more mad at Konstantine. If she let her mind carry on like this, she was going to believe that it was Konstantine's fault she hadn't gotten a good night's sleep last night. That, perhaps, it might be his fault for Riku still being alive.

She loosed a slow, controlled breath, bringing her thoughts back under control, and threw back the covers.

The apartment was cold. The skin along her arms and especially her fingers and toes was icy to the touch. She pulled off her night clothes and inspected her wounds. They were already healing. The underarm area was still tender, but it did not ache as it had the night before. And the hole at her hip was only a little sore to the touch.

The feeling of heat had just begun to return to her fingers and toes when Piper crossed her mind.

Lou stepped from her apartment into the linen closet that smelled of cedar and lavender. One slip through the dark and she found herself in Piper's tub.

She pulled back the curtain, stepped out into the empty bathroom, and immediately heard the crying.

She followed the sound to the living room, where Piper sat on the sofa with her face in her hands. Dani sat beside her, a tissue box cradled awkwardly on her lap as if she weren't sure if she wanted to hold it or put it down. All around them, wadded-up tissues littered the floor.

"I knew it would happen," Piper wailed. "This is why I didn't tell him about Adkins attacking me. I knew he was just looking for the first reason to doubt me. He doesn't believe I can do it. He doesn't believe in me."

"He never said that," Dani said. "Don't get carried away."

Lou looked to Dani.

"King fired her," Dani said.

"He didn't *fire* me," Piper said through the snot and the tears. "He just told me to go home for the week and that he was taking me off all the cases. I'm just supposed to do —*what*?"

"You'll work for Mel," Dani said encouragingly. "You love working for Mel."

Piper lifted her head and for a moment seemed as if she

might be okay, but then her lip began to quiver again. "I love working cases *more*."

Dani shot Lou a pleading look.

"I'll talk to him," Lou said.

Dani mouthed the words *thank you*, before Lou returned to the bathroom and slipped through the dark.

KING WAS ON HIS SOFA, LOOKING AT BUT NOT SEEING THE football game playing out in front of him. Mostly his mind kept replaying the last week of Jack Thorne's life. He wasn't sure why Piper's lie had brought these old memories to the surface, but something about what she'd said or did transported him back fifteen years to the night he got the call.

I'm so sorry, Robert. Jack is dead.

Jack and his wife were shot and Lou was made an orphan. All in a single night.

Why couldn't he stop thinking of that now? More importantly, why did he keep revisiting his last conversation with Jack in a strange overlay with today's fight with Piper?

The moment he'd pulled down the collar of her shirt and saw the blood-stained bandage and the moment Jack told him, *You worry too much, old man.*

Back and forth. Back and forth. Piper to Jack, Piper to Jack. Why was his mind playing it on a loop like this?

"Why am I doing this to myself?" he asked the flashing television.

The pressure built between his ears then popped suddenly. He shook it out, trying to head off the annoying ringing sound, just as Lou stepped forward from his bedroom.

He noted everything about her appearance. The change of her clothes and the color in her cheeks. She looked better than the last time he'd seen her. Then she'd been a sickly yellow. Now the color was right, and she looked like she'd slept more, even if she did seem pretty pissed about something.

"What's going on?" he asked. "Trouble in paradise?"

He didn't really want to hear about her relationship with the mob boss, but he knew that Lucy would want him to feign an interest once in a while.

"You made Piper cry," Lou said.

Maybe that anger is for me then.

He shrugged. "She lied to me. I asked her if anything happened, she said no, and then it turns out she'd almost got her throat slit."

"She didn't tell you because she knew you'd react like this. And you did."

King threw the remote down on the table. "Do I need to tell you what happens to little girls who fight bad guys? *You*, whose parents are both in Bellefontaine Cemetery. She's playing a dangerous game, and if I can't even trust her to tell me the truth—"

"You can trust her. You know you can. That's not what this is about," Lou said simply. She didn't raise her voice. She didn't try to talk over his escalating tone. She'd interrupted his momentum with a simple fact.

That's not what this is about.

And she was right.

King ran a hand down his face. He took several slow, steady breaths, trying to center himself again. Finally he said, "She's going to get herself killed. You realize that, right? You didn't make it to her in time with this bastard, and there will be another time when you don't make it."

"She's capable of taking care of herself."

King sprang to his feet. "So was Jack. Jack was one of the smartest people I knew. The toughest. A damn good fighter, but he's dead. He's fucking *dead*."

Lou said nothing.

King took a deep breath. "I'm sorry. I shouldn't be yelling at you. If anyone is aware that Jack is dead, it's you. I...I don't know why I said that."

"You're scared of losing her," Lou said, in that same frustratingly placid way of hers.

"Aren't you?" King asked, the grief in him so strong, like a fist at the base of his throat. "Doesn't it terrify you, the idea that you're going to see her pumped full of bullets someday?"

"Yes."

"Then why are you standing up for her? Why in the hell do you want her to keep doing this?"

"It's important to her."

King heard the unspoken *like it's important to me* that hung in the air. And why not? It made sense. Lou would no sooner stop what she was doing than King could. He'd tried to retire, and look at him. Some retirement. As for Lou, it was personal. It was cathartic.

He understood Lou's drive. He didn't understand Piper's.

When King didn't speak, Lou said, "If she wants to hunt, she'll find a way to do it. With or without your help, she'll find a way."

"Not if I call every agency from one coast to the other and tell them not to give her a job."

Lou's eyes darkened. "If you do that, if you block or hinder her, then I'll teach her my way."

King's heart kicked in his chest. The air left him. If Lou saw the panic rising up in him, she didn't care.

"You wouldn't," he said.

Her smile made his blood run cold. "Watch me."

25

Lou was gone, but King was still pouting on his couch when his phone went off. He recognized Detective White's phone number immediately. "King here."

"You're going to want to get down here. We've got Zoey Peterson."

A horse kick to his chest sent King's heart thumping. "Is she hurt?"

"Not yet. But it don't look good," White said, his voice tired. The chatter of a crowd filled the phone. Wherever he was, there was a great deal of commotion.

"Tell me where you are and I'll come now."

"We're on the riverwalk, just beside the French Market."

"The French Market?" he repeated slowly, hoping he'd heard White wrong.

"Yeah. I'll see you down here."

The call ended.

King slid his phone into a pocket and hastily pulled on his shoes. When he threw open the apartment door, he could see down into the shop below. Melandra was behind the register, making a list on her yellow legal pad.

She knew something was wrong as soon as she saw him at the foot of the stairs.

"What's happened?" she said, her hand hovering above the page. The pen trembled in her grip.

"They found Zoey. Come on."

Mel didn't even grab a coat. She just ran out behind King into the early evening with Lady on their heels. King got to the Buick and turned the key in the ignition, trying to will the old heater to life while Mel fussed with the shop's door.

Lady stayed by her side, her ears flicking as Mel locked the doors, her smart brown eyes looking up and down the street for any signs of trouble.

Good dog, King thought. *Damn good dog.*

"Let's go," Mel said as soon as she'd opened the Buick's passenger-side door.

She held the seat up for Lady so she could jump into the back before swinging her own legs into the car.

The drive was done in tense silence. Mel was fidgeting beside him, moving her weight from one hip to another as she couldn't find a comfortable spot. Lady, noting her master's unease, kept flicking her ears.

"You're scaring the dog," King told her as he hooked a left past Jackson Square.

"*Désolée, ma grande*," she said. "You're driving straight for the French Market."

"She's at the French Market."

Mel swore. "My dream—"

"I know." No need to let her whip herself into hysterics. "But we'll be there in a moment."

Mel fell into prayer, her hands clasped in front of her. "Please don't let me screw this up, Jesus."

King made a silent prayer of his own. Not to Jesus, but to Lucy.

If you've got a minute, baby. We could use a bit of your luck and grace.

A cool breeze blew across the back of King's neck. Or maybe that was Lady breathing on him.

The crowd by the market was thick when they arrived. King had no choice but to pull off, half blocking the street, because there was nowhere else to put the Buick. He managed to get her mostly off the road, and that would have to do.

He'd barely got the car into park before Mel was throwing open her door and leaping out into the crowd.

"Mel, wait!"

King turned off the ignition and held the door open for Lady to jump out.

White spotted him and shouted over the commotion caused by the gathered bystanders.

"*Move*, people. Get him through here!"

Two officers worked to push the crowd back and make a path for King to get to the center of the storm. When the final line of it broke open, King finally saw what they were dealing with.

Zoey Peterson was standing on the very edge of the walk with her back to the Mississippi River. The winter waters flowed unhurriedly behind her, unaware of the commotion above.

Zoey's face was tearstained and red from crying.

She was holding Mel's gun to her chest, pressed right up against her heart.

Mel, it seemed, hadn't needed help to get to the front. She was only eight or ten feet from Zoey, her hands up in a surrender position as she tried to get closer to the girl.

"Don't!" Zoey screamed. "Don't come any closer to me or I'll shoot."

King looked to Dick White, whose face was a mask of

exhaustion and fear. King understood. Dick had two daughters near Zoey's age, and one had gotten into drugs and had almost killed herself. There was no way White was going to be able to look at this girl and not see his own kid.

Their eyes met.

It don't look good, he'd said on the phone.

King had to agree.

This was bad.

MELANDRA WAS CERTAIN SHE'D NEVER BEEN SO SCARED IN her life. She knew that this probably wasn't true. When she'd thought she'd killed someone. When she'd had to face her ex-husband, Terry, at the end of a gun. When she'd accidentally shot Lou and watched the girl bleeding to death before her eyes, absolutely helpless. All of these moments had terrified her.

But this moment, too, was right up there.

"Don't do this, Zoey," Mel said, ignoring the crowd behind her. "You don't have to do this."

"You're wrong," the girl said, sniffling. "I have to. It's all my fault."

"It's not your fault."

"You don't know that!" she screamed. The gun shook in her hand.

Mel had to draw a deep breath just to get the voice back into her throat.

"You're right," Mel said. "You're right, I don't know what happened to you. But I'm listening. If you wanna tell me, I'm right here. I wanna listen."

Zoey's lips trembled, her eyes bright with unshed tears.

"He was a good boyfriend," she said finally, and sniffed. "He didn't deserve to die."

"Who, baby?" Mel said. She kept her voice soft. Kind.

There was no point in showing how scared she was to this child so engulfed in her own fears.

"Zach. My boyfriend, Zach."

"What happened to Zach?" Mel asked gently.

Zoey licked her lips. "We were at a party. A stupid party. I didn't even want to go. If I hadn't gone, maybe he'd still be here."

"What happened at the party?"

"Stupid Chelsea. When I got there, she told me that Zach was cheating on me. That he was upstairs with another girl. And so I go up there, and he was alone in the bedroom with her."

Mel didn't think any of these names were important, but she didn't want to miss some critical detail. She did her best to keep up.

"We fought at the party, and I broke up with him and—" Fresh tears spilled over her cheeks. "It's all so stupid. I was *so* stupid."

"So he cheated on you?" Mel asked, trying to understand how they'd gotten from a cheating boyfriend to killing herself by the Mississippi.

"No. He never cheated, but I didn't know that until Chelsea told me at the hospital that she'd lied. That she made it all up. Zach was talking to Hannah because Hannah was super drunk and these guys were bothering her, and Zach stepped in and took her somewhere quiet so that they'd leave her alone and—"

She dragged her nose across the sleeve of her jacket.

"What happened to Zach?" Mel pressed.

"He died," Zoey sobbed. "He was a good guy and he died because I broke up with him."

Mel was fairly certain this was not Zach's cause of death.

King said, "Zach wanted to talk it out, so he drove over to your house the next night to explain what had really happened at Hannah's, only he never made it. A drunk driver ran a red light and hit Zach. Is that right?"

Mel hadn't seen King maneuver through the crowd and had no idea how long he'd been standing beside her.

But Zoey was nodding, wiping at her eyes again with her sleeve. "It's all my fault."

"No, baby," Mel said. "It's not your fault."

"Yes it is!" Zoey pointed the gun at Mel. "You don't know me. I should've known that Chelsea was lying. I should've known that Zach would never do that to me. He was a really good guy. And she blames me too. She blames me for everything!"

"Who?" King asked.

Mel caught sight of Lady then. Lady was inching forward, slowly, almost imperceptibly.

Mel was about to order her to stop when King's hand clamped down over her wrist, giving it a firm squeeze.

"Zach's mom," Zoey said, sniffing. "At the hospital right after Zach died, she told me she was going to find a way to punish me for what I did. And she's right. This is all my fault. If Zach is dead, then I should be too. I don't deserve to keep living if he's dead."

Mel understood now. With blinding clarity, Mel understood why God had sent her *this* girl. It was because Mel *was* this girl.

How many years had she blamed herself for what had happened the night she drove her ex-husband's car? How many years had she believed his lies and thought she'd killed someone? How many times had she felt—as this girl felt now —that she didn't deserve to be alive?

"The person responsible for Zach's death was the drunk driver," King said calmly. "Nothing you said or did or didn't do makes it okay for him to get behind a wheel and drive drunk.

He chose to do that, and it cost Zach his life. That's on him. Not you."

Zoey's arm shook from the effort of holding up Mel's gun.

Mel thought she was going to lower it finally. But instead, fresh determination overtook her as she pressed the gun to her own heart again.

"You're wrong," she said. "It's my fault. I know it is."

Zoey glanced down then and noticed Lady. Lady gave a hopeful wag of her tail, and Zoey's face crumpled. Her aim slackened, the dark eye of the pistol pointing to the ground at last.

The distraction was just enough for King to dart forward and seize the girl's gun hand. He wrenched it to the right, tearing the gun out of her grip and letting it clatter to the pavement. Mel picked it up, unloaded it, and slipped the bullets and gun into separate pockets of her coat.

Then her arms were around the girl.

Zoey sobbed as Mel rocked her.

She sobbed as if she was trying to empty her very soul of its torment.

"I know, baby. I know. You let it all out," Mel said, tears springing to her own eyes. "Everything is going to be all right."

When Mel pressed her face to the top of the girl's soft hair, something red caught her eye. A bird cut across the crowd, flying off into the sky.

It was fast, but Mel knew what she'd seen.

A cardinal, bright and darting.

26

———

Lou stood in her armory and considered her choices. As she always did, she looked longingly at her flamethrower, wishing *this* would be the moment she could put it to good use. She quickly had to abandon this idea. If Riku was as well guarded as Konstantine believed, Lou would have to rely on her stealth to get to him. She couldn't move through the darkness as swiftly or as silently with a flamethrower in her arms.

She decided on four harnesses. One for her shoulders that would allow her to wear her twin Glocks close to her ribs. Another for her hips. She'd put two Berettas and extra ammo there. Then she could strap a gun to each thigh too, the Hi-Power Browning pistols given to her by Konstantine.

She decided to put silencers on everything. She was tired of getting lectured by King that if she didn't start wearing ear plugs or something, she'd be deaf by forty.

She picked through her box of knives, then fingered the S&W blades she kept hanging from a hook, but decided against them. She went with her black blades instead. They were no less sharp, and the black metal meant that she could thrust them without them catching and reflecting light. She decided against the machete and grenade belt, but at the last moment thought she might take one grenade. Something to get the party started, should she walk into a room with a great deal of firepower. It could cause enough chaos and distraction to turn the situation in her favor. She could do the same with tear gas canisters, but that meant masking up herself, and she wasn't in the mood.

Her weapons plus the bulletproof vest and Kevlar sleeves completed her ensemble.

In the full-length mirror, she looked herself over, satisfied with her work. She didn't like how exposed her neck was with her hair pulled back out of the way, but there was little she could do about that. The alternative was to risk her hair falling in her face at a crucial moment.

IN THE LIGHT OF ALL HIS *LYING*, LOU DECIDED TO GIVE Konstantine a chance to explain himself. He could thank Piper for that. She'd seen how desperate Piper had been to protect herself from King's reaction. Perhaps Konstantine was no different. Had he refused to tell Lou about the microbial difference because he'd feared some reaction from her?

There was only one way to find out.

He was alone in his office, staring into his lit fireplace, his gaze transfixed on the dancing flames. He didn't even look up at her until she was quite close.

"Louie," he said softly when he saw her.

She could tell he wanted to touch her. He'd come forward as if he would reach out but stopped himself.

So he is afraid then.

His voice and face were deceptively calm when he said, "You're going to fight him tonight? Have you healed?"

"Yes," she said, then, deciding it would be as good for her as everyone else to be more honest, she added, "More or less."

"I'm sorry," he blurted. "I'm sorry I lied to you."

Something in Lou's stomach unclenched. She thought it might be the desperation in his eyes that had softened her.

"Why did you?"

He fell back against his chair and squeezed his eyes shut. "It was stupid of me."

She waited.

"I didn't want to tell you that I suspected you had to have an open wound in order for the microbes from that lake to enter your blood. You get shot. You get stabbed. Anything. Anything with an open wound, and then you cross over and that is how they get into your body. That is how they heal you."

Lou leaned her weight against the desk but still didn't speak.

"But lately you've been more careful. You haven't gotten hurt, and so when you cross—I guess you aren't getting this transfusion. I don't think that is why you got a cold, but I also didn't want it to be the excuse you need to keep getting hurt."

"You know, there is such a thing as a paper cut. Or I could nick my hand with the tip of a blade. If you'd told me. It's not like I would let someone shoot me just to get a microbial *boost*."

"I know. Forgive me." He placed his head against her stomach, and when she didn't push him away, dared to wrap his arms around her waist.

Lou ran her fingers through his hair, enjoying the silky feel of it, loving how it tightened the muscles low in her body and the delicious, heated thoughts that came to her mind.

She wanted him. But it could wait. She still had unfinished business with Riku Yamamoto.

Lou snorted. Then, unable to contain herself, laughed fully.

"What?" Konstantine looked up at her, his chin still grazing her stomach. His smile grew, hesitant. "What is it?"

"*Blood* Lake," she said. "And all this time, I thought my name for it was just about its color."

He smiled. "Clever."

She withdrew then, untangling herself from his hold.

"Are you going to him now?" he asked.

"Yes."

"Wait," he said.

Her irritation rose. "Konstantine—"

"Just a minute, I promise." He pulled his cell phone from his pocket and pressed the keys on its screen. He held up a finger, begging for her patience. "Yes, it's me. Is it done?"

A pause.

"No, I can't make any promises. Especially if you choose not to honor the initial terms of our agreement."

Another pause. Lou shifted her weight from one foot to another. What game was this?

"Very well. I wish you luck."

He ended the call and met Lou's gaze. "They're ready for you."

"Who was that?"

"Watanabe. Riku's second-in-command."

Her hands went to the Berettas instinctively. "Do I need more guns?"

"I don't think so," he said.

"You said they were ready for me. I have grenades and—"

"No, *amore mio*," he said. He took her hands and brushed kisses across her exposed knuckles. "That isn't what I meant."

"Then what did you mean?"

His smile was wicked. "Go and see for yourself."

"Konstantine," she said in a low warning.

But his smile didn't falter. Instead, he said, "Happy birth-day, *amore mio.*"

LOU WASN'T SURE WHAT TO EXPECT. GIVEN THE DEVIOUS way Konstantine had smiled at her, she'd imagined a surprise. And still, she never would have guessed what awaited her in Tokyo.

When she stepped from Konstantine's shadowed office into Riku's apartment, the bedroom was dark. There wasn't a soul in sight.

With a Beretta in each hand, she eased open the bedroom door and walked into his living room.

It was a sight to behold.

In the center of the room, Riku had been gagged and hog-tied. The gag appeared to be a silk scarf of deep scarlet red. Both his wrists and feet had been zip-tied. A cord connected the two and was wrapped around his body for good measure.

Finding her nemesis wrapped up tight was strange enough, but now she understood why Konstantine had wished her happy birthday. It was stranger still the way his men fell to their knees and prostrated themselves before her.

"Forgive us," one of the men said. He lifted his head, only to dip it low again.

Lou had learned in aikido that deep bows like this were meant to signify respect. She just didn't understand why they were bowing to *her.*

"He has offended you and we offer our sincerest apolo-gies," the man added, before sitting up. He didn't rise. He remained on his knees, but he did lift his gaze. It hovered somewhere near her chin. Maybe her lips.

"You're giving him to me?" she asked.

"Yes," he said with another dip of his head. "We are very sorry for the trouble he has caused you and the innocent people he has hurt. We swear to you that we will not violate the terms of the agreement."

The terms of the agreement? Hadn't Konstantine said something to that effect? The situation began to take shape in her mind, but she didn't lower her gun.

"Are you Watanabe?" Lou asked.

"Yes," he said with a dip of his head.

"And you will be the leader of this group now?"

"If you will permit it."

She bit back a laugh.

She understood now. Konstantine had been clear that he wouldn't tolerate any group that dealt in trafficking. Riku had violated that contract, but Watanabe was ready to honor it. More than that, it was clear that he believed Lou to be the deliverer of retribution for that violation.

Riku was screaming through the silk scarf stuffed in his mouth, though it absorbed most of the sound.

"Who's this guy?" Lou pointed her pistol at a second man hog-tied beside Riku.

His face was bloody and his eyes swollen shut. He hadn't been given the same care as their former leader.

"He is the one who shot you," Watanabe said.

One of the men prostrating themselves had peeked his head up, trying to get a look at Lou. When Lou saw this, his head snapped back down to the carpet. She resisted the urge to laugh at the absurdity of the scene. They had even kept the lights low for her, as if to make her more comfortable.

"Why would you do this?" she asked. "You're betraying him."

"We have been horrified by his actions for a long time," Watanabe began.

"Because he fucks children," Lou said.

Watanabe winced, and that was the reaction she'd wanted. She wanted to force them to look at the ugly truth of what they'd allowed. Sure, maybe they didn't have the opportunity or means to stop him before, but it was hard to believe that, seeing as how Riku was now conveniently tied up at her feet.

"We do not want it to go on," Watanabe said. "We want to be better."

What did that mean? Lou wondered. What ambitions could a crime organization have for *being better*? Her mind went to Konstantine, to all he had done to try to elevate boys like Matteo out of poverty. She could see that he was trying to be better than his father, Fernando Martinelli.

Has he hurt children? Lou asked her compass, her gun passing over Watanabe's crouched form. *Has he been complicit in their pain?*

The compass didn't stir.

Maybe I shouldn't be so quick to judge, she thought. After all, Watanabe *sounded* sincere.

"I accept your offer," Lou said. "But I don't want him."

She gestured to the second man. This was simply a practical choice. Lou wanted to give Riku her full attention, and she wasn't as offended that someone had shot at her in the heat of the moment as she was by the atrocities Riku had committed.

"You can do what you want with him."

"As you wish."

"But, Watanabe..." She pitched her voice low, filling it with quiet menace. Here she crossed to him and put her gun under his chin. She forced his face up so that he had no choice but to look her in the eyes. "If you hurt a woman or child, I *will* come back. For you."

Watanabe swallowed. "I understand."

She released him, and an audible exhale escaped his lips.

Lou kept her gun up even as she bent down in front of Riku and took hold of the rope at his back.

"Thanks for the gift," she told them. And with a wink, she

was gone.

Lou regarded Riku on his side in the snow and considered how she wanted to handle this. It was a first for her. She'd never been *given* her target gagged and bound. She'd gotten so used to fighting her way to them that this felt wrong. She pulled a knife from its sheath and knelt beside him. She slid the blade between his cheek and the silk and pulled, cutting the gag free.

Despite the fact she hadn't meant to cut him, blood welled up on his cheek instantly, reminding her just how sharp she kept her knives.

He spat the silk onto the ground.

"You must've been a *really* bad boss," Lou said.

"Only a coward would kill a man like this."

Lou only smiled. She had nothing to prove to this one. Rapist of children. She could think of few more cowardly actions.

"I could cut out your eyes," she said thoughtfully. "I could remove each of your fingers one by one. Or perhaps something more important to you."

She pressed the tip of her blade to his dick.

He went very still beneath it.

"Have you no honor?" he asked. "Fight me on my feet."

Would she? It would be giving him what he wanted, which she loathed to do. Then again, it might also demoralize him, if he was beaten so completely at his own game only to lose his life anyway.

No, she thought. Men like Riku never lost their high opinion of themselves, whoever bested them or how badly.

"No," Lou said at last, her breath fogging white in front of her face. "I think you've been getting what you want for long enough."

Riku screamed. He thrashed and writhed on the ground but to no avail. He couldn't free himself.

Lou waited until he quieted to say, "The only question left is which piece of you I should cut off for Mai. Which do you think will make a more appropriate present?"

Riku's eyes doubled in size, the whites made brighter by the moonlit snow around them.

"Didn't you know she was alive?" Lou asked, enjoying his surprise. "She's a beautiful young woman in her thirties, living in Canada."

"No," Riku hissed, his jaw working.

"Oh yes," Lou said, kneeling down again. "I can't be sure because I haven't asked, but I think maybe it was Hinato who helped her fake her death and escape you. Of course, you didn't know about it, or Hinato would be dead, am I right?"

"No," he said again with a sharp shake of his head. "No, she died. She was reborn, she'd be a child, a—"

"I mean, that certainly fits your sick delusion, but no. Mai isn't a child. She's a woman."

Lou reached into her pocket and scrolled for the picture she'd taken. She never really used this phone for anything, much less for photography, but the photo was clear enough.

Lou held it up for Riku to see. The glow of the phone illuminated his twisted face in the dark.

"See?" she asked. "You'd never guess by that beautiful smile what had happened to her. Or what a monster her brother was. But it's her."

His mind was clearly dilating from the shock. His eyes remained wide and unblinking, his jaw slack. Even after she pulled the phone away, he stared at the night sky without seeing anything.

I guess my fun is over, she thought, and grabbed the rope at his back.

Given his shape and weight, he sank beneath the water

even before Lou could get to a point deep enough to submerge herself.

I'm going to drown him before I ever get him across, she thought.

Yet he was sputtering and choking when Lou hauled him onto the twilight shores of La Loon.

Lou hardly noticed. All her attention was fixed on a single black shape placidly sitting on the beach, waiting for her as if it had been there all along.

And the eyes were yellow. Not red.

"Jabbers," she breathed, and dropped Riku on the embankment.

The beast let out a sound that could be mistaken for a purr, though it sounded as if it belonged to ten lions. Lou didn't care. She pressed her forehead to the beast's, with one hand on either side of its huge head. There were no injuries or wounds from what Lou could see. Either Jabbers had healed herself in the waters or she'd done a better job of protecting herself than Lou had given her credit for.

"I missed you," she said. The scales were cool against her cheek. "I'm so sorry I pissed off your boyfriend. When I didn't see you, I thought you were hurt. I didn't realize I was —interrupting."

The beast chuffed. A sharp snort of air.

Lou laughed.

That was when Riku began to scream, his head twisting from one side to the other. When his eyes fell on Jabbers, however, his screams dried up.

Jabbers slid around Lou and went to stand over him. The rumble from her throat turned from a friendly purr to a menacing growl.

"Do you still want me to cut you free, Riku?" Lou asked him. "Because I have to tell you, it won't matter. She'll only hurt you more if you run."

27

King asked Piper to meet him at Café du Monde on Sunday. He'd warned Mel in advance that he would need her for an hour or so, and Mel said she was closing anyway because she wanted to go to the psychiatric hospital and talk to Zoey before her family picked her up.

What he hadn't expected was to see how miserable Piper looked when she showed up five minutes after he'd sat down with two coffees and a large order of beignets.

"Hey," Piper said. She looked at the coffee and beignets then at the clock on her phone. "I'm sorry I'm a couple minutes late."

He noted the dark circles under her eyes and her chapped lips. It didn't look like she'd even brushed her hair this morning.

"Are you okay?" he asked, genuinely concerned.

"I'm fine," she said blandly, and pulled her coat closer around her. "What did you want to talk about?"

She didn't touch the coffee or the beignets, which surprised him. He knew she loved both. Obviously, yanking her off the case had hurt her more than he'd realized it would.

I better get to apologizing then, he thought.

"Have I ever talked to you about Jack? Louie's dad?" King asked.

Piper shook her head. A faint interest returned to her eyes, but she was still far more subdued than he wanted her to be.

King took a sip of coffee and said, "Jack Thorne was brilliant. He was one of the smartest recruits I'd seen in ages. He was a hard worker, never turned his nose up at the dirty or unglamorous parts of the job. He brought a hundred percent of himself to everything he did, and I admired the hell out of him for it. It's why I fought so hard to get him transferred to St. Louis. I wanted to keep working with him. I was learning as much from him as he was from me."

Piper nodded, but still said nothing.

King's heart clenched.

"Two days before he died, before Angelo Martinelli murdered him and his wife and almost Louie, I talked to him for the last time."

Piper searched his face. He had her attention, at least.

"I asked him how he was. I asked how his case against the Martinellis was going, and he said, 'Fine, fine. Don't worry so much, old man,' and so I let it go. What he *didn't* tell me was that a week before that, he'd gotten a warning. They'd slashed all the tires on his car. They sent someone to beat the shit out of him. They made it perfectly clear that if he didn't stop, they were going to end him. You see my point, right?"

Piper ran her hands through her hair. "Are you telling me this story to prove that you're right? That I'm a total freaking idiot?"

"No," he said, and put the coffee cup down on the table. "I want to say I'm sorry."

She frowned.

"Whatever reason you had for not telling me about Adkins attacking you must've been the same reasoning Jack had," King pressed on. "And I've spent almost every night of my life since wishing that I'd been the kind of mentor that Jack could've talked to. There were a hundred things I could've done to keep him safe, if only he'd let me know what was going on. But he hadn't, and that's on me."

"Look, I'm sorry I didn't tell you—" Piper began.

King held up his hand. "I'm the one apologizing here. Let me finish."

Piper finally reached for the coffee closest to her. King pushed the container of sugar packets and creamer toward her.

He took that moment to reach down and pull out the case files Piper had made for him out of the leather satchel at his feet. He slid them across the table toward her.

Her hand froze mid-stir. "Why are you giving this back?"

"I can't use it."

She groaned. "I worked so hard on that."

"I know," he said.

"If it's because I didn't tell you, I—"

"It's because the DA has decided to charge Brock Adkins with murder instead of stalking."

Piper dropped the creamer she'd been holding. "What?"

"The lock of hair they found in Brock Adkins's place matched the girl we pulled out of the river. Turns out that she also reported a stalker a couple of months before she disappeared."

"Holy shit."

"Yes, holy *shit*," King said. "Sometimes it's like that. We're following a guy that we think is a basic bad guy only to find out he's a *very* bad guy. That's how a lot of killers, rapists, and the like get caught. They make mistakes. They get taken down for something small, and only later do we discover they've done far worse."

"So to be clear, you're telling me this story because I *am* an idiot," she said.

He shook his head. "I'm telling you because I want you to know that it's not that I don't trust you. It's that I want you to treat every case like they could be a murdering psychopath, because sometimes they will be."

Piper swallowed, her eyes downcast. "You say that like you're ever going to let me work a case solo again."

"I am," he said. "Not just because Louie threatened to teach you to hunt her way if I don't."

Piper laughed. "Glad to know she has my back."

"I will support you in this," he said. "But you should know some things."

"Oh no." She leaned back in her chair. "You're gonna tell me about freaky hazing rituals in the cop world now?"

"Do you want to be a cop?" he asked.

"No," she conceded. "I'm thinking FBI, maybe, or someone who hunts killers."

King suppressed the wave of overprotectiveness threatening to consume him. After a slow breath, he said, "It's not easy to be a woman in this line of work. There are a lot of good men in the field, but there's also a lot of misogynist pricks who will give you twice the shit for being both a woman and a lesbian. You're going to need a bachelor's in criminology at least. A minor in psychology or forensic pathology, whatever interests you. It would help if you spoke Spanish, and you do realize that there is a fitness test you have to pass, right?"

She swore. "Is that why you made me do all that walking?"

"No. But now that I know you've got your sights on Quantico, I'll know how much harder to push you."

She frowned. "I don't know if I like this."

King was smiling, and after a pause, so was she.

"We'll put you on cases that will give you the valuable work experience they'll be looking for, and I've got connections I'll use to get you the interviews. I'll do what I can to help you get where you want to go, Genereux."

"Genereux!" she cried. "You've never called me by my last name before."

"Get used to it. All us cop types go by our last names. Unless you're an *Allendale* by then."

Piper wrinkled her nose. "Doubtful. The Allendales are old money, and I'm but a humble American mutt."

She finally went for the beignets and stuffed one into her mouth, leaving a ring of powdered sugar on her lips. She looked like a kid, and King realized that she wasn't much younger than Jack had been when he'd met him.

Please, he thought. *Please don't let anything happen to her.*

"I've just got one question," King said.

"Shoot."

"I get why Lou can't stop what she does. And we both know I'm a lost cause. But I don't get why you want this. You could be anything. Literally anything."

She put down a second, half-eaten beignet and looked out over the square, watching a carriage pulling a family of four down the street, the horse's hooves clopping loudly.

Finally, she said, "It was really hard for me to watch my mom live how she lived. The men she dated treated her like shit, and there was never anything I could do about it. I just wanted to protect her, you know? I just wanted to keep her safe."

Her gaze remained distant a moment longer before she looked back at him.

"When I told Samantha that we got her stalker, she hugged me *so* tight. Before we got him, she was terrified. But after I told her that he was gone, out of the picture, it was like this huge burden was off her shoulders. I felt so *good*. So important. It was like I could actually do something that mattered to help people. It was such a different feeling than the helplessness I'd had with my mom all those years. So I guess that's it. I just—I just want to help people. Does that make sense?"

He tried to relax against the bittersweet ache in his chest.

"It does," he said. "It really does."

28

—————

Zoey Peterson sat by the bright window with a cup of Jell-O and a spoon. She seemed oblivious to the cheerful red dessert, her gaze fixed instead on something outside the window, in the distance.

Mel took the seat opposite her at the table.

"Hey there." Mel fussed with her bangles and the placement of her wrists on the table. "Do you mind if I join you for a little while?"

Zoey looked relieved. "No. I was hoping I would see you one more time."

This surprised Mel. "Really? How come?"

"I wanted to say I'm sorry for stealing your gun." Zoey's gaze fell to her lap. "You were so nice to me. You let me stay with you and you gave me money. You fed me. And then I just—"

She exhaled a shaky breath.

"Why did you do it?" Mel asked.

"I don't know," she said. "I just—Everything got to be too much. I just kept telling myself what a piece of shit I was for letting Zach get hurt like that and that I deserved to be dead."

"That's not true, baby," Melandra said, her bangles clinking against the tabletop, momentarily blocking out the sound of the hospital's dining room around them. "I hope you know it's not true."

"I don't *know* it yet," she said, licking her lips. "But I have a feeling I might be wrong."

"That's a fine place to start."

Zoey finally met Mel's gaze. "Did you just come here for an apology?"

"Not at all. I wanted to see that you were all right and to give you a piece of advice."

Zoey's eyes widened. "Did you have another vision?"

Mel resisted the urge to laugh.

"No. This advice just comes from being old and living for a minute or two." She tugged at her head scarf. "A long time ago, I was driving a car when I shouldn't have been and I hit something. In fact, I thought I'd killed somebody."

Zoey gasped. "Did you?"

"No," Mel said, struggling against the shame clogging her throat. "It was a fox. But the point is, I carried this guilt and false belief for *decades*. For most of my life, I went around believing I was the worst person in the world. Do you understand? I tortured myself for something that didn't even happen the way I thought it did. That's no way to live. I want better for you."

Mel reached across the table and pushed the Jell-O and spoon aside. She clasped Zoey's hand.

"I want better for *you*."

Tears welled in Zoey's eyes before spilling down her cheeks. "But it's so hard."

"Don't I know it. But if I've learned anything, it's that this is the work worth doin'. So don't you give up on yourself.

Promise me you won't *ever* give up on yourself, no matter how hard it gets."

Zoey pulled her sweater down over her fists and dabbed at her eyes. "I promise."

"Good." Mel squeezed her free hand gently. "*That's* what I came to hear."

PIPER STOOD ON A CHAIR, TRYING TO PIN THE BANNER TO one side of the wall with tape. Jim, the owner of Jim's Jambalaya and the generous soul who'd allowed this party to commandeer a corner of his restaurant, stood back and offered instructions.

"A little higher on the left side," he said.

Piper raised her corner of the banner while Dani held her side in place. "Like that?"

Jim gave her a big thumb and forefinger OK and a wink. "Lookin' good."

Piper and Dani had just climbed off the chairs to join Mel and King at the table when Lou walked in, her eyes covered by mirrored shades, her leather jacket snug across her shoulders.

"Happy birthday!" said Piper and Dani.

"Surprise!" said Mel, turning to see her.

King hadn't managed to say either of the greetings because his lips had been wrapped around a balloon he was trying to inflate. Instead, his hand lifted in a limp half-wave.

Lou regarded the decorations and gave Jim a nod before taking the fifth seat at the table, leaving only one empty chair.

"Where's Konstantine?" Dani asked.

"Working," she said flatly. No one pressed her on this.

"I'll get the dishes out here," Jim said, and left the dinner party alone.

"We already ordered family style," Piper said. "Hope that's okay."

"You didn't have to do all of this."

"Of course we did," King said. "It's not every day you turn—"

"Twenty-seven," Piper whispered into his ear.

"Twenty-seven," King finished. "Ah, to be in my twenties again."

Mel snorted. "Spare me. I wouldn't go back if you paid me all the money in the world."

Piper arched a brow. "That's a bold claim. I'd be willing to do a lot for 'all the money in the world.'"

Dani shot her a look. "Really? Because you'd think you could take some of my money then."

"Don't fight," King said. "This is Lou's day."

Lou wasn't bothered by the squabbling. Her eyes were fixed on the television suspended in the corner, just to the left of the birthday banner. She recognized the photo of Elliot Simpson on one side of the screen and the photo of the charred remains of a vehicle on the other.

"They found his car," King said, after turning around to look at the screen himself. "They're saying Elliot must have wrecked it trying to escape the authorities."

"My question," Piper began under her breath, "is how the heck did you get the Honda from New York to Arizona. I didn't realize you could, you know, with a whole car."

"I can," Lou said. "I did in Baltimore once too."

Though that had been in water. Lou didn't feel like explaining that she hadn't known she could move a whole car through the dark until she'd tried with Elliot's.

"That's *awesome*." Piper shoved a paper straw down into her iced tea and swirled it several times for good measure. "But let the record show that next time the opportunity arises, I'd rather burn a car than dig up a b—Beautiful food incoming. Would you look at that."

Jim began placing dishes on the table. Piper forced a smile, accepting the bread basket with both hands.

When Jim left, Dani nudged her with an elbow. "What Piper *means* is that we are always available and willing to help you with whatever you need, Louie."

"Yes," Piper said. "That."

"Genereux, pass the rolls," King said.

"On it, boss." Piper slid the basket down the table toward him.

"Should we eat first or do presents?" Mel asked.

"Eat," everyone said.

"Alrighty then," Mel said, and began spooning rice out onto her plate. "Eat we shall."

Lou's eyes slid to the gifts collected at the end of the table. They'd been stacked neatly in front of the empty chair. Colorful paper with bright patterns stood out against the white tablecloth. Some of the wrapping jobs were tidy, others haphazard. Lou could guess who had given her what based on the prints and the state of the wrapping.

She had never been big on receiving gifts, and yet, seeing that little pile there, waiting to be enjoyed while everyone around her ate heartily and talked, left Lou's heart feeling quite full.

"Aren't you going to eat?" Mel asked her. "Honey, give me your plate if you aren't going to fill it yourself."

Mel loaded her plate and Lou managed to eat her way through half of it before Piper leaned back and groaned. "God, I love the food here."

"I want to see what you got," King said. "Open your gifts."

He reached into the pile and slid a small box wrapped in shiny blue paper toward her.

"This one is from me," he said.

Lou unwrapped it, peeling back the paper and opening the cardboard flap to discover a small silicone rabbit. She raised her brow at King.

"It's like my stress penguin," he said. "But yours glows in the dark."

Lou gave it a few squeezes, watching its face expand and contract. "Thanks."

"Me next," Mel said.

She slid a medium-sized box across the table to Lou. The paper smelled like incense and repeated a mandala design of green and purple across its surface. Lou tore it open and found a statue made of black stone.

"It's black tourmaline," Mel said. "For protection."

"Who is the woman?" Lou asked.

"Kuan Yin," Mel said. "She who hears the cries of the world. I thought it was fitting for you."

"It's beautiful." A shiver ran through Lou as she turned the black statue over in her hands. "Thank you."

"Now us!" Piper said.

After the biggest box was placed on the table in front of Lou—the paper resplendent with unicorns and rainbows—Piper continued to lean forward expectantly.

"Come on," she said. "I'm the worst at keeping presents a secret. If you don't open it in two seconds, I'll just tell you what it is."

"What is it?" Lou asked, slowly peeling back the paper.

"It's—"

Dani clamped a hand over Piper's mouth. "Just open it."

It was a waterproofing kit. Lou opened the wooden box and inspected each of the containers, brushes, and cloths in turn.

"We had to hunt for one that was as good for leather jackets as it was for boots and gloves, but *voila*." Piper grinned triumphantly. "Do you like it?"

"It's great," Lou said. "I'm almost out."

With a proud smile on her face, Piper went back to eating her jambalaya.

When Jim brought the dessert menus and everyone was distracted for a moment, trying to decide between praline sundaes, pecan pie, or warm bread pudding with whiskey sauce, Lou had a moment to herself.

She searched the faces around the table, and a sense of peace as deep and steady as the waters of La Loon settled in her chest.

"What are you smiling about?" King asked her after lowering the dessert menu.

Her smile only deepened. "It's been a good day."

THE SECOND MAI SAW HER BROTHER HINATO SITTING ON the stone bench beside the temple's pond, she called his name softly, as if this might be a dream and she would wake up any second.

Hinato must have also felt he was dreaming, because he could not have risen from the bench any more slowly, hesitating to speak her name.

The spell broke and they ran into each other's arms and began to cry.

Lou kept her distance, not wanting to intrude on the reunion. She would have left them like that if not for Hinato catching sight of her and waving her forward.

"I don't understand," he told her. "How—"

"Riku's dead," Lou said. "You don't have to stay away from her to protect her anymore. He won't find you. You're both safe."

Then it was Lou's turn to be crushed in their embraces. She held them both, but her eyes were on the blue heron in the water. The way its wings opened wide before launching itself up into the gray-white sky.

KONSTANTINE WAS ON HIS BED, FEELING SOLEMN AND petting Octavia, when Lou separated from the shadows of his bedroom.

"I didn't see you on your birthday," he said, his hand stilling on Octavia's back. "I missed you."

Why did I say that? he thought. *I promised I wouldn't pout like this.*

"I was in New Orleans," she told him.

"What did you do?" he asked, without looking up from the cat.

"We ate at a restaurant and then I went back to Piper's to watch a zombie movie marathon. There was also bread pudding involved."

"And Riku?" He didn't really need her to tell him that Riku was dead. Watanabe had called Konstantine just after she'd taken Riku. With Riku gone, it was left to Konstantine and Watanabe to finalize the details of their agreement. He was more than a little glad to be working with Watanabe now, given how much more reasonable the man seemed than his predecessor.

Only, he'd expected Lou to come to him afterwards.

When she hadn't, what followed was a long, sleepless night in his bed. Alone.

"Dead," Lou said, leaning her weight against the bed post. "And Jabbers is back. It looks like she sent the boyfriend packing. Maybe you were right about the temporary nature of their relationship."

Octavia leapt from the bed and sauntered away, making it clear that she wouldn't accept half-assed pets from a distracted Konstantine.

Without the cat, Konstantine had no choice but to look up.

He found Louie watching him, her dark eyes searching his face.

Could she tell how much he'd missed her? How desperate he'd been to see her again? How hard it was for him when she was away?

"What about us, *amore mio*?" he asked. He resisted the urge to reach out and pull her to him. "Are we also of a temporary nature?"

Lou shrugged out of her leather jacket and threw it across the foot of the bed. She removed her shoes and climbed on top of him.

She buried her face in the crook of his neck and softened completely when he dared to envelop her in his arms.

A knot in his gut loosened. He held her closer.

"No," she said against his skin, before kissing him on the hollow of his throat. "Not at all."

Did you enjoy *Overkill*? Louie's story continues in *Silver Bullet (Shadows in the Water #8)*

GET YOUR THREE FREE STORIES TODAY

Thank you so much for reading *Overkill*. I hope you're enjoying Louie's story. If you'd like more, I have a free, exclusive Lou Thorne story for you. Meet Louie early in her hunting days, when she pursues Benito Martinelli, the son of her enemy. This was the man her father arrested—and the reason her parents were killed months later.

You can only read this story by signing up for my free newsletter. If you would like this story, you can get your copy by visiting ➜ www.korymshrum.com/lounewsletteroffer

I will also send you free stories from the other series that I write. If you've signed up for my newsletter already, no need to sign up again. You should have already received this story from me. Check your email and make sure it wasn't marked as spam! Can't find it? Email me at ➜ kory@korymshrum.com and I'll take care of it.

As to the newsletter itself, I send out 2-3 a month and host a monthly giveaway exclusive to my subscribers. The prizes are usually signed books or other freebies that I think you'll enjoy. I also share information about my current projects, and personal anecdotes (like pictures of my dog). If you want these free stories and access to the exclusive give-aways, you can sign up for the newsletter at ➜ www.korymshrum.com/lounewsletteroffer

If this is not your cup of tea (I love tea), you can follow me on Facebook at ➜ www.facebook.com/korymshrum in order to be notified of my new releases.

ACKNOWLEDGMENTS

My twentieth novel, over and done. Eight years ago (almost to the day), I published my first novel *Dying for a Living* and now here we are with *Overkill*. What an adventure! Thank you to everyone who has taken this unpredictable journey with me.

A gracious bow to my first readers: Kimberly Benedicto, Kathrine Pendleton, Angela Roquet, and Monica La Porta. *Extra* special thanks to Monica in particular for her help with the Italian translations. *Grazie!*

Professional assistance included the always charming Toby Selwyn from across the pond. Thank you again for making sure my sentences make sense. Another gorgeous cover from Christian Bentulan who is just amazingly talented, and of course, a shout-out to the lovely Alexandra Amor, my super helpful assistant, who takes my manuscripts and turns them into the books you read. Not to mention she also helps keep the business machine running while I keep writing.

Last but not least, there's my amazing street team. You guys are always spotting those last minute typos and leaving the first reviews—two critical tasks required for each book's launch and subsequent success. What would I do without you?

ALSO BY KORY M. SHRUM

Fiction

Dying for a Living series

Dying for a Living

Dying by the Hour

Dying for Her: A Companion Novel

Dying Light

Worth Dying For

Dying Breath

Dying Day

Shadows in the Water: Lou Thorne Thrillers

Shadows in the Water

Under the Bones

Danse Macabre

Carnival

Devil's Luck

What Comes Around

Overkill

Silver Bullet

Castle Cove series

Welcome to Castle Cove

Night Tide

The City / 2603 novels

The City Below

The City Within

The City Outside

Jack and the Fire Eater

Poetry (as K.B. Marie)

Birds and Other Dreamers

Questions for the Dead

You Can't Keep It

Non-Fiction

Who Killed My Mother?

Learn more about Kory's work at: www.korymshrum.com

ABOUT THE AUTHOR

Kory M. Shrum has published over twenty books including the bestselling *Shadows in the Water* and *Dying for a Living* series. She has loved books and words all her life. She reads almost every genre you can think of.

In 2020, she launched a true crime podcast "Who Killed My Mother?", sharing the true story of her mother's tragic death. You can listen for free on YouTube or your favorite podcast app. She also publishes poetry under the name K.B. Marie.

When not writing, eating, reading, or indulging in her true calling as a stay-at-home dog mom, she can usually be found under thick blankets with snacks. The kettle is almost always on.

She lives in Michigan with her equally bookish wife, Kim, and their rescue pug, Charley.

Learn more about Kory and her work at
www.korymshrum.com